JAVA SEA

Also by Stanton Swafford

China Sea

JAVA SEA

A Novel

STANTON SWAFFORD

KING HARBOR PRESS

REDONDO BEACH, CA

Published 2016
King Harbor Press
Redondo Beach, CA

ISBN: 978-0-9964028-2-8

Book design by Stacey Aaronson

Printed in the United States of America

For my ninety-seven-year-old mother and confidante, Meri Swafford

Life is uncertain ... eat dessert first.

1

BALI, INDONESIA

THE MOST URGENT TASK FOLLOWING THE EXPLOSION was to remove the critically burned survivors and place them in nearby hotel swimming pools to relieve their unbearable pain. Other injured men, women and a few children were taken to Denpasar's hospitals which were soon overwhelmed. Eventually many of the victims were flown long distances, one thousand to two thousand miles, to receive specialized treatment.

The driver of the van had never learned how to drive. Jeko Rusdiana taught him only how to steer in a straight line. That's all he needed to know to guide the van on the road that ran past the five-star hotel. The van was rigged for detonation by remote control—in case the suicide bomber got cold feet. Jeko had stood on the roof of a building overlooking the hotel and held a trigger, a cell phone, in his hand for that eventuality.

The Mitsubishi L-300 van incinerated in the explosion along with its driver.

The six overseers of the plot, led by Ghazali, escaped from the area in the small hours of the morning on rented motorbikes which they ditched before boarding the boat that ferried them away from Bali.

The half dozen perpetrators separated when they arrived in East Java. Ghazali ordered them to limit future communications among themselves. When necessary they would employ the secure techniques he had taught them. Chances were they would never meet again.

2

THE BOY'S SCREAM WAS LOUDER THAN THE ONE HE'D
heard a minute earlier. The child's weeping was followed
by a curse and a hard slap. Marine Corps Captain Marc
Mancini, the duty officer that night, heard it all one floor below
the victim. The officer glanced at his wristwatch. It was one-thirty
in the morning.

A few of the Marines on the ground floor had learned to
sleep through the abuse of the young boys. And like Mancini,
many more could only grit their teeth, and privately seethe. Marc,
as always, lay awake grasping the metal frame of his bunk while
the young boy was being raped.

Another scream from above, followed by a muffled punch.
And a sharp command in Pashtun.

"Flores," Mancini called to the Marine on duty in the hallway.

"Yes, sir."

"Come here. I've heard enough of this shit. It's time to civi-
lize that pervert," the captain said in a lowered voice. He threw

off the bed sheet, stood and flexed the fingers of both hands. He was barefoot, wearing boxers and a white T-shirt. "The goddamn colonel is fucking another virgin *bacha bazi*. Follow me."

"Sir, we've been ordered to ignore . . ."

"I don't give a shit about the order. Follow me."

When they heard the Humint Exploitation Team commander's voice several Marines raised themselves to observe what was happening in the darkened room. "About time," one of them called out.

"Yes sir. Lead the way," the enlisted Marine on fire watch said.

The two of them walked to the foot of the stairs that led to the second floor.

"Let's roll," Captain Mancini said in a calm voice. He rushed up taking two stairs at a time, the lance corporal running right behind him.

The half-naked Afghan army colonel was bent forward with his back to the onrushing Marines as he sodomized the naked, crying eleven year old boy in the pitch dark barracks room.

Marc Mancini charged at full tilt across the room and tackled the Afghan officer around the waist. He hauled him off the boy and threw him violently to the ground. The small boy wailed and continued to cover his face with his arms.

The powerful American wrestled the Afghan onto his back and ordered Lance Corporal Flores to hold the man's bare legs on the floor. He straddled the man and raised his right fist above his ear and drove it with blinding force into the middle of the Afghan's face, breaking his long beaked nose with a crack of cartilage. He continued to punch the bloody face over and over until the Afghan senior officer's head fell sideways, unconscious. The Afghan soldiers in the room looked on in anger, or disbelief, as the Marine captain shoved their unconscious commander against a wall.

When the two Marines returned to the ground floor, the captain ordered Flores to be vigilant and not hesitate to shoot any armed Afghan that came down the stairs to avenge the Marines' treatment of their commander.

"We should feed all those fuckers to the Taliban," Marc Mancini said aloud as he returned to his bunk.

3

BALI

TRAVEL MAGAZINES DECLARED BALI THE "BEST ISLAND in the World." Readers' surveys said so, with Maui a distant second. As a result the American Association of Travel Agents, known as AATA, elected to hold their annual convention in March 2003 on the "island of the gods." No less than two hundred American travel agents, spouses and partners joined in the weeklong junket to Bali. Few attended the formal meetings and seminars throughout the week. Most members of the group wrote off the trip as a business expense while they enjoyed the vacation of a lifetime in quaint Ubud, on the white sand beaches of Sanur, Seminyak and Kuta, and at the Bali Sea Resort in Amed on the island's east coast.

The group was scheduled to depart from Bali on Thursday. Several of them had extended their stay for a few more days. Who could blame them? It's tough to leave paradise.

The final event of the week was the gala reception at the Grand Nusa Dua Hotel on Wednesday night, the last day of the convention. The lavish buffet in the garden was accompanied by throbbing Balinese gamelan music and ravishing local dancers. A jazz band played funk for dancing after dinner. The drinks flowed and the atmosphere was electric throughout the evening. Goodwill prevailed among the Americans and their thirty or so Indonesian guests. Some were heard to remark it was an evening to remember for the rest of their lives.

By ten-thirty some Americans and a couple of the less inhibited Balinese, fueled by the free-flowing French champagne, had shed their tropical attire, changed to bathing suits, and were frolicking together in the large swimming pool in the middle of the garden. The party was still going strong at eleven o'clock as the president of the association stood, clinked her wine glass, and gave a final toast to the Americans' new Indonesian friends and expressed her thanks for a perfect week in Bali. Her speech lasted precisely five minutes before it was cut off in mid-sentence.

4

BALI

MARC MANCINI HAD DIED AND GONE TO SEVENTH heaven. He caressed the bare brown hued hip and behind of the beautiful twenty-one year old Balinese woman who lay beside him. He was on his back, still breathing deeply. He stroked her hair with his other hand. Her warm thigh nuzzled his lingering erection. He could feel her soft wetness brush against his hip. They had made love, achieving screaming orgasms in concert, for the fourth time in as many hours.

Marc chuckled under his breath as he reflected on his recent life. He had been celibate during the entire seven month tour in Afghanistan. And now he compensated for those months of lost love with this gorgeous woman he held in his arms.

"Ayu," he whispered in her ear. "I've never had it this good."

"I think I'm in love, Marc." She raised her head and kissed him lightly on the lips and touched the length of the red scar that ran above his waist with a fingertip. Her dark, almond-shaped eyes opened wide when she said, "Stay in Bali. Don't leave me."

Marc smiled happily. He was one lucky man.

Ayu had been a flight attendant on his first-class journey from

Singapore three weeks earlier. During that two hour flight they'd flirted playfully with each other. As the plane descended into Denpasar, Ayu slipped her phone number to Marc and told him she would be home for the next two days. "I'll call you tonight," Marc had said to her in a low voice. "You can give me language lessons at the villa. One-on-one." They had thereafter spent every day and night together whenever Ayu wasn't flying.

Five weeks earlier Marc's father, Roy Mancini, had asked his oldest son if he'd join him in his coffee trading business. Marc returned that month to the family home in San Francisco after completing a four year hitch in the Marine Corps. He'd admitted to his father that he was looking for something to do with his life.

"No pressure, Marc," Roy had said. "But I'd like to bring someone into the business that I can trust. Give it some thought."

Two days later Marc told his father that he had given the idea a lot of thought—the pros and cons of working in a family business. "Don't treat me like a wet-behind-the-ears kid, like you do Lorenzo," he said, referring to his younger brother. "Deal with me like a partner." Marc suggested they give it a try for six months. They'd see if the chemistry was right. Roy had liked that answer, and they shook on it.

Marc's first assignment for Coffee Traders International was to go to Bali where the Mancini family owned a five-thousand square foot four bedroom villa. Roy explained, "Most of my Arabica bean purchasing is in Indonesia—Sulawesi, Papua, and Sumatra. You'll need to learn to speak the language there. Get to know the culture. Have some fun."

Marc Mancini was twenty-six years old. He was a handsome blend of both parents with black hair, penetrating brown eyes and a muscular six foot tall physique. His only blemish was a fresh scar across his torso from the IED that had exploded in front of him outside Kandahar during that final month in Afghanistan.

Ayu kissed Marc's chest and worked her sensuous, full lips and darting tongue along his stomach. He tangled her hair in his fingers. "I want you again, my love," she said as she crouched over him and prepared to take him into her mouth. They heard a slight rumble in the distance.

A moment later there was an explosion, a crack, far beyond the rice field that surrounded the Mancini villa. A dog in the field barked once. Then a ghostly stillness.

"What the fuck!" Marc gasped as he raised himself into a sitting position. He drew Ayu into his arms. He had a sudden reflection of Kandahar and of the soon-to-be-dead lance corporal sitting in front of him in the Humvee when the IED exploded.

"Marc, it sounded like a plane crash . . . in the direction of the airport," Ayu whispered. She stood and rushed to the window that overlooked the swimming pool and stared for several seconds in the direction of the sound. "I don't see anything."

The only light in the bedroom was from the half moon. Marc glanced at the digital clock on the bedside table. It was 11:05.

"Ayu, come back to bed," he said as she closed the curtain. "I don't like this. Something's wrong."

Marc drew Ayu close to him beneath the single sheet. They made love, cuddled, and Ayu fell asleep thirty minutes later. He remained awake, an uneasy sense of déjà vu prevented him from drifting off to sleep.

5

_____

MARC MANCINI WOKE AT 6:45 A.M. FOLLOWING A fitful sleep. He'd climbed out of bed to an eerie silence at three o'clock and stared through a bedroom window at the moon and starlit sky. He'd done this again a few minutes before sunrise. Now he lay on his side for several minutes caressing the ebony hair and watching the soft breathing of the sleeping beauty beside him. At last he rose, wrapped a sarong around his waist, and walked to the kitchen to pour coffee. The cook had arrived at the villa an hour earlier.

When Ayu awoke, neither of them mentioned the sharp crack they had heard the night before. They had plans for the day ahead. They'd ride their motorbikes to Ayu's family home in Ubud for lunch.

Ayu had that week decided to introduce Marc to her parents. She knew how awkward that was going to be. A young woman of Bali, as a rule, did not stray outside of her tight-knit Hindu community for intimate relationships. It was taboo.

Marc's cellphone rang at 7:50. He saw on the screen that the caller was his father.

"Hey, Dad. What's happening?"

"Marc, I just landed in Seattle. I'm at the airport, watching CNN in the terminal. The bombing . . . What do you know about it?"

A chill coursed through Marc. He touched the scar above his waist with the palm of his hand as he recalled the sound of the night before. "What?" he said in a hoarse whisper.

"You don't know?" There was frustration in Roy's voice.

"No, Dad. We . . ." He hesitated. "Ayu and I heard a loud bang last night. After that, all was quiet. We didn't see anything from the villa."

"Who's Ayu? Never mind. Turn on a TV now or listen to your radio broadcast in a few minutes. Call me back." Roy disconnected without another word.

At the time of the call Marc and Ayu were stretched out on lounge chairs on the villa's roof deck that overlooked the kidney-shaped pool and the ten acre emerald green rice field, drinking their second cup of coffee. Marc got to his feet and walked downstairs. He rushed to the bedroom and switched on the radio which was set to receive the BBC World Service.

The breaking news was of the American invasion of Iraq that same morning. After months of American posturing in Washington and at the United Nations, the war in Iraq was now being waged with maximum violence. They were calling it "Shock and Awe."

The next news item was of a suicide bombing the night before on the island of Bali in Indonesia.

"We go now to Bali, and our correspondent there, Colin Templeton-Praiseworthy. Colin, what can you tell us?"

"Jonathan, there were apparently two bombs detonated last night at 11:05 near the garden of the Grand Nusa Dua Hotel. At the time the hotel was hosting a reception in the garden for two hundred members of the American Association of Travel Agents and their Indonesian guests. The first bomb, according to police, was carried in a backpack by a suicide bomber. That smaller

12

bomb caused panic and several casualties. As guests fled from *that* explosion and toward the road adjacent to the garden, a second large bomb detonated inside a van as it drove along that road. Another suicide bombing."

"Do you have a report yet regarding casualties, Colin?"

"Tentatively, yes. There were one hundred and fifty Americans killed in the blasts. The second bomb, the one in the van, was massive. There were many Indonesians killed—party guests, hotel staff and passersby. The injured and burned have been transported to local hospitals. Some of those burn victims, we are told, are being airlifted out of Indonesia for specialist treatment. The hotel is a crime scene, Jonathan, and the area is in chaos. Members of the press have not been allowed to get anywhere close. So the information we have now is still a bit sketchy. All we know is that there has been a devastating terrorist bombing here in Bali that targeted a reception for American travel agents and that about two hundred people have been listed as dead and more than one hundred people have been injured, many seriously."

Ayu listened, open-mouthed, and held Marc's hand. At last he grabbed his cell phone and dialed.

Roy answered after one ring. "Yeah, Marc. Talk to me."

"We heard the news. The bombing was at a hotel in Nusa Dua. The explosion we heard late last night."

"Have they identified any of the casualties?"

"No. Only that most of the dead are Americans, here for a convention. A group of travel agents."

"That's what worries me. I'm thinking of Putu and Komang."

"Dad, give us time to get more information. Right now you know as much as we do. I'll phone you later, after we check it out."

Marc terminated the call and turned to Ayu. "Change of plans. Ubud will have to wait."

"I can be ready to go in thirty minutes," Ayu replied.

A dirt road threaded its way from the villa along the rice field and to a main highway that ran south to Nusa Dua. Marc and Ayu traveled at high speed on their Honda motorbikes, arriving in Nusa Dua before ten a.m. The sky was redolent of smoke and debris. Police and army units had cordoned off a perimeter of five hundred meters around the area of luxury hotels.

LATER MARC ROAD HIS HONDA INTO THE CITY TO LEARN what he could about the bombing before phoning his father with an update. Ayu had traveled to Ubud to be with her family. He bought a special edition of the English-language Bali Times at a downtown supermarket. Grief and fear were palpable on the faces of the Balinese in Denpasar. This was being referred to as Bali's 9/11. Marc returned to the villa to study the newspaper reports.

He read the news and made notes. And he perused the list of names of deceased Indonesians.

"Ah fuck. *No, no!*" he shouted. The startled cook and a housemaid rushed from the kitchen to the living room. Marc stared at the inside page of the newspaper, an index finger underscoring a column. He read the short article again.

> *A prominent and popular couple from Amed, Putu and Komang Surya, who were directors of the East Bali Tourist Association and owners of the Bali Sea Resort were killed Wednesday night by the terrorist bombing while attending the AATA reception at the Grand Nusa Dua Hotel. Putu Surya had been the keynote speaker at the garden party. Putu and Komang are survived by their children, a son, Wayan and daughter, Kadek, who have been assisting their parents in managing the family's various tourist businesses in Amed.*

Marc recalled when he'd met Putu and Komang's kids for the first time. He'd been in San Francisco on vacation from the Naval

Academy. The Balinese siblings were visiting the Mancini home on Pacific Heights over a weekend. The two were undergraduates at Berkeley. He and his father had taken them sailing that Saturday afternoon on the Bay in Roy's Catalina 30. There had been a fresh wind and a strong current. The Balinese were quick learners and by the end of the day proved to be a proficient crew. Marc, a lifelong sailor like his father, had been impressed. The three had established a friendship that hadn't waned in six years.

Marc had planned to travel with Ayu to Amed the next weekend to visit Wayan and Kadek, and their parents, Putu and Komang. And now the elder Suryas were dead, murdered in a terrorist bombing in their own land.

Marc agonized over the imminent phone call to his father. The Mancini and Surya families had become close. Because of that trust and friendship, Roy had listed his villa and the ten-acre rice field under the Surya name. The two families went back a long way, twenty-nine years.

Roy answered the phone immediately. It was after midnight in San Francisco. He'd been expecting the call.

"Dad, this is difficult. I have very bad news." There was a brief silence.

"Tell me, Marc."

"Putu and Komang were at the hotel. The paper says they were killed in the bombing. I'm sorry."

"No!" Roy Mancini gasped. "Could it be a mistake, Marc? Not Komang Surya. Not Putu. Those are common Balinese names. Perhaps it's someone else."

"The newspaper, the Bali Times, mentions Amed."

"And the kids? Wayan and Kadek?"

"The news report says only that Putu and Komang were victims. They were survived by their children."

"Marc, I'm hanging up," Roy said. His son had never heard

such anguish in his father's voice. "I'll call the Suryas' resort. I pray there is an error in the report you read. I'll get back to you." The phone went silent.

Marc waited in the living room, staring at the ceiling fan that rotated above his head. The melancholy movement of a Ravel piano concerto played on the stereo. Twenty minutes passed. At last the phone rang. He muted the music. "Yes, Dad."

"Marc, I'm going to ask you to drive to Amed. I spoke with Wayan. The family is devastated. Yes, Putu and Komang were killed in the blast. No remains found . . . Seems they were consumed in the explosion. It's difficult for me to grieve with the kids over the phone."

"I'll leave right away."

"Thanks. Get back to me when you can."

When Marc arrived at the resort hotel in the early evening he was met by a deathly silence. A soft breeze blew from the placid sea. A waiter served dinner to a solitary guest in the outdoor dining area. The grief-stricken receptionist stood at the front desk and bowed her head as Marc approached.

"My name is Marc Mancini," he said in a somber tone. "I'm a friend of Kadek and Wayan. Would you inquire if they are available to see me?"

The receptionist made a phone call and spoke softly in the Balinese dialect.

"Please take a seat Mr. Marc. *Pak* Wayan will meet you here in a minute."

Wayan Surya arrived in the lobby in less than a minute. Marc stood, and Wayan walked over to him. The two men grasped each other's hands with both of their own. Although Marc had never been a hugger, he put his arm around Wayan and drew him close.

"It is kind of you to come, Marc. I spoke with your father earlier today. This is difficult. Kadek is grieving in her bedroom.

She . . . is so sad. Let's sit on the beach." Wayan motioned for a waiter to meet them at the lounge chairs spread out along the sand in front of the hotel.

"I'll order iced *cendol* for us. Have you tried it? Or would you prefer a beer?" Wayan asked.

"No. *Cendol* will be fine." Wayan ordered, and the two men sat on the edge of their chairs. Both men stared at the dark sea for several minutes without saying a word. The sun had set behind them.

At last Marc spoke. "Wayan, you and I know how close my parents have been to Putu and Komang. I want you to know we'll help you in any way we can. Tell me what you need."

Wayan was silent as he continued to gaze with a stoic expression at a darkening sky and the half moon.

"Find the killers," he replied at last.

6

THE WHITE HOUSE

"MR. PRESIDENT, HER CHIEF OF STAFF SAYS PRESIdent Hartono is not available to take your call." The senior secretary's voice was neutral. In fact, she was flabbergasted. Never in her two years at the White House had a foreign head of government refused to accept a phone call from the President of the United States. This was precedent setting

"Damn it, Joyce. What time is it there in Jakarta?" The president was doing his best to contain his anger.

"It's past nine o'clock in the morning, sir."

"What? Is she sleeping in?"

"Her aide said she was in a meeting and couldn't be disturbed. He told us to phone back in an hour. He's still on the line, sir."

"All right. Tell 'em we'll call back in an hour," the president replied. He shook his head and glanced around the Oval Office at the others in the room—the national security advisor, the secretary of state, and his chief of staff.

Joyce Ingebretsen phoned the Indonesian president's direct line sixty minutes later. The chief of staff in Jakarta answered the phone after five rings and put her on hold. After four minutes, President Hartono, the first female president of Indonesia, came on the line.

"Good morning, Madam President," the American president drawled. "I imagine you have a pretty good idea why I'm calling you today."

"Yes, Mr. President. The bombing. Terrible," the Indonesian said. "Let me put our interpreter on the line. Give me a minute."

"Sure, sure. Do that."

"All right. She is here now. Go ahead Mr. President. Miss Fatmawati will translate for us. What is it you wish to discuss?"

It occurred to the Americans in the Oval Office who listened by way of speakers that President Hartono spoke fluent English.

"The bombing in Bali is on my mind. One hundred and fifty Americans and many Indonesians were killed. I want to help you, Madam President, in any way I can."

A few moments passed as Fatmawati translated the English to Indonesian. The Americans could hear the Indonesian president reply in her own language. The translator spoke in English. "My condolences, Mr. President. We are still trying to get our heads around the event. Rest assured, we will do all we can to bring the culprits to justice."

"Well, Madam, that's what I'm calling about. My government, our intelligence and law enforcement branches, are prepared to assist you in any way we can. Say the word."

There was a long pause on the Indonesian end, with some mumbling in the background, which a State Department linguist would later amplify and translate. At last Fatmawati spoke. "We appreciate your concern, Mr. President. However, we will conduct the investigation ourselves. Your assistance is not required."

The American president replied immediately. "President Hartono, I recommend in the strongest terms you take advantage of the resources that we can contribute to the investigation. Experience with these terrorist killings informs us that speed is of the essence. I can order the full force of our intelligence community—the NSA, CIA—to identify and locate the terrorist bombers. And our FBI has unsurpassed forensics. We could have them working with your team in Jakarta in a matter of hours."

President Hartono took the phone herself now and replied. There was, as everyone in the Oval Office suspected, no real need for an interpreter. "Let me speak candidly, Mr. President," Hartono said. "Following September 11th and the terrorist attack on your country there was sympathy for the United States in Indonesia. We admired you—your country and the American people.

"Keep in mind that we are the largest Muslim country in the world with a population of close to three hundred million. Indeed the majority of well over one billion Muslims throughout the world sympathized with you and understood why you would seek justice and wish to neutralize Al Qaeda.

"Your invasion of Iraq this week has changed that positive perception of your country in the Muslim world. I do not exaggerate when I say you are, or soon will be, despised by most Muslims for your gratuitous invasion of a country, a Muslim nation that did not attack you. Take my word for it, you have opened, as you Americans say, a can of worms.

"What I want to get across, sir, is that I cannot afford to be seen cooperating now with America. I cannot risk the political impact if someone in the opposition were to reveal that we invited Americans to interfere in our investigation.

"Furthermore, Mr. President, if it were ever discovered and made public that America meddled in our forthcoming investigation, I could not guarantee the safety of your citizens or of your institutions in my country. So I implore you, do *not* get involved. We Indonesians are capable of identifying and prosecuting those responsible for killing your countrymen in Bali. You must leave it to us. Is there anything else you wish to discuss?"

There was a stillness in the Oval Office. The American president laid the phone onto his desk, lifted a pen, and looked around at each of the members of his team. The three of them were as dumbfounded as the president by what they had heard from the Indonesian president, a rejection of America's offer of assistance. At last the president lifted the phone and spoke.

"I hear you loud and clear, Madam Hartono. And no, there is nothing else I have to say. Have a good day." The president hung up.

"God damn, sonofabitch!" the president shouted, slapping his hand on the table. He pointed at his national security advisor. "Harvey, schedule an NSC meeting. Make it tomorrow, early as possible. My gut reaction is to tell Hartono to take a long walk on a short pier. But I suppose I should listen to what members of the council have to say. Time for bed. See you all tomorrow."

7

JAKARTA

AT THE SAME TIME THE PRESIDENT IN WASHINGTON, D.C. was ordering an NSC meeting for the next day, President Hartono scheduled a cabinet meeting for after lunch. The various ministers arrived at the presidential palace and took their seats at a table in a soundproofed conference room. Hartono entered the room after all were present and sat at the head of the table.

"I took a phone call earlier this morning from the American president. He offered to commit his government to the investigation of the Bali bombing. I told him we do not need him to meddle in this affair. Our national police force will conduct the investigation and apprehend the criminals. Any comments?" Hartono, never quick to smile, glared around the table at her ministers. Some of the men and women in the room shifted in their seats. The two in uniform, the heads of the army and the national police force, maintained grim expressions. After a long silence, the minister of foreign affairs spoke.

"Madam President, I concur that we are fully capable of running this investigation ourselves. However, I believe it would be counterproductive to offend the Americans. We do not want to jeopardize our trade and diplomatic relations. Perhaps there is a way we can give them some assurance without compromising our independence in the matter."

Hartono paused before replying. "You have a point. There is no good in alienating them to the extent that we harm our own interests. The Americans call it 'cutting off your nose to spite your face.'" She quoted this final aphorism in English, which most at the table understood. Although some considered the metaphor grotesque.

"General Supardi, do you have any suggestions short of involving the Americans?" Hartono gestured toward the commander of the national police force.

"Yes, Madam President, I do. I have a man who could run the investigation. He's a talented brigadier general. His name is Ida Agung. He comes from the higher caste in Bali. Currently he is in command of the South Sumatra region. And he is due for promotion. I would give him a second star and appoint him to run it."

"A Balinese? So he is a Hindu?" the president asked.

"Yes, Madam. He is a Balinese Hindu. And his performance has been stellar, such that I can recommend him to carry out the investigation without reservation," the general replied.

The president frowned at General Supardi. At last she said, "I suppose there is some merit in appointing a non-Muslim to the job. All right, it is decided. Appoint General Agung to run the investigation." She motioned to her minister of foreign affairs. "Helmi, I want you to inform the American ambassador in advance, before Agung's appointment is announced. Tell the ambassador I have selected a Balinese to lead the mission. He should inform his president. That should soothe any hard feelings the Americans might have.

"Meanwhile, I have no intention of visiting Bali any time

soon, as more than one of you have suggested I do. After all they were mainly foreigners and Hindus that were killed in the bombing. Relatively few Indonesian Muslims were victims. I don't mean to sound insensitive, but that is politics. And politics is how we win elections in our young democracy. I cannot be seen as sympathetic to the Americans.

"I have nothing else to discuss. You may all go back to work." President Hartono stood and walked out of the room.

8

THE WHITE HOUSE

THE MEMBERS AND SENIOR STAFF OF THE NATIONAL Security Council gathered in the cabinet room adjacent to the Oval Office at nine o'clock in the morning. The presumption was that the president wished to discuss the war in Iraq which was in its third day.

"Good morning, all." The president grinned and waved as he entered the room. As soon as he sat he said, "I need some advice. It's about Indonesia and Bali. You know, the bombing."

Several of those at the conference table and the ones sitting behind them glanced at one another in surprise.

"I know, I know. You're prepared to talk about Iraq," the president said. "Well, there is nothing new to discuss. It's going well. This is about the terrorist bombing this week in Bali where one hundred and fifty Americans were killed and many more terribly injured. Again, as in East Africa five years ago, the Cole in Yemen, and 9/11, our citizens have been killed, this time in Indonesia, by radical Islamic terrorists.

"I offered our assistance to President Hartono. She turned me

down. Doesn't want the U.S. involved. Says it would be bad politics. My gut tells me to launch a covert mission in Indonesia, capture those jihadis, kill 'em or send them to Guantanamo. Any
ideas?"

The secretary of state raised his hand. "Mr. President, I was
in the room when you phoned Hartono. The odds are we could
not keep a covert mission in Indonesia secret for long. Indonesia is
the largest Muslim nation in the world. It is also one of the most
nationalistic countries on earth. In the best of times we would
inflame anti-American hostility among their people if we were
caught running a man-hunt in their territory. And now with the
invasion of Iraq, this is not the best time to offend a large Muslim
nation. As much as my gut tells me to get involved and seek
vengeance for the bombing, I believe the disclosure of an American
covert mission in an important country like Indonesia would be
disastrous. We are going to need the international support, or at
least the ambivalence, of moderate Muslim nations like Indonesia
and Malaysia as we pursue these wars in Iraq and Afghanistan."

"So what can we do about it?" The president was frustrated.

The director of central intelligence spoke. "The secretary has a
point about Indonesian nationalism. They are a sensitive people
when it comes to foreign meddling in their affairs. That has been
the case since the early days of Sukarno and is no less so now.
They'll riot in the streets at the drop of a hat if they sense American interference. I suggest, Mr. President, that we monitor their
investigation from here. We have the capability to do that by
means of cyber espionage. And if the terrorists ever flee from Indonesia and travel to another country, that is when we pounce.
They'd hardly be in a position to blame us if we snatch their people
in Pakistan."

The president looked at his national security advisor. "Harvey?"

"Mr. President, as much as I'd like to coordinate a full court press inside Indonesia and bring those terrorist bombers to justice, I have to concur with Stan and Gerald. We need Hartono and her government on our side in the global war on terrorism. We can't afford to piss off the president of a country with three hundred million Muslims. Let's monitor their investigation from a distance and see what it leads to. It's possible this terrorist attack was directed from somewhere outside Indonesia."

The president smirked. "All right. I've been overruled. So it's hands off Indonesia. Meeting adjourned."

9

SAN FRANCISCO, CALIFORNIA

ROY MANCINI WAS SPENDING THE MORNING AT HOME. His office was on the second floor in the five-bedroom house in San Francisco's Pacific Heights district. If his people downtown needed to get in touch, they knew where to find him. His younger son, Lorenzo, was serving as an apprentice manager, and the company's experienced staff could handle the day-to-day coffee trading business.

After receiving his MBA from Stanford, Lorenzo had asked his father if he could join the business. Roy couldn't refuse. Though he would have preferred that Lorenzo become an officer in a branch of the military and serve a few years to get some seasoning, like his brother Marc, before embarking on a business career. Roy Mancini could tell the guys who had served in the armed forces from those who hadn't. The former gained a maturity at a young age that the latter didn't possess.

Roy dialed the unlisted number for the *Institute*, the Defense Department's super-secret HUMINT task force. He was put through to Biff Foley, the East Asia desk officer. The two were acquainted due to the freelance work Roy was performing for the outfit.

"Hey there, Biff. This is Roy Mancini."

"Roy, good to hear from you. How goes the coffee trade?"

"A good year so far. Say, I wanted to discuss the situation in Bali with you. We're on an insecure line, so I'll make it quick."

"Well now, that's a coincidence. We had a meeting this morning about the goings on in Indonesia. What's on your mind?"

Roy was prepared to make a succinct pitch. "You're aware of my contacts and area knowledge. I want to offer my services to the *Institute* full-time, Biff. There's going to be an investigation. Right?"

"Roy, we were briefed on this earlier today. The word has come from on high that there will be no American involvement in Indonesia. Something to do with the politics over there. Anyway, I'll be sure to inform the deputy director that you called."

"You have got to be kidding, Biff. No American mission to capture the bombers? There were one hundred and fifty of our people massacred there! What's going on?"

"Those are orders, man. Comes to us from the highest level, if you get what I mean." Neither spoke for a few seconds. Roy supposed Foley was referring to the White House, and he was stunned. "But, Roy, let me take this opportunity to thank you for all the good work you've done for us over the years. Is there anything else you wanted to discuss?"

"Good-bye, Biff."

Roy leaned back in his overstuffed leather armchair and stared out the floor-to-ceiling window at a large container ship as it steamed beneath the Golden Gate Bridge into San Francisco Bay. He closed his eyes and massaged his temples with his fingers.

The sudden violent death of his two best friends, and silent business partners, Putu and Komang Surya, saddened him like no other event in his life.

He had his doubts that the government in Indonesia was capable of tackling the radical jihadists in their midst. He suspected the Hartono government would not pursue a thorough investigation and the prosecution of the radical Islamist terrorists. The Indonesian president had welcomed those same jihadists back to her country from Pakistan and Malaysia after the demise of President Suharto. Roy doubted she would acknowledge the folly of that policy.

Between the NSA, the CIA, the FBI, and the *Institute*, the United States had the skill and resources to track the terrorists in Indonesia and bring them to justice. Justice being a euphemism for their fate once captured. That appeared to be off the table.

HE WAS ROUSED FROM HIS DEPRESSING REVERIE BY THE SOFT hands of his wife, Cynthia, as she slipped behind him and massaged his shoulders.

"What is it, my love?" she asked. "It's Bali, isn't it?"

Roy opened his eyes and took her hands in his. He was still in love with his beautiful Filipino-American wife. They had married twenty-six years earlier after Cynthia had become pregnant with their first child and while they were living undercover in a Manila safe house, both of them employed by the *Institute*. Roy's cover was that of a single, entrepreneurial coffee bean trader. Her legend then was that she was 'Maria Soriano', Roy's elegant and sexy housekeeper. It didn't take a brain surgeon to figure out how that undercover relationship would evolve.

"Yeah. I can't get Putu and Komang off my mind. And Kadek and Wayan. I'll fly over there."

"Would you like me to join you?"

"Better you stay behind, Cyn, and keep an eye on Lorenzo and the office. It'll be a short trip. I'll ask Marc to go to Malacca and run our purchasing operations."

"When will you leave?"

"I'll phone the office in a minute and ask Melanie to book the first available Singapore Airlines flight." He raised his head to Cynthia, and they kissed deeply.

10

MALACCA, MALAYSIA

ROY MANCINI HAD DONE SOME OF HIS BEST PLANNING on long flights. Back in the day, as a peripatetic spook, he'd figured it was because of all the free drinks. He didn't drink on flights anymore, save for the odd glass of champagne on takeoff.

During the following day's first-class trip from San Francisco to Singapore Roy concocted the nucleus of a plan. Long story short—if the United States government wasn't going to pursue the terrorists that killed one hundred and fifty Americans, he would take on that assignment himself. And what's more, he needed some excitement. Life was a tad too comfortable. And predictable. He'd been happiest when he found himself on the edge, and was compelled to use his wits. Before he landed in Singapore, he had devised a covert plan to locate and assassinate the leaders of the Bali bombing, one-by-one.

He would recruit the best operatives in Asia he could find. Men and women who were adroit at working undercover and who were not squeamish about putting a bullet through the back of the head of a fellow human being.

He had phoned his oldest son and asked him to fly to Malaysia. Roy hired a car and driver at the airport in Singapore and drove north on the super-highway to Malacca. Marc arrived the next day. They met at the family's condominium penthouse overlooking the Straits of Malacca and the Portuguese Settlement.

The following day, Roy and his son went for a jog on *Bukit China*, Malacca's four hundred-year-old Chinese cemetery. Paths laced the hill among the scores of ancient tombstones and the few lavish mausoleums. Roy had not used *Bukit China* for a clandestine meeting since his boss at the *Institute*, Tom Hiatt, concocted the master plan to recruit a KGB double agent in Manila, twenty-seven years earlier. The ageless Chinese graveyard hadn't changed a bit since that day.

As he and Marc ascended the hill at a fast pace, Roy explained to his son what he wanted him to do. "I need you to move to Malacca, Marc. The language lessons in Bali can wait. I'll put the bean-purchasing operation in your hands. We've got good staff in the Malacca office. You won't be in the dark."

"Why the sudden change, Dad?"

Roy had debated with himself as to how much of his plan he should reveal to Marc. On the one hand, he should keep his private mission in Indonesia compartmented, for Marc's safety, so he would not be at risk if the shit hit the fan and the operation was exposed. In short, Marc and Lorenzo could run the coffee business together in the event Roy was apprehended and sent to prison.

On the other hand, Marc Mancini had been a professional, a Marine Corps intelligence officer in Afghanistan. He'd faced the Taliban head on and had the scar to prove it. Truth be told, Roy suspected that Marc regretted leaving the Marines and his brotherhood of warriors. His son had matured immeasurable during that four-year tour. Marc had his act together, and could be an asset in Roy's plan to track and kill the bombers.

"I'm going to flip a coin," Roy said as they stopped to catch their breath at the top of the hill. He didn't have to tell Marc why. That was easy enough to prevaricate if it went one way instead of another. Roy pulled a U.S. quarter out of his pocket and flipped it. It landed on the trail. He lifted the coin and saw it had landed on 'heads.'

"I'm going to let you in on a secret plan, Marc. That's why we're outside and not discussing this matter at home or in some café. You have a choice, though. You can join me or you can stay out of it. The latter route would be safer for you."

"Fuck safety. What's the plan?"

Roy paused and collected his thoughts. "You remember what Wayan replied when you asked him what we could do for him and his sister."

"Yeah, he asked us to find the killers."

"Bingo."

Marc looked his father in the eye and gave a wry smile. "And?"

"And the U.S. government has opted out. The powers-that-be have no stomach for pursuing this, despite the number of Americans killed and wounded."

"How would you know that?"

"Let's make another round." They had arrived at the bottom of the hill. "I've never told you what I was doing when *I* was twenty-six years old."

As they increased their pace heading uphill, which was a walk in the park for the fit Marine Corps captain, Roy explained how for seven years he had worked as a case officer for the *Institute*, the DOD's clandestine intelligence agency. Marc had never heard of the *Institute*. Barely anyone had.

Roy explained how Komang Surya had been one of his clandestine agents. The Balinese was the radio operator on a cargo ship chartered by the government of North Korea.

"Komang, in concert with a Navy SEAL team, foiled a horrific plot where terrorists were planning to fire a lethal surface-to-air missile at an American jumbo jet after it took off from Tel Aviv. Putu operated a shortwave radio, and she was the communication cutout between Komang and me. The three of us remained close friends ever since.

"I have worked off and on for the *Institute* as an access agent since resigning as a case officer. I've done the odd job in China for them. Introduced their case officers to leads—politicians and businessmen around Southeast Asia. That sort of thing. Back in the eighties, I befriended a Russian intelligence officer at a cocktail party in Tokyo. An *Institute* case officer met the Russian spook later and turned him. So when I phoned the *Institute* desk officer last week and offered my services to hunt for the bombers, he knew who I was. And the instruction was to stay out of it because the United States wasn't going to get involved. And that's where we are, Marc. Leaving it to the Indonesians to solve the murder of one hundred and fifty Americans."

They walked in silence for several minutes. Marc was digesting what his father had revealed to him. His face was expressionless.

Finally he asked, "And what makes you so sure the Indonesians won't solve the case and bring the bombers to justice?"

"Because of the politics in the country. Pundits over there are declaring that the bombing was a conspiracy instigated by the CIA to shame Muslims. Conspiracy theories like that will confuse the people. And now, because of Iraq, I'm not sure how vigorously the Indonesians will pursue the investigation. Their president, Hartono, hasn't visited Bali yet. A bad sign, an indicator of how seriously she *doesn't* take the bombing."

"And your plan is?" Marc asked.

"My plan is to do the job that the U.S. intelligence community and our Special Forces units should be doing, but won't be.

As Wayan asked us to do, I'm going to find his parents' killers and terminate them—one terrorist at a time—until they've all been dispatched to meet their seventy-two virgins in the sky."

"And you believe you have the resources to do that?" Marc frowned. His expression revealed doubt.

"I spent most of my sixteen-hour flight planning it. Now it's you and me. That is, if you decide to join me. If you don't, I still need you here in Malacca running the business because I'll be busy."

"And that's what your flip of the coin was all about?" He grinned.

"Yeah."

"Count me in."

"Right. I want you to base yourself in Malacca for now. I'll need you to work on the coffee business while I travel and arrange the pieces. After I've contacted some people, we'll meet again and I'll explain what I've done. Fair enough?"

"You're the chief. Let's do it."

They continued to walk along the trail at a fast pace. Neither man spoke for a while.

"Dad, there is something I haven't told you, haven't told anyone." They had arrived at the top of the hill for the second time. They stopped there and their eyes met. "You see this slight bruise on these knuckles?" Roy squinted but didn't see much of a bruise.

Marc continued. "It's nearly disappeared."

"Well, what is it?"

"It's a long story. I was asked to leave the Marine Corps because of something I did. I had every intention of staying in the Corps, making it a career."

"I suspected you wanted to stay in the Marines, Marc. I was surprised when you left. Want to tell me about it?"

"I beat the shit out of an Afghan army colonel when he was

raping an eleven-year-old boy in our barracks. A Marine lance corporal held the colonel while I battered him unconscious."

"What the fuck."

"Yeah, this stuff was going on all the time. Our commanders told us to ignore it because pedophilia was part of their culture. They said we needed these perverted senior Afghan army and police officers on our side. Well, I got sick of hearing the children's screams at night. They were on the floor right above us. So I kind of lost it. I ran up the stairs and hauled the colonel off the boy and beat him senseless.

"That week the regimental commander called me to his office and told me I was in deep trouble. I'd attacked a senior officer in the Afghan army and thereby put our company in danger. The Afghan brass had made a complaint. He told me the Marine Corps brass at Helmand were reviewing the case and that I would hear from them. Meanwhile I was restricted to base.

"Ten days later I reported to the battalion commander. The colonel told me the way I could avoid a court martial or less-than-honorable discharge was to resign when my time was up. It would all be forgotten. I reminded him that we were fighting the Taliban, who were evil, yet we ignore our so-called allies when they commit a worse evil, raping young boys on the base and young girls in the villages. He said orders were orders, don't rock the boat. So ended my career as a Marine Corps intelligence officer."

"Their loss, my gain, Marc. If this scandal ever comes out, there will be a firestorm."

"Well, it won't come out. The colonel warned me that what was going on under the sheets was classified. Any Marine or soldier who reveals it would be prosecuted for exposing a military secret."

Roy paused for a moment before speaking. "You know, the wars we're foolishly fighting in those foreign cultures are going to destroy us. How soon we forget."

11

CHARLOTTESVILLE, VIRGINIA

OY'S FIRST OBJECTIVE WAS TO SECURE FUNDS FOR his mission. He could have financed the hits himself. That wasn't the problem. But he needed to obtain money that would not leave a paper trail to his doorstep, funds that were undetectable. Each of his bank accounts was either under his or his company's name. He hadn't fiddled with undercover banking since his days as an *Institute* case officer.

There was one individual he trusted and respected above all others in the business of human intelligence collection, one who knew the ins and outs of espionage finance: Tom Hiatt.

Hiatt had been the Deputy Director of the *Institute* when Roy worked for the outfit. He'd retired over fifteen years ago. The two had never lost touch. Roy knew that Hiatt continued to keep his finger in the pie as a consultant for the *Institute*.

Roy phoned him after returning to San Francisco the following week. They agreed to meet at Tom's home in Charlottesville two days later. Roy had mentioned over the phone that he was contemplating a new venture and needed Tom's sage advice. Hiatt had laughed and said, "Bring it on."

He explained his dilemma over dinner. Hiatt lived alone.

"Have you met the new Deputy Director at the *Institute*?" Hiatt asked. Roy hadn't.

"He's Walter Sarkies. I pirated him from CIA when I was running things at the *Institute*. He'd been an Agency case officer in the Middle East. Lebanon and Egypt. Indonesia later on. Speaks fluent Arabic and Armenian. His parents are from Lebanon. We met in Cairo during one of my trips to the Middle East. Remember how I used to visit each of our stations once a year?"

What Roy remembered was that Tom Hiatt used to run circles around the military personnel at the *Institute*. The senior officers would come and go every three years or so, get promoted and move on to new assignments. Tom Hiatt, a civilian, was the one permanent honcho for over fifteen years.

"So I pinched Sarkies from the Agency and assigned him to the Middle East, where he performed miracles for us."

"And now he's deputy director?"

"Yep. He might be able to help you. I'll give him a call tomorrow."

Hiatt continued, "The *Institute* has an untraceable black account. Two people, the admiral and the deputy director, are allowed to operate it. They're the only ones there who know of its existence. The money in the account is replenished annually, if need be, from some other fuzzy, undeclared Pentagon fund. There is a limit to the amount Sarkies can remit at any one time. You'd have to work that out with him."

"Why would he agree to send me black money?"

"Walter owes me . . . for who he is and what he's become. If I whisper in his ear that agent Roy Mancini is working on a project critical to our national security . . . Anyway, he can cover his ass under the Patriot Act if anyone asks. Which they won't."

Roy woke early the next morning in his motel room to the

customized ringtone of his cell phone—the twelve-bar theme of Miles Davis' Freddie Freeloader. He saw that the caller was Tom Hiatt.

"Morning, Tom."

"Meet me in the lobby in an hour. I want to give you the number for Walter's direct line."

"Will do." They disconnected.

Later, as they shook hands, Hiatt handed Roy a slip of paper with a number on it. "He's expecting your call."

"Thanks, Tom. I owe you."

"No you don't. Let me know how it goes. That is if I don't read about your arrest in the newspaper."

"Let's hope you never do."

Before leaving Charlottesville Roy purchased four prepaid throwaway cell phones and twenty-five thousand dollars' worth of prepaid credit cards at seven different shops.

12

WASHINGTON D.C.

LATE THAT AFTERNOON, ROY CALLED THE NUMBER TOM had handed him. Walter Sarkies answered the phone after two rings.

"I've been expecting your call, Mancini. When can we meet?" Sarkies asked after Roy introduced himself.

Roy told him he'd arrived in Alexandria that afternoon and that he could meet at a time and place of Sarkies' choosing. There was a long silence. Finally Walter Sarkies spoke. "Meet me at Clyde's in Georgetown at 8:45. Get a table in the back. I'll recognize you."

"See you there."

Roy arrived at the well-known M Street restaurant five minutes ahead of schedule. He took a table set for two in the back room and sat facing the entrance. He ordered an Arnold Palmer and waited. At 9:05 he sensed the presence of someone standing behind him. He turned his head. The man had entered through a back door that Roy hadn't seen.

"Mr. Mancini?" The man stared into his eyes.

Roy looked the man over. He had a Mediterranean mien. He was about six feet tall, had a full head of black wavy hair, a five o'clock shadow, a prominent nose, thick brows and less-than-friendly brown eyes. Even in his business suit he appeared to be the type who worked out at a gym.

"Walter?" He stood, shook the man's hand, and removed a business card from his wallet. The man likewise took a card from his pocket that identified him as Walter Sarkies, Vice President of Christopher Maier & Associates in Alexandria, Virginia. Roy knew the *Institute*'s front company had changed its name and moved from Springfield to Alexandria sometime in the 1990s. Presumably their cover had been blown.

Sarkies sat, facing Roy. "We won't stay long. Finish your drink and we'll make a move."

Roy had anticipated something like this and had already paid for his drink and left a tip. "Let's go," he said.

"Follow me." Sarkies motioned toward the rear of the room and led the way into an alcove. They exited through a back door.

They climbed into a late-model BMW. Sarkies drove through an alley and on to M Street heading east and eventually onto the Rock Creek and Potomac Parkway. Roy recognized that they were driving inside Rock Creek Park. He waited for Sarkies to speak. He was still waiting as they drove north through the park. Had Roy not been engaged in this business years ago, he might have been unnerved by Sarkies' silence. As it was, he knew the man was concentrating on countersurveillance, confirming they were not being followed.

At last he spoke. "There are those in the opposition who would recognize this car and the plates. We're clear."

"Good to know," Mancini replied.

"I'll pull over soon." They continued driving along Ridge Road. Sarkies made an abrupt right turn and they entered a cul-de-sac. He made a U-turn at the end and parked facing out. He kept the engine running.

"So, agent Mancini, Tom Hiatt tells me you have a project you wish to discuss with me." He gave a thin, humorless smile.

Roy asked him how much Tom had revealed of the plan.

"He mentioned that you were engaged in a private mission to avenge a recent terrorist event. One can assume that would be Bali. Your neck of the woods."

Roy had made the decision not to mention his personal motivation in the case, his anger over the killing of the Suryas.

"Right. My plan is to bring the bombers, the organizers, to justice for the murder of the many Americans and Indonesians, and the horrible injuries to scores more. Many of our countrymen and women at the hotel are unaccounted for. They were vaporized by the car bomb. I'll arrange the assassination of each of the terrorists—one hit at a time."

"What you may not know, Mancini, is that the U.S. government, on orders from the White House, has opted not to get involved in the Indonesian investigation or capture of the local organizers. The politics are too dicey. Your project is in direct contravention of that order. So you know the risk you're taking. You could go to prison for a very long time if you're caught engaging in a private, unauthorized enterprise like this."

"I assure you I will not recruit any Americans to my team."

Sarkies appeared to disregard this comment. He bobbed his head from side to side. Roy imagined a cobra as it was preparing to strike.

At last Sarkies turned to Roy and spoke. "I worked as a case officer for three years in Indonesia for the Agency before Tom hired me. I have a special fondness for the country. Made some good friends.

"And I've read your files, Mancini. There are two files—the one where you were under contract years ago as an *Institute* case officer, and the file where you have served for the past twenty years as a freelance access agent. Had I not read them, and been impressed, we wouldn't be having this conversation in Rock Creek Park. I'd buy you a drink at Clyde's as a favor to Tom and call it a night."

"Thanks."

"Your recruitment in the Philippines of the KGB officer, Sasha Popov, turned out to be fortuitous. He was a clever devil, and over the years, he introduced us to an abundance of Soviet defectors in North America. We put him in witness protection, changed his identity, and gave him cosmetic surgery. And we continued to task him until the end of the Cold War when he was murdered. The Russians found him. One of CIA traitor Aldrich Ames' victims."

"Happy I could help." Roy had recruited Popov in Manila in 1975 and had helped him escape from the Philippines a year later. He was saddened to learn of his demise.

Sarkies continued. "If there was one fuck up from my point of view, it was when you retired from the *Institute* and revealed your true name to your former agent, Komang Surya."

"There's not much you *don't* know, is there?"

Sarkies ignored this.

"Let me update you on what we do know and what we suspect. The Indonesian authorities believe that military C-4 was the explosive material in the Bali bomb. Our experts say there is no way C-4 could have caused such a massive explosion. The Indos are stalling the investigation. This blast was similar to a thermobaric explosive. Some of the victims would have been consumed by the blast. We doubt even the Indonesian terrorists knew how powerful that bomb would be.

"Second, we suspect there were some Indonesian army and police officers of a high rank, including generals, involved in the bombing. The quality and quantity of the explosives, plus the sophistication of the plot, were far above the pay grade of some wannabe Indonesian jihadists and their bearded guru in Central

Java. The Indonesian investigators no doubt know this by now. This could explain their objection to the U.S. meddling in their affairs. They don't want the complicity of military higher-ups to be revealed. The FBI bomb lab at Quantico would figure all this out before the end of a month if we had access to ground zero.

"Finally, we're certain there was foreign involvement in the plot—Al Qaeda money and bomb-making technique. We've monitored chatter. Osama bin Laden is said to have transferred a sum of money to Jemaah Islamiyah to buy the explosives from corrupt military sources. An Indonesian terrorist named Hambali is OBL's conduit for Indonesia. We suspect he's lurking around the periphery of this."

Sarkies paused so Roy could digest these facts and conjectures. At last he continued speaking. "Your plan to bring the bombers to justice will not get anywhere near the organizers, the ones at the top. You may be able to hit some of the middlemen. That'll be the best you can do. Now, what is it you want to discuss with me?"

"Funding for the operation. I can't risk financing this project. I can afford it, but I can't gamble that our government won't follow the money trail back to me. Tom said maybe you could help. Something about a black fund that you operate."

Sarkies looked like he was about to choke.

"I could reimburse you, Walter. I'm going to terminate those so-called middlemen in the plot, and without any direct American participation. Absolute plausible deniability for the U.S. government."

"Good old Tom. Now there are four of us who know about that secret account. He must be getting senile." Sarkies shook his head in disbelief.

Roy continued. "This discussion goes no further. If you can assist me, I'd be grateful. If not, I forget we ever met."

"All right. Two things. If Hiatt trusts you, that counts for something. Second, I can see how this mission of yours, assassinating the Bali bombers, could be viewed as a national security imperative. Get the bad guys off the streets. How much do you need?"

Roy hesitated for several seconds. He had a rough figure in mind. But there were others he needed to meet before determining a fixed amount. "How much can you send at one time?" he asked, recalling Hiatt's advice that there was a limit.

"That *is* a secret you don't need to know, agent Mancini. Let me tell you how this is going to work."

"I'm listening."

"Don't write anything down. First you will establish a shell company on Labuan Island, Malaysia. That's an offshore tax haven near the west coast of Borneo. Sort of a Southeast Asian Cayman Islands. A lot of dirty money passes through the banks there. We use a law firm in Panama to set these companies up. Or you can register your company with one of those accounting firms on the island. You will list the law firm or accountant as your nominee shareholder and director. Your name remains off the books. Open the company's bank account at one of the Swiss banks on the island. Finally, you inform me how much you need for one, repeat *one*, hit. I will pay you for one kill at a time. We limit it to a total of four. That is sufficient to eliminate the Indonesians who got their hands dirtiest in the bombing."

"How do I communicate with you?"

"You will communicate with me only once. We'll use pre-paid throwaway phones. Our brief conversation will be in code. Yours will be a one-time request for money. After the first one, don't ever call me again. I'll call you. There need be no further communications between us about black funding. I will learn of your first success one way or another. And I'll replenish the Labuan bank account three more times. No more than that."

They agreed on a simple but clever code.

"Any questions?" Sarkies asked.

"I need some tools. You may be in a position to help. I can't carry the stuff with me through Indonesian customs."

"What do you need?"

"The gun. A 9-mm Beretta with a silencer. I'll need two encrypted laptops. State-of-the-art."

Again Sarkies jogged his head from side to side, as though weighing the alternatives and the risk. "I'll send it all to our man in Singapore. You figure out how to move the stuff from there. Perhaps you can charter a boat and send the packages at night to a small Indonesian island. Use your wits and your contacts. I'll instruct our commander there that the containers are to remain unopened. Plan to collect them two weeks after you send me the request for funds."

Roy wasn't sure how he should take Sarkies's comments about "wits and contacts." Was he being sarcastic? Smuggling these items, the pistol and silencer, into Indonesia would be high risk.

After a moment of silence, Sarkies asked, "Is there anything else I need to know to make this work for you?"

"Do you need me to reimburse the black funds?"

"No. As long as the amounts are within my authority to disburse, I'll take responsibility." He paused and scratched his jaw. "Listen, Mancini, I'm inclined to agree with this mission of yours. I've mentioned my fondness for Indonesia, and Bali in particular. You're doing the right thing, hunting for those killers, assassinating them before they flee the country. So I'll fund it. You keep my involvement between us—you and me, no one else. And remember, never again communicate with me after your initial request for money. I don't expect to ever see you again."

Walter Sarkies put the car in gear and drove off. "Where shall I drop you?" he asked. Roy told him where he'd parked his rental car on Wisconsin Avenue.

As Roy climbed out of the car onto the sidewalk a block beyond the parking garage, Walter Sarkies leaned over and said, "Good hunting, Roy." Roy turned as Sarkies sped away.

13

SAN FRANCISCO, CALIFORNIA

ROY FLEW FROM D.C. TO SAN FRANCISCO THE DAY after his meeting with Sarkies.

During the flight, he considered his next steps. First he needed to identify and locate the bombers. That's where his old friend Jack Chapman might help. Jack was now the CEO of Cain, Acheson, and Carpenter, better known as CAC, the largest and most influential private consultant to the U.S. defense and intelligence communities, and in particular the NSA.

Their high school class would celebrate a fortieth reunion in ten days. Jack and Roy had been classmates as well as rivals and partners on the San Luis Obispo High School tennis team, and had remained good friends over the years.

The first thing he did upon returning home was make passionate love to Cynthia. Since their earliest days together, when they had cohabited in the Manila safe house, they had invented fantasies to embellish their passion. At that time, it was fun and games. They continued with the play acting throughout their married life. Both of them, in their mid-fifties, delighted in inventing these scenarios now as much to enhance the lust as to get a good laugh.

When Cynthia met Roy at the front door she was stark naked. He had phoned her after leaving the airport to say he would arrive home in thirty minutes.

"Oh my god," she cried out to him as she opened the door. "I was expecting my husband."

"Ma'am. I'm a struggling encyclopedia salesman. May I come in and show you everything I have to offer?"

She looked over his shoulder, pretending to make sure no one could see them, and invited him into the house. As soon as he closed the door and dropped his suitcase on the floor, she got on her knees, loosened his belt, unzipped his pants, and pulled them and his boxers to his ankles.

"Ma'am, you're beautiful. Your husband is a lucky man," he said. And she was, and so was he. She stood five-foot-seven—and still had the face and body of a forty-year-old supermodel. Her long black hair was now tied into a long ponytail. Her firm body was as lithe as it had been back in the day. Proportionate breasts, magnificently shaped hips and legs. A rear end to die for.

Roy had raised a semi-erection in the taxi ride home in anticipation of what Cynthia might have in mind. She had placed a thick carpet on the floor. As she stroked and sucked him, she commented on how big he was getting. How right she was.

"It's your turn," he said at last. He placed her on her back on the lush carpet, placed a pillow beneath her butt, spread her legs wide. He dropped to his knees to lick her moist pussy.

"Hurry. He'll be home any minute," she wailed. Roy gave her the yes-yes, no-no treatment with his tongue.

"Now, now," she groaned. "Give it to me hard, you bastard."

He lifted her legs until they were straddling his shoulders and entered her. The foreplay had brought them both near the limit, and they climaxed within seconds of each other. Afterward they lay together, speechless, for a full minute.

"So compared to this, how was your trip?" Cynthia asked with mock seriousness.

"I've had better," he replied.

She pinched the head of his cock playfully.

"Ouch!"

"You really know how to hurt a girl." She laughed, and they embraced and kissed each other deeply.

After Roy showered and shared a bottle and a half of Napa Valley chardonnay with Cynthia on their back porch overlooking the bay, he phoned Jack Chapman at his home. Jack worked and lived in the D.C. area because of his position with CAC. Roy had put off a meeting with him until they could get together later in California. He knew Jack planned to attend the class reunion. The event would give them an opportunity to visit their parents, see old friends, and have a private tête-à-tête.

"Hey, Jack. It's Roy. Are you still planning on the SLO trip?"

"Sure am. Don't forget to bring your racquet. We'll play at the club."

"I'm planning on it. Say, I need to discuss something with you when we meet. Let's plan on breaking away where we can talk."

"Oh, oh. This brings back memories," Jack said with a snicker under his breath.

His intuition was right. He and Roy had engaged in a secret project years earlier in Asia, which they never spoke of because it had been illegal.

"Well, yeah. I want to run something by you. It can wait till then."

"Right."

"See you in ten days."

"You got it. Give my regards to Cynthia."

"And mine to Marguerite." They disconnected.

14

San Luis Obispo, California

Roy Mancini booked a court at the San Luis Obispo Country Club for seven o'clock in the morning the day after the reunion party. Jack and Marguerite Chapman needed to fly back to D.C. later that afternoon. And Roy figured early morning would guarantee the privacy he needed.

They played one hard set of tennis which Jack won in a tie breaker. After the game, they moved to an unoccupied area on the deck where they sat undisturbed at a table beneath an umbrella.

"So, partner, what is it you want to discuss with me? I must say I'm intrigued by the hush-hush," Jack said after they'd ordered drinks. "Something tells me this harks back to an earlier era."

"You're perceptive, Jack. I've undertaken a quiet mission. And I'm going to request your help . . . again. Hear me out."

"Like old times. How long has it been?" he asked, referring to 1975, when he monitored NSA intercepts of phone calls made by the arch-terrorist, Wadi Haddad, and passed the information on to Roy.

"Twenty-eight years. Let me tell you what I need."

Roy explained that not only were one hundred and fifty Americans killed in the Bali bombing, but that Komang Surya and his wife Putu were among those murdered. So the mission had become personal. Jack Chapman was aware of the roles Komang and Putu had played in thwarting the horrendous terrorist attack over the Mediterranean Sea.

He told Jack that the position of the United States was to not get involved in the investigation or in the capture and prosecution of the bombers.

"Why the hell not?" Jack asked in a loud, angry voice. Roy motioned with a finger to his lips that they needed to speak quietly.

"Apparently the White House believes it's too risky. I suspect the Iraq and Afghan wars have something to do with it. They can't afford to get caught interfering in the affairs of another Muslim country like Indonesia."

"Well, that's bullshit." Jack spoke again with a voice that was a shade louder than Roy would have liked. "All of those Americans killed by terrorists in Bali and we sit it out? Where are our priorities, Roy? And what's your plan?" He hesitated for several seconds and looked his friend in the eye. Finally he asked, "Didn't you get out of the covert business years ago?"

"Right. And now I'm back. This time it's private and I need your help. We'd have to keep it secret, the same as we did back then."

He stared at Roy for a moment without speaking. "Tell me about it," he said at last.

"The NSA has the capability to track cell phone calls in Indonesia."

"So?"

"I'll need that to set my project in motion. One cell phone.

I'm not talking about doing anything as massive as vacuuming every phone call in Indonesia."

Jack chuckled and replied, "You'd better not be. Even though the NSA *is* capable of that. You know, most international communications made throughout the world are routed through U.S. equipment, fiber optic cables, switches, and servers at some point. But I can't ask anyone to scoop up every call in Indonesia. What do you want?"

Roy had contemplated during the past few days what he would ask Jack Chapman to do for him. He could not ask him to risk his position at CAC by flagrantly violating the law. However, as Roy suspected, his old friend was outraged by the American government's reluctance to pursue the Bali bombers, and so he might be motivated.

Jack continued. "Roy, once upon a time . . . what, twenty-eight years ago? We had a similar conversation. And I told you if it were not for our friendship and trust we would not have had that discussion. The same goes now."

"I remember it well. We were in the Manila safe house. You, me and Cynthia. I said the same to you. Our cooperation was personal."

Jack shifted gears. "Do you remember my brother Bill?"

"Vaguely. Isn't he a lot younger than we are?"

"Ten years. He's now a colonel in the air force, and he heads up the Signals Intelligence Directorate at the NSA. He'll retire next year, and I've offered him a job at CAC. He's brilliant."

"I'm listening."

"All right. When I return to D.C. I'll talk with Bill and see if he's willing to track *one* cell phone in Indonesia. If he agrees and you can provide me with the one phone number, he can insert spyware into the phone and lock into it, locate it, and tear apart its history of calls for several months before, during, and after the bombing. Likewise for their email. Identify one of the bomber's computers, or the server if they're using an internet cafe."

This assistance would be priceless. Roy assumed the bombers used aliases during their phone calls and emails. But penetrating that one phone, the proverbial needle in the haystack, would be half the battle.

"You're lucky, Roy, that I have a brother I trust with this kind of access. You'll have to give us the one phone number and we'll work out the contacts chain. How you find that number is your problem."

"I couldn't ask for more, Jack. I suspected you needed a bit of excitement in your life anyway." Roy grinned.

"Go to hell," he answered with a smile. "I need a comfortable retirement in a few years. And I don't mean in some federal prison as a result of violating the Espionage Law."

15

MALACCA, MALAYSIA

TWO DAYS LATER, ROY MANCINI ARRIVED IN MALAYSIA. He hadn't alerted Marc about the precise time of his arrival at the Malacca penthouse. So when he unlocked the door and entered the foyer, he surprised both his son and the beautiful Asian woman he was holding in his arms. She was wearing a colorful blue batik sarong and was naked above her waist. Her figure, with her firm, uplifted breasts, was jaw-dropping.

"Oh, sorry guys," Roy said, feigning to cover his eyes with the splayed fingers of one hand. "Let's try this again."

He walked back out and closed and locked the front door. He waited thirty seconds before unlocking the door, and again he entered the room.

"I'm home," he called out. "Anyone here?"

The three of them laughed. The young woman had put on a white blouse that contrasted with her dark brown complexion.

"Hi, Dad. Meet Ayu. She flew in yesterday from Bali. When you walked in the first time, she was demonstrating how Balinese women were attired in the good old days."

"Hello, Mr. Mancini," she said in unaccented English. "It is nice to meet you. I apologize for the surprise."

"No. It's my fault. Next time I'll phone ahead." Roy smiled as she offered him her hand. "I recall Marc mentioning an Ayu over the phone. Could it be . . .?"

Marc replied before he could finish. "One and the same, Dad. Ayu and I have been seeing each other since the day I arrived in Bali. She knows I'm based in Malacca now to run the coffee-purchasing end of the business."

Ayu continued in a somber voice, "We were together at the villa the night of the bombing. We heard the blast. You phoned Marc the next morning."

"Yes, I remember. Marc mentioned your name on the phone that day."

Roy spoke to her in Indonesian. He wished to put her at ease after the awkward first encounter. "A pleasure to meet you, Ayu. I see my son inherited my good taste. Welcome."

"All right you two," Marc said. "Until I learn the language, let's stick to English."

"I'll freshen up. It's been a long flight," Roy said as he walked to the master bedroom. "We can head downtown for an early dinner."

During the thirty minutes that he was showering and unwinding from the trip, he considered how he would brief Marc on the covert operation he had launched. He'd decided to codename the project *Operation Java Sea*.

Without seeming unwelcoming to Ayu, he needed to know when she would leave Malacca. He and Marc required privacy to map out his plans. He had a certain momentum now with *Java Sea* that he did not wish to interrupt. Roy had determined on the flight from the U.S. that he needed Marc's participation, and energy, in the operation.

As if he'd read Roy's mind, Marc said when he joined them in the living room, "Ayu needs to go to Singapore tomorrow. She has a flight in the evening back to Denpasar. She'll return to Malacca next week."

Roy said, "As they say in Spanish, Ayu '*mi casa est su casa.*'"

She laughed. "And that means?"

"Make yourself at home."

16

MALACCA, MALAYSIA

R OY MANCINI HAD NEVER DISCUSSED CLANDESTINE
operations within four walls whenever he was overseas.
So at seven-thirty the next morning he and Marc walked
to *Bukit China*, a pleasant twenty minute stroll from the condo.
They were the only ones on the hill at the time. Roy decided that
Marc would need to know the essential parts of the plot to assas-
sinate the bombers. With one exception—Roy would not identify
Walter Sarkies or the secret source of funds to anyone, including
Marc.

"Now let me explain where we are," Roy said to him as they
walked along the trail. He told him what he had accomplished in
the States with Jack Chapman. Jack, as his brother Bill had now
confirmed, would pinpoint the location of a terrorist's cell phone
once they provided him with a phone number. How they'd un-
earth that number was now the sixty-four million dollar question.

The day before he had flown out of San Francisco, Walter
Sarkies had phoned. He informed Roy that a General Agung had
been appointed as the Indonesian police commander in charge of
the Bali bombing investigation.

He explained with circumspection that he and Agung, a Balinese, had become friends during the former's CIA tour in Jakarta.
At that time, Agung had been a colonel in the national police
force. Sarkies did not recruit Agung. However, the two of them
met socially on occasion and Sarkies elicited confidential information from the police officer. Toward the end of Sarkies's tour,
Agung invited the American to his home in Ubud, Bali. And from
there they spent a week exploring the island. Coincidentally, they
had spent one night in Amed at the Bali Sea Resort.

Listening between the lines, Roy gathered that Walter Sarkies's
attraction to Indonesia, and Bali in particular, was a result of that
weeklong journey with Agung. The two men had stayed in touch
by way of birthday greetings and the like after Sarkies left Indonesia.

Walter Sarkies offered Roy an introduction to General Agung.
Sarkies would inform Roy when his introduction letter had been
emailed to the general.

Roy and Marc had arrived at the top of the hill and were on
their way along the side with a view of the Straits of Malacca
when Roy completed his briefing about what he had accomplished so far. They continued to thread their way among the
Chinese cemetery's centuries-old tombstones.

"Marc, there is one matter that keeps me awake at night.
Someone will send our tools—the gun, the silencer and encrypted
laptops—by diplomatic courier to the *Institute*'s Singapore office.
They won't risk sending the pouch to the Jakarta military attaché
because it would be outside the *Institute*'s control. They don't have
an office there. We need to use our ingenuity to smuggle those
items from Singapore to Indonesia."

Marc didn't comment. They jogged on in silence for a minute.
Something was on his mind.

"Any ideas?" Roy finally asked.

"I'm thinking of Ayu," he replied.

"Yes, she's a beautiful woman. But can we please remain on point?"

Marc hesitated for another minute before speaking. "She disclosed to me that her colleagues on trips to and from Singapore, Bangkok, and Hong Kong smuggle consumer products and luxuries into Bali. The flight attendants have a nice little sideline going: garments, electronics, jewelry, and cosmetics. The Indonesian government normally charges a hefty import tax for that stuff. They all have fences in Denpasar that distribute the smuggled merchandise throughout Bali and East Java. They pay off the airport customs examiners to make them look the other way when they pass through the inspection lines. Ayu has one Balinese inspector that she works with. He knows her flight schedules, and he's there to cooperate. She pays him an advance every month."

"And you expect . . .?"

"Ayu's smart. She'd know this was something more sensitive than the usual luxury goods. I can't tell her I'm collecting perfume from the U.S. Embassy in Singapore. The undercover officer at the embassy must allow me to collect the unopened parcels. I'd pass the package to Ayu in Singapore that same day. She'd have to pack it into her checked luggage."

"You believe you have a relationship with Ayu where you can ask her to take this risk? Smuggle the gun through the airports in her suitcase?"

"As long as it's certain her Balinese customs examiner is there to wave her through without an inspection, this is doable. I would need to reveal to Ayu that we're bringing in a prohibited weapon. She'd have to be involved . . . and motivated.

"I'll fly to Denpasar on an earlier flight from Singapore and meet her at the airport, beyond the customs inspection area. I'll take the parcel from her and leave it unopened at the villa. How does that sound?"

Roy replied, "This subterfuge has got to be built on the trust between you two, Marc. Swear her to secrecy. You may have to tell her the equipment she's smuggling in from Singapore will be used for the purpose of bringing the bombers to justice. Motivation enough?"

"We'll see."

They walked along the jogging path again. Roy continued, "I don't have a problem involving Ayu in that part of the operation. Don't reveal any more than you have to. We keep all the moving parts compartmented. In fact, you and I will be the only ones who know every facet of this mission. And in the end there *will* be several parts. Ayu would play a vital role. Go ahead and run it by her, Marc."

17

NEW YORK CITY

APRIL, 2003

W ALTER SARKIES THOUGHT OF THE ADAGE TAUGHT
to him by his father: *It takes five gentiles to beat a Jew,
five Jews to beat a Greek, and five Greeks to beat an Armenian.* He speculated where the Persians might fit into the equation.

He sat in his home office in Falls Church and reflected on
that week eighteen years earlier when he'd been a rookie working
on the CIA's Middle East desk. He'd traveled to New York for the
ostensible purpose of recruiting a diplomat who was known to be
working for *VEVAK*, the Ministry of Intelligence of the Islamic
Republic of Iran. It was peculiar that the Company had selected
him for that mission instead of a more experienced case officer.
Perhaps the division head needed to give him street cred before
dispatching him to Beirut. The recently bombed mission in Beirut
had needed replacement staff with experience.

He'd waited for two days outside the United Nations Headquarters building. At about four-thirty p.m., he spotted a bearded,
middle-aged Iranian diplomat leaving the building, wearing a suit

and no tie. Sarkies followed the man into a nearby subway station. He boarded the train through a different car than the diplomat and, after thirty seconds, walked back to the car where the Iranian was sitting. Sarkies stood in front of the man and appeared to ignore him. Several stops later, in East Harlem, the Iranian exited. Sarkies followed him out of the car and station and east along 116th Street. At last his target was alone.

"Pardon me," Sarkies said as he walked up beside the man.

"Yes," he replied in a Farsi accent. "You follow me? For what?"

They continued to walk side-by-side, now at a faster pace.

Sarkies replied, "I wish to offer my services to the Islamic Republic of Iran. I am prepared to make a commitment." He handed a piece of paper to the diplomat. "Here. This is my name, the hotel, and room number where I'm staying." The Iranian pocketed the note.

"I can stay in New York for two more days," Sarkies continued. "Pass this to the appropriate *VEVAK* officer. I will wait for his call at nine in the morning and again at three in the afternoon, tomorrow and the next day. If I don't hear from your man by that time, I will leave New York. And *VEVAK* will forfeit an opportunity, through me, to penetrate the Central Intelligence Agency." Sarkies turned and walked away.

At three in the afternoon on the second day, the phone rang.

"Sarkies."

A man with a slight foreign accent said, "A colleague says you wish to meet. Is that correct?"

"Could be," Sarkies replied. "What language do you speak?"

"Farsi, of course."

"Say something in Farsi," he demanded.

The man obeyed and spoke rapidly. Although Sarkies did not speak the language, he did speak fluent Armenian and Arabic, and he had an impeccable ear for Middle Eastern languages. He knew on hearing the sound of the man's voice that he was indeed speaking Farsi.

Sarkies continued, "When can you meet?"

"I'm in the vicinity of your hotel. Is it convenient that I come to your room?" he asked.

"No. Meet me at the Russian Tea Room in fifteen minutes. Take a table in the back. I'll recognize you." He disconnected.

The Iranian introduced himself as Afshin as Sarkies joined him at a table in a dark corner of the room.

"Last year I graduated from the farm," Sarkies began in a low voice after ordering drinks. "I work in the operations directorate, Middle East division. And I have been sent to New York on a mission to recruit *you*, an Iranian intelligence officer working undercover as a U.N. diplomat."

"Are you trying to make me laugh?" the Iranian chuckled. "What are we doing here?" He raised a hand to a waiter gesturing for the bill.

"I'll tell you my story. How much time do you have?"

"I have no time for games like this. But good try." The Iranian stood.

Sarkies intercepted the bill from the waiter and placed it on the table, out of the Iranian's reach.

"Listen to me, Afshin. I'll tell you my story. You can, at the end, decide."

The Iranian sat again and stared for several seconds at Sarkies. Finally he said, "Go ahead. Amuse me."

"My father was an Armenian immigrant to Lebanon and my mother was Palestinian, a Shi'ite Muslim. She lived in southern Lebanon. They immigrated to America in 1956, and I was born in Fresno, California in December 1957. I speak Armenian and Arabic. My parents were old school, and proud of their cultures.

My mother barely spoke English. She raised me to be a good Shi'ite Muslim. No one, however, is aware of that. I haven't been inside a mosque in over ten years."

"And you were sent to recruit me to spy against my country."

"That's *not* the reason I contacted you . . . through your colleague. I am offering my access to *VEVAK*."

"Go on."

"Fast forward. My mother traveled to southern Lebanon to visit her mother two and a half years ago, in September 1982. Does that ring a bell?"

"Why should it?" The Iranian glanced at the bill as though he intended to grab it and run.

"Sabra and Shatila," Sarkies said quietly.

"You don't mean . . . !" Afshin sat straight, grasped the edge of the table with both hands, and stared into Sarkies's eyes.

"My mother and grandparents were killed, massacred, by Phalange, the fucking Israeli proxy. I was studying for a law degree at Stanford at the time. I dropped out for a semester to grieve. They understood."

Afshin asked Sarkies to continue.

"I got my law degree and passed the bar, half-heartedly. I did not want to disappoint my father. He suffered enough with the murder of my mother. However, I'd lost all interest in practicing law. Since September of 1982, I've had one objective in life. *Revenge*."

The Iranian remained silent.

"I decided to commit myself to undermining Israel, from the inside."

"So you joined the CIA? You do not make sense," Afshin remarked and drummed his fingers.

"I met a recruiter on campus as an undergraduate. We stayed in touch. At last I was hired, trained, and assigned to Operations, the Middle East desk. I'm scheduled to go to Beirut next month to work as a case officer. As you know, many of our staff were killed in the embassy bombing last year. My assignment has been accelerated because of that. I could be stationed in Lebanon for three years."

Afshin smiled for the first time. "So you are telling me your motive for working for the CIA is to seek vengeance for the murder of your mother and her parents?"

"Yes."

"And how do you plan to do that, Mr. Sarkies?"

"Mossad."

"Ah, I see . . ." Afshin now stared at Sarkies with a wide grin. "And you wish to report on your dealings with Mossad to my organization?"

"Is there another way?"

"Perhaps not. If what you say is true—and believe me, my organization will find out who you are—we may have something in common after all."

"The ball is in your court, Afshin. You'll know when I arrive in Beirut. I'll be under diplomatic cover at the new embassy. You need to assign a recognition signal and code words."

Afshin grabbed the bill on the table. "You see the amount on this bill for our drinks?"

"Yeah, $8.68."

"My colleague in Beirut will identify himself to you by saying something about eight dollars. You will reply to him by saying sixty-eight cents. Clear?"

"Clear enough. We'll both know who we are dealing with. And I'll know that you have vetted me and you are convinced of my *bona fides*. Is there anything else, Mr. Afshin?"

"No. But I will let you pay for the drinks, Mr. CIA, in cash. Keep the receipt for the future. Someone may ask for it. I will leave now. You remain behind for ten minutes."

Walter Sarkies never met Afshin again after that day in 1985. He had worked with several *VEVAK* handlers over the next eighteen years—in the Middle East and in the United States. Currently he was reporting to an intelligence officer under U.N. diplomatic cover. Sarkies' task, however, had shifted beginning in the late 1980s and with the war between Iran and Iraq. The enemy, and Sarkies' target, were the Sunni Arabs, the Saudi military in particular.

The pretense was that the Persian diplomat in New York was a double-agent handled by Sarkies and that the Iranian spy, code-named *Filibuster*, passed information regarding Iran's military readiness to the American. In reality, Sarkies was passing information to the *VEVAK* officer that had been gained from the *Institute*'s penetration of Iran's arch-enemy: Saudi Arabia.

Walter Sarkies considered the latest twist. He had agreed to send discretionary funds to Roy Mancini, a former *Institute* case officer and current freelance access agent, so that Mancini could privately track and assassinate Sunni jihadists in Indonesia. Sarkies had hard intelligence that the Bali bombing had been organized at the highest level by Osama bin Laden and Al Qaeda. OBL had said in an audio tape that the bombing in Bali was to punish America for its "Global War on Terrorism."

There was also credible intelligence that Saudi Arabia was providing financial support to the radical Muslim elements in Indonesia, including Abu Najib, the Islamist imam in Surakarta, Central Java. Sarkies suspected that *VEVAK* would have an interest in neutralizing the Saudi's insidious influence in Indonesia, the largest Muslim country in the world. And nothing would delight his Iranian masters more than the termination of the Sunni radical, Abu Najib. So he had agreed to Mancini's request for black funds.

Walter lifted the phone and dialed a number in Brooklyn. When the Iranian cutout answered, Sarkies identified himself as Mortimer. By way of code, he requested a meeting with his handler for the following week. The continuously changing time and location for the meeting was programmed well in advance.

18

NEW YORK CITY
APRIL, 2003

THEY MET AT 3:15 IN THE AFTERNOON AT MCSORLEY'S Old Ale House on East Seventh Street. Walter Sarkies arrived first wearing Levis, tennis shoes, a sweatshirt, and a cap pulled low over his eyes. He took a table in the back room and ordered two glasses of ale. The mid-afternoon crowd at the bar was sparse.

The saloon had opened in 1854, and not much had changed over the years. Women had finally been allowed inside New York's oldest Irish tavern in 1970.

The casually dressed clean shaven Persian entered the bar five minutes after Sarkies. He sat across from his American agent without saying a word and lifted the full glass of ale to his lips.

"I know you enjoy your cold beverages, Ramin," Sarkies said as he watched his Persian handler quaff his drink.

"Living my New York legend, my friend," the man whispered in clear English and wiped the froth from his upper lip. "So why the urgent meeting? We are not due to meet until next month."

During their last clandestine meeting three weeks earlier,

Ramin had revealed to Sarkies that *VEVAK* had an asset who'd penetrated the Saudi Royal Compound located in the National Guard Base, north of the port of Jeddah. This was one of the large compounds in the country where the king and various and sundry princes and their ministers met occasionally for business and pleasure. The Iranian asset was a Palestinian technician who worked on the communications equipment inside the buildings. He had of course been thoroughly vetted prior to being employed by the Saudi royals. Only later was he approached by a *VEVAK* case officer during a visit to his family home in Jordan. The Persian operative had made the Palestinian an offer he couldn't refuse: a vast sum of money for providing information about the doings of the Saudis inside the compound.

Ramin had described to Sarkies how the technician had been called at his home on September 11, 2001 and ordered to report to the royal compound to repair a defective television set. He'd arrived at 4:25 in the afternoon and had found that the set required a simple wire reconnection. As he was preparing to depart at 5:00 he heard loud cheering in an adjacent suite. Curious, he walked gingerly toward an open door and glanced inside. There he witnessed a crowd of royals and their guests raucously celebrating as they watched the Twin Towers disintegrate on CNN.

"Finish your ale, and we'll take a walk," Walter Sarkies told his handler.

Sarkies was aware that the Iranian diplomat and spy code-named *Filibuster* was under constant FBI surveillance and that they would be followed now, at a distance. Given the subterfuge that Sarkies was running the Iranian, receiving classified military information from him, he was not worried. He paid the bill, and they left the pub together.

Sarkies spoke in a low voice as they strolled along the streets of the East Village. "I have agreed to provide black funds to a rogue operator whose mission is to assassinate the Indonesian Sunni plotters of the Bali bombing."

"Rogue operator?" The Iranian frowned and glanced suspiciously at Sarkies.

"Yes. The operation is being plotted by an individual, a former *Institute* case officer. The U.S. government can't be involved in an assassination in a moderate Muslim nation like Indonesia. I agreed to fund the plan because it satisfies *your* objectives of neutralizing Sunni Wahhabis. Indonesia is important to your ministry. Am I not right?"

The Iranian did not answer the question. "You say the United States government is not involved? You're providing funds for a *private* mission? This is bizarre, Walter."

"Yes. It is unusual. I do, though, have confidence in the plotter. He knows the territory well. Given your support, I can predict success."

"*Our* support?"

"Ramin, I have committed money for the mission from an unaccountable fund. The truth is, no funds are ever unaccountable. I will have to explain to the people upstairs where the money went. And that is where I believe you could and should help."

The Iranian stopped in his tracks, turned his head and stared into Sarkies' eyes. "And you believe I can justify . . . ?"

"I know you can. For two good reasons. One, *VEVAK* has, over the years, valued my work for the Islamic Republic of Iran. I am providing you with highly sensitive intercepts of Saudi communications. And during my earlier CIA days, I furnished your people with information on the workings of Mossad. I never charged you a dime. And two, your country should have an interest in curtailing Sunni influence in a large Muslim nation like Indonesia. The Saudis, with their petrodollars, are funding the Indonesian madrassahs, which, as you know well, spread hateful anti-Shia propaganda."

Ramin interrupted, "Yes all of that is true."

"Listen to me, Ramin. This operation is underway. I have committed to the plotter that I will send funds to him, one kill at a time. And I intend to do that until the leading Sunni imam, Abu Najib, is terminated."

The name Abu Najib caused the Persian to stop walking and turn his head toward Sarkies.

"And neither of us wishes to have my position at the *Institute* compromised because of unexplained black fund remittances. Correct?"

"Of course, Walter." Ramin replied.

"The amount of money to pull off the four assassinations, including Abu Najib, is mere pocket change for the Islamic Republic of Iran. Look. You may never be able to replace the Sunni ideology in Indonesia with your Shia brand of Islam. But you will put a brake on the further expansion of their radical jihadists. This is an unexpected opportunity, Ramin. Don't pass it up."

"How much?"

"I should have a figure for you within a month. The deal is we send enough funds for one assassination at a time until we reach four. I've insisted on receiving photographs of the murdered terrorists. That should send a message to the Saudis and their Indonesian clients. I'll provide you with the amount and the banking details shortly. Send the funds from one of your untraceable offshore accounts."

Ramin bowed his head, stared at the ground, and continued to walk in silence. At last he replied, "I will make the proposal to Teheran. My superiors will need to know how much they have to pay for each hit. And Walter, be sure Abu Najib is on the list."

"Of course. And let them know that I will consider this as full payment for all of the favors I have done for them over the years."

"You *are* a clever devil." Ramin smiled.

"I'll leave you here," Sarkies said. "Contact me when you receive the go-ahead from Teheran."

Walter Sarkies turned into Washington Square Park and was soon lost in the crowd.

19

DUMAGUETE CITY, PHILIPPINES

MARC HAD ASKED ROY A FEW WEEKS EARLIER TO treat him like a partner. Roy was now prepared to do that. And his son would be more than a junior partner in the operation. Marc would run the operation in Indonesia. He would guide the assassins to their targets. Roy had decided to work in the background, arranging the finances and providing intelligence.

As they walked back to the condo, Roy explained the next step. "We're going to the Philippines this week."

"Manila?"

"No. To a spot that's a lot more pleasant than Manila."

AFTER THEY LANDED AND DEPLANED AT THE AIRPORT ON the island of Negros, Roy noticed a large sign above the terminal building: *Dumaguete—The City of Gentle People.* He pointed it out to Marc. "You're gonna like this place."

Roy had first visited Dumaguete City twenty-three years earlier. Not a lot had changed. Now, as they motored down the

Boulevard he saw the calm blue-green sea and a large island, Siquijor, fifteen miles offshore to their left. On their right was the lineup of Spanish mansions—some in apparent disrepair, others recently renovated. There was an atmosphere of calm, in stark contrast to the numbing traffic and pollution of faraway Manila. The small city had reminded Roy of the tranquil Macao of yesteryear, with its seaside Esplanade.

Perhaps that was what had compelled him to move one-time Macao resident Anthony D'Rosa to Negros Oriental. Five years earlier, Anthony had needed to get out of Macao in a hurry, and Roy had assisted him with his escape to the Philippines.

Marc and Roy took penthouse suites at the Bethel Hotel along the seafront. Roy had last stayed in the hotel four years earlier. The hotel's receptionists still remembered him by name. A nice homecoming.

Looking out his window, Roy saw islands in the distance: Cebu, Bohol, and Siquijor. He watched as a passenger ferry from Cebu docked at the port on the northern end of the Boulevard. He phoned Marc.

"This is heaven-on-Earth," his son said.

"Agreed. Let's take a stroll along the Boulevard and talk things over. Meet you in the lobby."

The sun was setting behind the mountains west of the city. The cool temperature now brought Filipinos of all ages out to play and promenade along the seaside—parents and children, young couples from nearby Silliman University. The two men found an area with some privacy. Roy needed to tell Marc about Anthony D'Rosa.

He began the story. "Tony had registered a shipping company in Hong Kong in the early '90s. The company operated feeder vessels. They loaded containers in the smaller Asian ports and delivered them to Singapore and Hong Kong. I needed Tony's ships to move my coffee beans from Makassar, Belawan and Sura-baya. Our cargoes were transferred from Tony's feeders to the mammoth container ships in Singapore that carried the beans onward to Europe and to the east and west coasts of the U.S.

"Tony had elected to live in Macao rather than Hong Kong. He liked the ambiance. He and I would dine at Portuguese restaurants along the Esplanade and drink too much Portuguese red wine, *vinho tinto*. Often we'd finish off the night at a floating casino.

"Tony would ride the ferry boat from Macao to Hong Kong once or twice a week to check on business at his office in the Prince's Building."

Roy and Marc found a bench at the southern end of the Boulevard. "Let's sit, and I'll tell you the rest of the story about Tony D'Rosa, the second and third acts."

The street lamps had been turned on and so had lights inside the large mansions on the other side of the street. There was a mild offshore breeze. The moon and stars now festooned the darkening sky. Marc pointed out the North Star to his father.

Roy continued his story. "Tony often traveled to China. He'd cross the border from Macao and go south to Hainan, Guangxi and Yunnan. And as I learned much later, he would occasionally cross the border from Yunnan into Laos.

"Now, I was performing as an access agent for the *Institute*. I still am. So when I learned that Tony traveled into Hainan, I informed an *Institute* case officer in Hong Kong. They did their background check and asked me to recruit him. I asked Tony to collect intelligence on air force and naval activity at Hainan. Long story short, Tony agreed to do it for a price. And one of his conditions was that he would only deal with me. He refused to meet with the *Institute*'s case officers. This was in 1996. About seven years ago."

"The plot thickens," Marc remarked.

"Indeed it does. So for over a year Tony and I met in Macao and Hong Kong. He passed me written reports and photographs of Chinese fighter jets, warships and naval port construction in Hainan. It was good humint. Although one never knows if it's redundant given our satellite coverage. Anyway, the *Institute* was happy, and we paid Tony a retainer of three thousand a month, which he blew in the casinos because he didn't need the money. I recall he paid a hundred bucks a month to a Chinese sub-agent who snapped the photos in Hainan for him."

Roy suggested they stop for a beer at a disco-and-karaoke joint on the Boulevard. The music hadn't started, so it was reasonably quiet. Roy ordered a couple of bottles of San Miguel at the bar, and the two sat out on the terrace for thirty minutes and chatted about the coffee business.

When they returned to the seaside, the bench they'd used was occupied by a young couple. So they strolled north and Roy continued the saga of Tony D'Rosa.

"One day Tony gives me a call. That was unusual. I always called him. He's in a panic. He tells me he needs to meet me in Macao ASAP. I was in Malacca that day. So I flew from Kuala Lumpur to Hong Kong and then rode the ferry to Macao the next morning. We met at a cafe on the Esplanade."

"'I'm up shit creek,'" he tells me. "'I need help from your guys. I gotta get outta here. *Pronto.*'"

"I didn't know what he was talking about. He seemed terrified. His passport had been stolen, so he couldn't travel. I knew whatever it was, 'my guys' weren't going to go out of their way to help him. At that time, I was clueless about his hidden underworld activity. I knew him only as a rather eccentric Italian-American shipping executive."

MARC AND ROY HAD DINNER AT A CHIC SPANISH RESTAURANT. "Try the paella, Marc," Roy suggested. The cuisine was fantastic, the waitress was gorgeous and the flamenco music soothing. Marc commented with a wide grin that he was ready to transplant himself to Dumaguete. "Are there coffee beans in the Philippines?" he asked, half in jest.

After dinner they continued their stroll.

"As you know, Marc, I've been racing sailboats all my life. I've skippered boats in the South China Sea Race from Hong Kong to Manila twice. And I won the race fifteen years ago in a chartered forty-five-foot sloop. So I'd been there, done that."

"I can guess where this is going."

"Right. The only way I could figure of getting Tony out of Macao, without travel documents, was to hide him in a sailboat. He'd need to leave everything behind, and he couldn't tip anyone off that he was leaving. I couldn't charter a boat in Hong Kong because I'd have to return it. So I bought a thirty-six-foot, thirty-year-old wooden sloop in Manila, hired a Filipino boat boy at the yacht club to crew for me, and set sail across the South China Sea. Took us six days to get to Macao. When we arrived, I paid off the Filipino and gave him enough money to buy his plane ticket back to Manila."

Roy asked Marc if he wanted him to finish the story the next day so he could get some rest.

"Negative," he replied. "Let's hear it."

Roy continued his story.

20

MACAO

FEBRUARY, 1998

ROY AND HIS CREW MEMBER SAILED HIS WOODEN sloop, *Mistral*, into the marina a few minutes after midnight. They were surrounded by a fleet of fishing boats and the odd Chinese cargo junk at anchor. As agreed, Anthony D'Rosa was waiting, out of sight, on the dock with no more than the clothes he wore and a backpack. Roy noticed him in the shadows as he motored up to the pier.

Tony had a muscular, broad-shouldered physique without an ounce of fat. Remarkable for a guy in his mid-sixties. He was six-foot-two and weighed around two hundred pounds. He had a full head of light gray hair bordering on white that was cut fashionably long. There was a scar on his tough-guy face along his right jaw. His eyebrows resembled two large gray caterpillars. He could be called handsome in a Sicilian sort of way.

Roy had instructed Tony to ignore his arrival at the dock until he had paid off his crewman and sent him on his way to a hotel. He made sure the Filipino hadn't forgotten his passport, that he had plenty of cash for expenses and that he remembered the instructions on how to get from Macao to Hong Kong to book his flight back to Manila. Tony trotted across the dock and hopped aboard as soon as the crewman had disappeared in a taxi.

"Go below, get comfortable, and stay out of sight," Roy commanded as he cast off and backed the yacht away from the pier. This was the risky first chapter of the voyage back to the Philippines. If he was ordered to stop by the harbor patrol before they got into international waters, he'd have a devil of a time explaining why Tony had no documentation.

The wind was light, and so Roy motored due south toward the South China Sea, figuratively crossing his fingers that they would not be pulled over by the Macao harbor patrol, or later by a Red Chinese gunboat.

There were a myriad of lights on the rolling sea—white, red, and green. He knew from his experience sailing here at night, in the busy shipping lanes, that a collision with an enormous container ship or supertanker was the greatest risk they faced once they were at sea. The two of them would stay alert, on the lookout for large ships passing in the night.

Roy lashed the tiller, hoisted the sails, and shut off the engine when they were abeam of Huangmao Island. He hollered to Tony, telling him he could come topside. No response. He was sound asleep.

The voyage from Macao to Negros Island was uneventful. Fine weather. No near collisions with any of the dozens of ships they passed. And they only ran out of food and drink after they arrived at their destination, ten days after departing from Macao.

Roy had taught Tony how to steer as they sailed on a straight course south-southeast, with the wind abeam, until they arrived at the south end of Palawan Island.

It was during the early morning of the second day of their voyage, as the two men lounged in the cockpit with mugs of Sumatra coffee, admiring the sunrise over the South China Sea, that Anthony D'Rosa revealed to Roy Mancini what he had been engaged in during the past eight years.

"I got a story to tell ya, Roy," said Tony.

Tony explained that in 1990 Vincent 'Chin' Gigante, also known as the Oddfather, the boss of the Genovese organized-crime family in New York, decided that *globalization* was the new name of the game.

"So he calls me to his office at the Triangle Social Club in Greenwich Village at two o'clock in the morning. We decided I would set up a Genovese family business in Asia. By the way, I was Chin's *capo*, you know."

"No shit!" Roy thought at first D'Rosa was trying to lighten up the voyage with a tall tale.

Tony explained, "Vicente played the part of the fool—walking around the Village during the day in his fuckin' bathrobe and mumbling to himself. That was all a ruse, to confuse the cops so they'd believe he was insane. He was anything but crazy. He'd done his market research."

Tony went on to explain that he and Gigante put their heads together during those early morning meetings at the Greenwich Village social club and concocted a plan. They would establish a shipping company in Hong Kong as a cover. The real business was to build factories in China and establish a supply chain for crystal methamphetamine and ecstasy for emerging markets throughout Southeast Asia. And the other New York families wouldn't know a thing about it because they'd a hire a wise guy from Sicily as their enforcer.

Methamphetamine used thirty chemical ingredients—all but one of them tightly regulated in the United States and elsewhere. But in China, none of it was controlled. And the Chinese government had no incentive to curb either the manufacture of the drugs or the export of the finished products. The environment was a mobster's paradise.

Tony moved to Macao and built meth and ecstasy labs in Guangxi, Yunnan, and Laos. He established his cover company, East Star Shipping Limited. The drugs were trucked from the factories north to Hong Kong. From there he shipped the meth and ecstasy on his own ships to Singapore and to the out ports in Southeast Asia. The mafia guy from Sicily oversaw the distribution of the drugs and collected the family's money in the Philippines, Singapore, Malaysia, Indonesia, and Thailand.

Chinese mobsters of the *Tiu Chiu* clan handled the local distribution and retailing. By 1997 the shipping and drugs operations were earning millions of dollars a month for the Genovese family, all of it laundered into offshore banks in the British Virgin Islands, Singapore and Hong Kong. And all of it was unknown to the other four Mafia families in New York. Gigante and D'Rosa had gone global and outsmarted everyone.

D'Rosa continued, "Now it's 1998 and there's the handover of Hong Kong from Britain to China. Coincidentally this year there's a fuckin' extradition treaty between the U.S. and Hong Kong that goes into effect. And the new chief of detectives in Hong Kong, a *Tiu Chiu* asshole, wants to take over my businesses, and he's aware of the legal problems I'd face if I was extradited to the United States. He'd done *his* research."

Tony told Roy a Genovese consigliere became an FBI informant and ratted on him in order to reduce his own prison term. So D'Rosa was now wanted by the Feds on a RICO beef plus murder charges. He whacked a DEA agent in Puerto Rico by mistake back in the eighties. He was looking at life in prison without parole.

The Hong Kong detective, a character named Liu Choy, traveled to Macao and met D'Rosa. He ordered Tony to sign over

East Star Shipping to his son, Liu Feng. He directed him to hand the drug factories in southern China over to his brother, Liu Ma. The *Tiu Chiu* distribution network was already in place.

And finally Liu Choy ordered Tony to stay forever out of Hong Kong. He made it clear to him that if he didn't play ball, D'Rosa would face arrest and extradition to the United States.

"My Sicilian enforcer, Bruno Cazadero, returned to Italy. Who knows what happened to that poor sap who took the pictures for me in Hainan."

Ten days before Roy picked up Tony in Macao, his apartment had been burglarized and his passport stolen. Liu Choy's handiwork. He was now stateless, though not penniless. And without a travel document, he couldn't leave. And finally, Portugal was to turn Macao over to China next year, in 1999. He'd be at the mercy of Liu's counterpart in the former Portuguese colony.

Vicente Gigante had been sent to prison for life. So Roy Mancini was Tony D'Rosa's only pal. And he'd needed Roy to get him out of Macao before the turnover to China.

"And so here we are, *paisano*. Cruising in the South China Sea together in a yacht. A new life!" Tony chuckled as he squinted at Roy.

"Ah, the fickle finger of fate." Roy shook his head in feigned disbelief.

Seven days later, off the tip of Palawan, Roy tacked the boat and sailed northeast into the pirate-infested waters of the Sulu Sea. He'd had the foresight to bring along a shotgun in the event they were attacked by Moro pirates—or worse, terrorists of the Abu Sayyaf group which had reared its ugly head and begun kidnapping foreigners for ransom. They managed to slip through undetected.

Tambobo Bay was a secluded and well-protected haven near the southern end of Negros Island in the Philippines where dozens of round-the-world sailing yachts found refuge from foul weather or anchored for R&R. The bay was populated with about twenty cruising sailboats when they arrived early in the morning. Roy had learned about the place from a skipper in San Francisco who'd sailed around the world and made it to safety in Tambobo Bay to avoid a typhoon.

Tony emerged from the cabin as they sailed from the Sulu Sea into the bay. He looked at the sailboats nearby and, for the first time during the voyage, had a cheerful smile on his face, a smile that exposed his set of large teeth.

"I'll never forget this, Roy. You saved me from a lotta hassle."

"A new life for you now, Tony. Meantime, you can live on the boat for a while and unwind. Figure out what you want to do next."

"Where are we again?"

"Tambobo Bay in Negros Oriental."

He looked around at the lush tropical shoreline that surrounded them on all sides of the bay. "I like it here," Tony remarked. "Let's make this work, Roy." Another toothy smile in his dark, unshaven face.

After anchoring *Mistral* in the bay, they sat in silence in the boat's cockpit with mugs of coffee, both men contemplating their futures.

The one benefit of being in Tambobo was that the bay was in the middle of nowhere. It was many miles south of Cebu. Odds were negligible that a Filipino immigration officer would make rounds among the sailboats at anchor. Tony could hide out on *Mistral* until Roy figured things out.

At last Roy made the decision to go all in and help his wayward friend. "All right. You've got a ten-day growth. I want you to grow a full beard. That could take a couple more weeks. Stay put on the boat. I'll go to the village later to buy groceries."

"Yeah, okay."

"We can't arrange a passport with your true name. Not with those federal indictments staring at you. I'll have to go to Manila to see what I can put together. Your makeover is going to cost you a lot of money, Tony. You're gonna need a new identity."

D'Rosa let a minute pass before he said, "I got a bank account in Singapore under a phony company. Name of the company is United Ship Chandlers, LLC. Vicente don't know nothin' about it. Anyway he's in the joint for the duration, so it don't matter."

"It's called a shell company."

"Whatever. No one knows about it except for me and that outfit in Panama that set it up."

"How much in the account?"

"About three million U.S. and change."

"You'll have to add my signature to that bank account so I can operate it."

"What the fuck?" He glared.

"Listen up. Because from here on you will no longer be Anthony D'Rosa from Brooklyn and you won't be taking a trip anytime soon to Singapore. You're gonna need someone to wire that money to you here in the Philippines. Unless you have someone else you can trust."

He interrupted, "Okay, okay. I get it. I write a letter to the law firm in Panama and to the bank in Singapore and put your name and signature on the account. You're gonna wire my money to me here. Right?"

"Yeah. You'll have a new name, a new passport, and a visa so you can retire here. The Philippines promotes retirement for rich foreigners like you. You'll have to prove you've got the money here in a bank. Under your new identity. And you gotta agree to make an investment in a small business."

Roy continued, "I'll sell you this boat, Tony, for what I paid for it. You'll need it to live on for a while."

"That's fair." Tony looked around again at the myriad craft at anchor. "Could be worse."

He grinned like a fat cat, reached into his backpack, and removed several large wads of hundred-dollar bills. "Here. I'll pay you for the boat now. How much I owe you?"

Roy raised his brows, dumbfounded by the amount of cash Tony laid out.

"What'd you imagine I had in this bag? Toothpaste and deodorant? It's my casino money." He laughed.

"Settle with me later."

The last thing Roy wanted was to walk around with thirty-thousand dollars in cash.

21

NEGROS ORIENTAL, PHILIPPINES
2003

S O NOW YOU KNOW ALL ABOUT AN EX-MAFIOSO KNOWN
as Anthony 'Tony Chops' D'Rosa." They were having breakfast on the patio at the seaside hotel in Dumaguete City.

"And his new name is . . . ?" Marc asked.

"I was about to get into that. It's Brewster Levey. Tony didn't
want an Italian name. He needed a complete makeover—new
name, new nationality, new passport, and a new look." He smiled
as he recalled the work he did five years earlier, creating the new
persona. Back then, Roy had had a discreet acquaintance in Manila, who had a contact who had another contact who specialized
in forged documents—drivers' licenses, national identity cards,
and passports. They negotiated the price (each middleman took a
cut) for a fresh Canadian passport. The intermediary passed Roy
the forger's requirements.

Next he had found a hairdresser in Dumaguete who agreed to
travel to Tambobo Bay to do a cosmetic restyling for Brewster.
She brought her equipment along to the boat and dyed his thick
beard black, cut his hair short, and dyed it to match. She shaved
his caterpillar brows to a normal length and likewise colored them
black. The scar on his face was hidden by the beard.

Roy made passport photos of the new Brewster Levey and delivered them to his contact in Manila. Within a week, he had an authentic Canadian passport, with entry and exit visas from around the region, valid for six more years.

Anthony D'Rosa had disappeared, never to return. All that remained was his Brooklyn accent. And Roy figured in this part of the world that defect would go unnoticed.

Brewster Levey, Canadian citizen, was about to take legal residence in the Philippines as a wealthy retiree. He opened an account in U.S. dollars with the local branch of the Bank of the Philippine Islands, where Roy wired his three million dollars from the bank in Singapore. Roy sold *Mistral* to him. And Brewster changed the name of the boat, at Roy's request, to *Jambalaya*.

At last, Roy Mancini said farewell to Brewster and left him to his own devices in Tambobo Bay. He returned to San Francisco to trade in coffee beans. He didn't expect to meet the fugitive former Mafioso ever again.

It had been five years. Roy learned from an officer at the local bank that Brewster Levey moved two years earlier to Apo Island, off the Negros Oriental coast, a few miles north of Tambobo. He'd set up a bar and a small scuba diving business on the island. Apo was a fish sanctuary with a reputation for having pristine diving conditions.

Roy explained his plan to Marc. "We'll hire a boat and have them take us to Apo. Looks like it would be about a thirty-minute ride in a *banca*."

"You've done your homework, Dad."

"I'm not leaving much to chance. I expect Brewster will recall the favor he owes me. No doubt it's still part of his Sicilian creed."

"Does he still have the boat, *Jambalaya*?"

"We shall soon see."

22

APO ISLAND, NEGROS ORIENTAL,
PHILIPPINES

THEY BOARDED A MOTORIZED *BANCA* AT A BEACH NEAR Zamboanguita, the shortest route to Apo Island. As the boat cut through the swells and got to within five miles of the island, Roy spotted a sailboat at anchor off the beach. He pointed at the yacht and directed the boatman to head for it. As they approached, Roy was now certain that it was the former *Mistral.* Soon he saw the name of the boat on the transom—*Jambalaya.*

Two astonishingly well-shaped, suntanned, and string-bikini-clad Filipino women emerged on deck and watched the boat approach. One of them called to someone inside the cabin when the boatman killed the engine and glided toward the yacht. Brewster Levey, shirtless, wearing shorts, dark glasses, and a cap with a logo of a red and green parrot labeled THE RUSTY PECKER, stepped into the cockpit.

He shaded his eyes in a salute for a moment. At last he hollered, "Hey, *paisano.* Is that you?"

"Yours truly," Roy called back.

"I figured this day would come." He laughed.

Brewster's long hair and full beard were now back to their natural white hue. His skin was tan and he was slimmer than Roy had ever seen him. The large teeth were well hidden behind the growth on his face.

"Meet my wives, Veronica and Sissy," he said as he threw a line to Marc. "Who's the stud with you?"

"My son, Marc."

"Well, hop aboard. Your *banca* can take the girls to the island, and we'll go sailing for the rest of the afternoon. You can tell me what you've been doing, Roy. And later, at the bar, we celebrate." Brewster pulled out a wad of *pesos* from his pocket, peeled off a few, and paid the *banca* driver. He gave instructions to the boatman in his Brooklyn-accented Cebuano dialect. The two young women, plausible beauty-contest winners, giggled and stepped off the yacht and into the outrigger. Marc and Roy hoisted themselves onto the sailboat.

The Mancinis were expert sailors. As they motored beyond the shallow reef Roy could see that Brewster had learned the ropes. They hoisted the two sails in seconds, cut the engine, and took off on a beam reach, heading around the island and south toward Mindanao.

"You've come a long way in five years. Fate has been kind," Roy said as Brewster handed him the wheel.

"Thanks to you, *paisano*."

"Careful Brew, you're gonna blow your cover with all that Italian lingo."

Brewster looked askance at Marc.

Roy said, "My son knows all about it. Don't worry."

The breeze was fresh, the noonday sun was high, and *Jambalaya* soared over the dark blue swells. When they were several miles south of Apo Island Roy turned the helm over to Marc and sat in the cockpit beside Brewster Levey.

"Good to see you, Roy. As you see, life has turned into a non-stop fiesta. I own a bar called the Rusty Pecker that keeps me busy enough. And I live on the boat with Veronica and Sissy." Brewster laughed and put his arm around his friend's shoulder. "Thanks to you, pal. You know, I should have done this many years ago."

"Brewster, I've got a favor to ask you," Roy said.

"Name it."

"You've heard about the Bali bombing last month?"

"Bombing? No, can't say I have. Didn't you have a home in Bali?" he asked. "I don't receive much news on Apo. No TV or newspapers. Which is okay with me. We have great scuba diving. What's it about?"

"A suicide bombing. There were scores of Americans killed in the blast and a lot of Indonesians, mainly Balinese. I lost two of my best friends."

"No shit!"

Roy explained what he knew about the terrorist bombing to Brewster before he made the request.

"You told me once that you had a tough Sicilian enforcer who worked for you back in the day."

Brewster frowned and glanced at Marc, who was concentrating on the boat's course.

"Marc's part of my plan," Roy explained.

"Yeah? Okay, what is it?" Brewster was obviously uncomfortable with Roy's reference to his earlier life and knowing that there were now *two* people in the world who knew his dual identities.

"You said you had one guy—the name was Bruno—who was especially good."

Brewster gave a wistful smile at the memory. "*Good* doesn't begin to describe Bruno. He was the best soldier I've ever known. I was sorry I had to send him back to Sicily when my Hong Kong businesses blew apart. In hindsight and for good measure, I should have ordered him to whack Liu Choy before we left town. What is it you need, Roy?"

"I need Bruno. I plan to kill the organizers of the bombing because the U.S. government refuses to do it. Can you arrange the contract?"

Brewster paused for a second. "The short answer is yes. I know how to contact Bruno if that's who you need. He's retired now in Catania. So fill me in."

Roy told Brewster he had arranged the secret intelligence and the funding for the operation. His son Marc would coordinate the mission and the "wet" work on the ground in Indonesia. They needed a professional assassin, Bruno, to make the hits. He'd work in-country with Marc.

Brewster asked, "Has anyone identified those terrorist fuckers?"

"No, not yet. That's *my* job. I suspect by the time you return from Sicily with Bruno I will be on my way to locating at least one of them."

Brewster removed his dark glasses and polished them with a cloth. He used the same cloth to wipe the sweat from his neck. He glanced again at Marc, who was listening while keeping the boat in perfect trim. He looked Roy in the eye and grinned. "*Paisano*, when I owe a guy a favor, I don't forget it. Let's talk about the details."

The specifics turned out to be pretty straightforward for old hands like Brewster Levey and Roy Mancini. Roy would pay Brewster Levey forty thousand per hit for a minimum of three kills. He was planning on four. Brewster would share his fee with Bruno, and he would cover Bruno's travel expenses. Roy's assumption was that the hitman would ask for ten thousand dollars, clear of expenses, for each guy he whacked. Roy would supply the weapon and communications equipment. Brewster told him Bruno's weapon of choice was a Beretta 9mm. Roy had anticipated an order for the Italian model.

Roy would pay Brewster twenty thousand dollars in advance of each hit. The balance was payable on photographic evidence of a dead terrorist. Brewster needed first to open an offshore bank account outside of the Philippines.

They decided to sail *Jambalaya* south the following week, through the Sulu Sea, to Labuan Island so as to avoid being traced through airports in the Philippines and Malaysia. Brewster had a new weapon, an assault rifle, locked aboard the sloop in the event they met pirates or Abu Sayyaf terrorists south of Mindanao. He'd traded in the shotgun.

Roy took the helm and sailed the boat back to Apo Island, giving Marc and Brewster time to get to know each other and discuss weapons.

When they arrived at Apo, and after turning the boat over to a couple of boat boys to de-rig, the three men climbed the stairs to the Rusty Pecker. They ordered San Miguel beers, smoked Alhambra cigars, and played a few rounds of liar's dice. The view from the bar was of the beach below and of the lush Negros mainland several miles to the west. Veronica and Sissy lit the men's cigars for them, served fresh mangoes and rambutan, and laughed at their jokes.

"If I'd known you were coming I would have prepared a *lechon*," Brewster commented as the Mancinis prepared to leave the island. He referred to the roasted pig that Filipinos feasted on during special occasions.

Before they left Apo, Roy told Brewster they'd return on Monday the following week. He should have the boat and provisions ready for the voyage to Labuan. "And Brewster, make sure you've got plenty of ammunition for that M-16 of yours. The sea to the south is patrolled by Abu Sayyaf. Kidnapping and ransoming Americans is how they make a living."

Brewster had purchased the rifle from a Filipino army officer who ran a black market weapons business in Cebu. Later in the week he would go to Cebu City and buy more ammunition. Marc was an excellent marksman, and of course the Marine Corps captain knew the M-16 like the proverbial back of his hand.

23

THE SULU SEA

THEY HOISTED ANCHOR AND GOT UNDERWAY ON *Jambalaya* at dawn for what they hoped would be an uneventful voyage south to Labuan Island in Malaysia. After rounding the southern tip of Negros Island, the course took them southwest across the Sulu Sea. This was not only the most direct route to Labuan, it also avoided the west coast of Mindanao and the islands of the southern Philippines—Basilan and Jolo—which were the homes of the Abu Sayyaf group.

The group was not to be confused with run-of-the-mill pirates. It was notorious for terrorist bombings, kidnappings of Westerners, multi-million-dollar ransom demands, and beheadings with bolo knives for fun and profit. If you were captured by this evil terrorist group of the Philippines, you could kiss goodbye any notion of Filipino hospitality. Your chances of getting out alive were worse than fifty-fifty. The group had fraternal ties to the Indonesian terrorist organization Jamaah Islamiyah, the prime suspects in the Bali bombing.

As they sailed across the Sulu Sea they encountered few craft. The wind was fresh and the boat made good time. All in all, it was a pleasant cruise on the deep blue sea and under clear or star-lit skies.

Marc and Brewster got to know, and trust, each other. The three shared the helm and a lot of laughs. They had good stories to tell—Brewster about the capers of the former Brooklyn Mafi-oso, Tony D'Rosa, and the hedonistic life of the fugitive Brewster Levey in the Visayan Islands, and Marc about his months of fight-ing the Taliban in Helmand. Roy told the story about the late Komang and Putu Surya and how they thwarted a terrorist attack by Wadi Haddad of the Democratic Front for the Liberation of Palestine. This carefree good vibe ended when *Jambalaya* passed Balabac Island at the southern end of Palawan.

It was nine o'clock in the morning. Roy was steering the boat and saw the fast-moving forty-foot craft first. Marc was catnap-ping below after driving the yacht for the previous six hours, Brewster was busy viewing porn on a laptop computer.

"Brew, call Marc. Fast. Have him grab the M-16 and the ammo." Roy pointed at the approaching craft. The boat was a motorized outrigger, a *banca*, which was used for fishing in those waters. This one, it was apparent, had a powerful engine. She was approaching at twenty knots.

Marc rushed out of the cabin and into the cockpit with the assault rifle. The *banca* was less than a mile away, off the star-board beam.

"You both go below," Marc ordered as he took the wheel from his father. At this point he was in command. He would shoot first and explain later. The two jumped into the cabin where Brewster opened his combination safe and removed a Glock 9mm handgun. Roy looked at him in surprise.

"I've had this with me all along. I never told you. I wasn't going to let those Chinese bastards in Macao catch me and send me back. It would have been me or them. You'd better stay below if you're not armed." He checked the gun's magazine before climbing the ladder to the cockpit.

Before Brewster lifted his head through the cabin entrance, Marc let loose with the M-16 on full automatic.

"One down," Marc shouted. "Nailed the helmsman. Stay below. They're armed."

At that instant an attacker shot at the sailboat, hitting the hull, the mast and the top of the cabin with semi-automatic fire. Marc, crouching inside the cockpit, took aim and fired back, this time on the semi-automatic setting. He grabbed another thirty-round magazine and deftly inserted it. He fired a burst. "Two in the water."

Brewster was now squatting beside Marc, aiming his Glock at the *banca*. They fired together.

"And that makes three," Marc said in a calm voice.

Roy couldn't resist. He climbed the ladder so that he could take in the action as Marc let loose with a burst. The *banca* was 100 meters away when it executed an abrupt change of course. Marc continued to fire on semiautomatic. He hit the *banca's* new helmsman in the back, between his shoulder blades. The motor boat, now out of control, steered itself in a large circle.

"Stay down," Marc ordered. "I'm not sure I've finished 'em off."

Finally they saw the *banca* hold its course and head due north, in the direction of Balabac Island.

Marc placed the M-16 on a cushion, took the wheel and main sheet, and adjusted the course due south. "There's blood in the water. Two of them fell over the side. Shark bait," he said as he trimmed the mainsail.

Brewster and Roy looked back at the retreating boat. The two ASG terrorists had sunk beneath the swells, to be devoured by hammerhead sharks.

The rest of the voyage, along the west coast of Sabah, Malaysia went without incident. Brewster and Roy looked on Marc with new respect. It was one thing to listen to him tell war stories, it was quite another to see him in action.

They sailed into the Labuan marina five days after departing Apo Island. Roy paid one week in advance for a dockside mooring. They agreed Marc would sleep on the boat at night. Brewster and Roy would move into a hotel downtown and remain until they finished the business of registering a shell company and opening two bank accounts.

24

LABUAN ISLAND, MALAYSIA

ROY HAD GOOGLED THE ACCOUNTING FIRMS ON Labuan Island and studied the websites for three of them. He selected William Ong & Sons because he liked the idea of a guy who worked with his sons.

While Brewster and Marc explored the attractions on Labuan Island together the next morning, Roy met Mr. Ong Sr. He wished to register an offshore company in Labuan and he needed Ong's firm to act as nominee—as shareholders and directors. Although Roy Mancini was the beneficial owner of the company, and the only person authorized to operate the company's bank account, he did not want his name to appear on the corporate documents. Confidential arrangements like this were the reason Ong & Sons, and tax havens like Labuan for that matter, existed. And Ong would also handle the accounting. Though, at the end of the year, the account was expected to simply show money coming in and money going out. Labuan bank secrecy was sacrosanct. And the tax rate on profits was three percent.

"So Mr. Mancini, what would you like to name your new company?" Old Man Ong, who appeared to be in his eighties, was taking notes. He had asked his oldest son, Reginald, to join them in the conference room. They both drank tea while Roy had coffee.

"We'll name the company Allegheny Resources Limited. We're consultants, and we plan to have all our offshore income deposited here in Labuan. Are there reputable Swiss banks on the island?"

"Oh yes. Each of the large Swiss banks has a branch here. Reginald can make some calls and set up appointments for you after we complete the paperwork." The son cocked his head but said little in the presence of his father.

Roy did not wish to reveal any more of his personal life to William and Reginald than he had to. There was no need for the Ongs to know anything about his coffee business or where he lived. They only needed to copy a page from his passport for the record. At least in theory, the government of Malaysia left Labuan Island alone so it could present itself as a bona fide tax haven and free trade zone. Ong said he would expedite the company registration, and they'd be ready to do business in three days.

In the meantime, Brewster Levey opened his personal numbered U.S. Dollar account at the same Swiss bank where Roy planned to open ARL's company account. Money transfers from the company to Brewster would therefore be quick, seamless and secure. Four days later, Allegheny Resources Limited was registered and both bank accounts on the island were live.

Roy used one of his prepaid 'burn' phones to call Walter Sarkies. Their code for the request for funds was simple. He perused that day's NASDAQ stock quotes and looked for one of the surviving dotcom companies that had a share price somewhere in the eighties. The company Roy selected, Comstar, sold that day for $83 per share. His call to Sarkies was brief.

"Buy two hundred shares of Comstar." He disconnected.

Walter Sarkies would check the quote in the Wall Street Journal for Comstar and know the request was for eighty thousand dollars per kill. Roy had added forty thousand per hit to cover expenses.

Five days later there was a deposit of eighty thousand dollars to the ARL account at the Swiss bank in Labuan. The sender was a shell company in Antigua: Livestock International LLC. Livestock International was a conduit for black money controlled by the director of *VEVAK*, the Iranian Ministry of Intelligence.

The same day, Roy transferred twenty thousand dollars to Brewster Levey's numbered account at the bank. And Brewster booked his first class flight from Labuan to Rome on Malaysia Airlines using one of the prepaid credit cards that Roy sold to him. He left for Italy the day before Marc and his father departed Labuan Island in *Jambalaya*.

The one-week voyage to Apo Island gave Marc and Roy time to review, revise, and war game *Operation Java Sea*. And it gave the father an opportunity to get acquainted again with his oldest son. Marc had been absent from his life for most of the past nine years—the four years at the Naval Academy in Annapolis, and another five when he'd been deployed on the east coast and overseas in the Marine Corps. In the meantime, he'd grown from a cocky high school boy into a mature, independent, and self-confident young man. Roy could not have had a better partner. And the chemistry seemed right, to use Marc's own metaphor.

Marc and Roy parted at the airport in Cebu. Marc returned to Malacca, where he would await further instructions.

Roy flew to Bali, with a layover in Singapore. Sarkies had asked him to drop in at the *Institute's* office in Singapore and meet the commander, an Air Force major named Sullivan. Sullivan would pass him a decoded document: a copy of the letter of introduction to Major General Ida Agung of the Indonesian National

Police. A petite woman, a Navy chief petty officer, greeted him in the embassy lobby and asked to see a photo ID. She handed him a sealed envelope. The woman seemed as bemused as Roy by Sullivan's refusal to meet him and by his peculiar order to hand the TOP SECRET document to him in the lobby.

25

BALI

A YEAR HAD PASSED SINCE ROY LAST STAYED IN BALI. He took a taxi from the airport and passed through Nusa Dua. The impression was surreal, though by now the smoke and stench from the bombing had dissipated. After thirty minutes, the taxi turned into the road that ran along the verdant ten-acre rice field and to the villa. The staff had heard the car approach, and they were waiting for him at the opened gate. Their smiles—infectious.

The next morning Roy phoned the number that had been listed in Sarkies' document: the direct line in Bali for General Agung. An aide answered and asked what his business was. He replied to him in Indonesian and gave him his name. He told the aide the call was personal. He was put on hold for five minutes, five minutes that seemed like half an hour. At last Agung came on the line.

He spoke fluent English. "Yes, Mr. Mancini. You've arrived in Bali?"

"General, I know you are busy with your investigation. I don't want to take too much of your time. Whenever it would be convenient to . . ."

Agung interrupted, "I *am* busy and I depart for Jakarta this afternoon for meetings. I received Walter's email and a phone call. So perhaps we can meet after I return. I'll be back in Bali on Friday. Let's pencil in a meeting for Friday night at eight-thirty."

"That would be fine, General. I'll meet you at eight-thirty, Friday night."

"My aide says you speak fluent Indonesian. Is that correct?"

"My mother is Indonesian. I spoke the language with her growing up," Roy replied.

There was a pause before the general continued. "Interesting. Do you know my office address?"

"Yes, sir. It is listed here on my copy of Walter Sarkies' email."

"Then we will meet here in my office. I'll tell my people to expect you. Good-bye, Mr. Mancini."

Roy passed the next three days inside the villa, much of that time in his office. There was, for one thing, the coffee bean business to run. His company, Coffee Traders International, had containers of premium Arabica beans loading that week in Belawan and Makassar and dozens of containers being discharged in Seattle, New Orleans, New York, and Rotterdam. He was on the phone continually with Lorenzo and Cynthia in San Francisco, and with Marc and the purchasing staff in Malacca. Due to time differences, emails were sent and received twenty-four hours a day. And he waited for a call from Brewster Levey to his "burner" cell phone.

The phone rang at six a.m. on Friday. There were only three persons who knew the number—Brewster Levey, Walter Sarkies, and Marc. There was no caller ID.

"Hello."

"It's me," Brewster said in a low voice. "Bruno and I are in Rome."

That was all he needed to know. Bruno was in. "See you soon." Roy said, and disconnected.

26

BALI

ROY RODE IN THREE TAXIS, AS HE ENGAGED IN ACTIVE counter-surveillance around the byways of Denpasar for an hour before arriving at General Agung's office at 8:20 p.m. on Friday. The office was located inside the National Police Headquarters of Bali.

A series of security guards rifled through Roy's briefcase and studied his passport, matching his photo to his face, before he was escorted to an office at the back of the building. The general's aide, a lieutenant colonel, met him outside the door. He greeted Roy in Indonesian.

Agung stood as Roy entered the room. A severe, dark-complexioned officer stood beside the general's large mahogany desk. The three shook hands, and the general introduced Roy to Colonel Hotman Pardede. The colonel, because of his slanting eyes, could have been mistaken for Chinese.

Agung was slim, of medium height and athletic. He appeared much younger than his rank would indicate. He had smooth, light brown skin, clear, alert eyes, and a smile that radiated kindness. Right away Roy was at ease.

"I am going to suggest, Mr. Mancini, that we speak Indonesian so Colonel Hotman can join our conversation. All right with you?"

Roy replied in Indonesian. "Yes. That would be fine."

Colonel Hotman had yet to crack a smile or say a word. He was muscular, had a severe demeanor, and a glare that appeared menacing. His sinister bearing was the antithesis of General Agung's warmth.

"Colonel Hotman is my senior officer investigating the bombing." The colonel and Roy looked at each other without expression.

The general continued, "Are you familiar with the *Batak* people, Mr. Mancini?"

"Not really." Roy had heard of them. He knew they were a tribe that inhabited the land surrounding the Sumatran coffee plantations.

"Colonel Hotman Pardede is a *Batak*," Agung stated.

"All right." He didn't know yet where this was going.

"The *Bataks* are a distinct ethnic group in Indonesia. Most of them, like Hotman, are Christians. They come from the area near Lake Toba in North Sumatra."

"I know the area," said Roy.

The two policemen glanced at each other. "We need to take a short ride and talk. Have you been to Ubud?" Agung asked.

"I have, General. It's been a while."

"That is my home, though I have not lived there for several years. Still . . ." Agung motioned to Hotman that it was time to move.

The three of them left through a backdoor. A civilian sedan was parked in the shadows beneath an acacia tree. Hotman got behind the wheel and started the engine. Agung invited Roy to join him in the back. They drove off and were soon lost in Denpasar's dense Friday night traffic.

Agung looked straight ahead. "Walter Sarkies phoned me

soon after he sent his email about your visit. Our discussion was confidential, outside official channels. I will not describe to you how Sarkies and I manage that. He's a shrewd operator. Suffice to say that he and I have had occasional private conversations over the years."

Roy was listening. Agung must have noticed him frown when he glanced toward Hotman.

Agung caught Roy's expression. "Colonel Hotman is privy to everything I will discuss with you tonight."

"Right."

Agung continued speaking, looking ahead. "Sarkies and I agree on at least one thing. President Hartono won't prosecute, to the full extent of the law, the terrorists who murdered so many of your countrymen . . . and mine. She will not, for political reasons, wish to alienate the Islamists. The effort to crack this case will be no more robust that it was in solving the eighteen Christmas Eve church bombings three years ago.At worst, she will order the plotters be jailed after they are found. And they will be found. You get my point?" He looked at Roy as he said this.

They drove north toward Ubud in silence for several minutes. Roy sensed Agung was weighing what to say next, and in spite of Sarkies' assurance, the Balinese was questioning whether or not he could trust the American.

"Why are you here in Bali, Mr. Mancini?"

Now it was Roy's turn to figure how much he could reveal to the general. This had the feeling of a veritable first date. "I am here, General Agung, to make sure those plotters get what they deserve, more than a slap on the wrist. I am *not* here to interfere with your investigation. I hope we can work together . . . share what we learn with each other."

"And you plan to be prosecutor and executioner?" He knew more than Roy imagined he did.

Colonel Hotman snickered. The rearview mirror showed him smiling maliciously, his eyes mere slits.

"In a manner of speaking," Roy replied.

"You know I am Balinese. May I call you Roy?"

"Please do."

"This bombing was an attack on Bali, Roy. Your people also suffered and were murdered mercilessly. But those jihadists targeted Bali as though we were an enemy nation. Indonesians, including many Balinese, were killed and many burned beyond recognition in the bombing. Can you appreciate my anger?"

"General, I lost two of my best friends. They too were Balinese. Putu and Komang Surya of Amed. Perhaps that is the real reason, the personal reason, I am here. Their murder is not an abstraction."

Agung showed surprise. "I knew Putu and Komang!" He now looked Roy in the eye. "They did not deserve to die like that."

"Of course not."

"And your government, your president, has been ordered by our president not to interfere. A pity. I might have benefitted from the National Security Agency and the FBI laboratory. Alas, we Indonesians object to any hint of neocolonialism. The Dutch were not kind to us. Good riddance. Hartono loathes the idea of American interference. My task is to solve the crime with no help from the outside."

"I assure you, General, my plan is not sanctioned by my government. To the contrary. This is a private enterprise."

"Can you be more specific?"

It was now crunch time. Time for Roy to lay his cards on the table. He hesitated for several seconds before he spoke. "I am putting together a team that will locate and identify the terrorists who plotted the bombing."

"And then?"

"My team will turn them into martyrs."

"A fitting understatement," Agung said in English. Hotman glared into the rearview mirror. Roy turned to look at the General. They both smiled.

"Can we work together?" Roy finally asked.

"Not directly. In fact, today will be the first and last day that we ever meet. If any foreigners are caught participating in your project here in Indonesia, I will have no choice but to have them arrested and incarcerated. Is that clear?"

Roy waited for what was coming next. The tension inside the car was palpable. Hotman was gripping the steering wheel with both hands.

Agung continued. "You will coordinate with Colonel Hotman and communicate only with him. Of course he will report to me. We will share intelligence when we can."

Agung saw the expression of displeasure on Roy's face when he said he needed to work with Hotman.

"Let me explain something," Agung said. "I mentioned the Christmas Eve terrorist bombings in the year 2000. We have proof that those bombings were plotted by Al Qaeda's affiliate in Indonesia, *Jamaah Islamiyah*. In a matter of a few hours on Christmas Eve, several churches, Catholic and Protestant, in eight different cities in Indonesia, were bombed. Many Indonesians were killed or seriously injured. Hotman lost his father, sister, and brother, all murdered, after jihadists planted a bomb in the HKBP Protestant church in Medan, Sumatra."

Roy heard Hotman utter a hoarse curse. He now understood why Agung had selected the *Batak* as his senior aide in the investigation.

"The bombers have never been apprehended. Their ringleader, Abu Najib, was tried and found not guilty. Not so much as a slap on the wrist."

"A clash of civilizations," Roy remarked in English, loud enough for Agung to hear him.

"Rather a clash within a civilization. And we must put a stop to it if Indonesia is to survive as one nation. We have no choice. I do not want to see my country suffer the same fate as the former Yugoslavia or become a radical Islamist state. We must cut off the snake's head."

They had arrived at the outskirts of Ubud. On either side of the road there were vast rice fields, fertile and ripe for harvest, and magnificent Hindu temples of various sizes. The real Bali, a land of peace.

Agung ordered Hotman to turn around and drive back to Denpasar.

"Tell me how this will work," Roy said. "I will work with the colonel. Where do we begin? This is your turf, General Agung."

The general didn't answer for several seconds. At last he looked at the American and revealed a late development. "Two days ago a farmer discovered an axle in the middle of his rice field. Had he not been harvesting his rice crop, we may never have found it this soon. The axle was over a hundred meters from the road. It was from the van. I will let Colonel Hotman explain. You two may as well learn to speak with each other."

"Hotman, tell Mr. Mancini what we discovered."

"The van's VIN. Imprinted on the axle," Hotman explained.

"The Vehicle Identification Number?"

"Yes," the colonel answered. "This week we traced records for the VIN and discovered where the vehicle was last sold. The seller is in Surabaya. A car repair shop. Tomorrow we will raid the place and I will interrogate the owner. We will fly to Surabaya tonight and I will lead the raiding party in the morning." As Hotman spoke, his lips and eyes were as cold and intense as they had been all night. A panther relishing the kill.

"Colonel, give Mr. Mancini his phone," Agung told Hotman.

The colonel opened the glove compartment and withdrew a cell phone. He glanced at it and handed it over his shoulder to Roy.

"This is the only phone you will use in Indonesia to communicate with Colonel Hotman. You speed dial him by pressing number three. The phone's SIM card is not traceable and it has been anonymously activated. Have no fear. Only Hotman and I know the number." He withdrew a scrap of notepaper from a pocket. "We are entering perilous territory, Mr. Mancini. Were it not for my trust in Walter Sarkies, we would not be discussing this. You do know the danger you are putting yourself in by running your operation in my country? Killers and drug dealers face the death penalty in Indonesia. I will not be able to help you if you are caught."

There was nothing to say in response.

"Oh, and one other thing. Walter needs you to transmit a photograph of each terrorist killed. You are to transmit the picture to Hotman after the execution. I will forward the photo to Walter. Clear?"

"Understood," Roy answered.

"All right. We'll drop you off on a side street in Denpasar. You are to remain in Bali for now. Hotman will phone you next week. He will inform you about the results of the raid in Surabaya. I don't believe you and I have any reason to meet each other again."

"I do need the phone number for the *buyer* of the van," Roy said. "I am working with a private contractor who will use it to locate the terrorist."

Roy looked into the rearview mirror, and for the first time that night, he saw the colonel grin. "I will inform you," Hotman said as he raised his own cell phone.

Hotman pulled over to the side of the road. Roy turned to Agung. "Thank you, General. I won't disappoint you."

Agung nodded and continued looking straight ahead. Roy got out of the car and watched as they drove off and were lost in traffic. He walked the streets for twenty minutes before hailing a taxi and returning to the villa after midnight.

27

COLONEL HOTMAN PARDEDE SPEARHEADED THE RAID on the car repair and body shop the following morning. His unit consisted of six black-clad commandos, comparable to an American SWAT team. They had hidden in the squalid neighborhood and kept the facility under surveillance since an hour before sunrise. Workers arrived at the shop at seven a.m. At 8:15 the Chinese manager arrived. He honked his car's horn twice and the front gate opened. The gate was closed right after he drove his late model Toyota inside.

Ten minutes later Hotman gave the order. The team's armored personnel carrier drove to the gate and blasted its horn several times. A bewildered security guard opened the gate and the unit's vehicle roared inside. Hotman led the six commandos, each carrying an assault weapon, inside a one story building. Colonel Hotman removed his black ski mask and marched into the owner's office. He pointed his rifle at the seated man with one hand and held his policeman's identification card before him with the other. He ordered the terrified boss to place both of his hands on the desk.

Hotman sneered at the man. "Let's make this quick, or I blow your head off. The white Mitsubishi van, the L-300, you sold on the third of February. Who did you sell it to?"

"How would I know . . . I don't. . ." That was as far as he got. Hotman raised his leg, placed his boot on the edge of the desk and shoved hard. The heavy hardwood table thrust into the man's midsection causing him to lurch backward, crack the back of his head against a wall, and fall to the floor.

Hotman stepped around the desk and stood over the man, a foot on either side of his head. He pointed his rifle at the man's face. "Call for the vehicle's paperwork. Now!" he ordered.

"Yes . . . yes, sir. Please, I beg you, don't point your gun like that. Call my secretary. What is this about? We run an honest business here." The man was terrified, his speech disoriented.

A petrified Chinese secretary, also Chinese, was led into the office at gunpoint by a team member.

"Tell her," Hotman ordered. "The Mitsubishi L-300 you sold on the third of February."

"Evi, find the paperwork. Early February. Did we sell a van to someone?"

There was a pause. "Yes, sir. I remember a man bought a Mitsubishi van that month. He paid cash. I made the deposit to the bank the same day." The frightened woman went to a filing cabinet along the wall and opened the bottom drawer. She thumbed through files and folders and removed some papers.

"Here." She started to hand the documents to her boss, who was now allowed to stand beside his desk.

Hotman intercepted them. "I'll take those."

He spread the papers out on the desk and compared the VIN on the document with the one found on the axle in the rice field. They matched. He pointed. "Was this the buyer?"

Both the secretary and the owner looked at the name. The woman replied, "Yes, sir. I remember. He's the one, Mr. Jeko."

"Jeko Rusdiana? And this is his home address, in Madura?" Hotman asked as he pointed again at the document.

"Yes, sir. It matched his KTP."

"Did you make a copy of his KTP? I don't see it here." Hotman referred to the national identity card that Indonesians had to carry with them at all times.

She replied, "I remember he asked us not to copy it. And because he paid in cash I thought that would not be a problem."

"It is a problem. You are in violation of the law. I don't see his phone number here. Where is it?" Hotman growled. He glared at the secretary and then at the owner.

"Wait, wait. Now I remember," the Chinese man said, shaking. "We needed to do some minor work on the engine before we could release the vehicle. I told Mr. Jeko that I would phone him when it was ready for him. He paid a small deposit. Evi?" The woman nodded and appeared ready to cry.

"So, where's the phone number?"

"If it's not with the papers, I will have to see if I still have it. Can you please tell me what this is about?"

"Do what you're told and stay out of prison. Same goes for her. You had better pray to God you find that phone number."

The trembling owner and woman searched through the desk drawers. Meanwhile, five masked members of the team kept a close eye on the shop's workers, who stood together in the yard, and guarded the gate to make sure no one attempted to make a hasty exit.

"I've found it." The owner held a stained and wrinkled piece of scratch paper in his fingers. "Yes, it has the initials JR written on it. This is the one." He handed the piece of paper to Hotman, who slipped it into a vest pocket.

"All right . . . Sugianto?"

"Yes, sir. That is my name. Sugianto."

"You don't mention what happened this morning to *anyone*."

"Yes, of course." The two Chinese replied in near unison.

"If you do, I will find out. And going to prison will be the least of your and Miss Evi's worries." Hotman glared at both of them with a fearsome expression on his dark face.

Colonel Hotman left the office without another word. He told his men to board the personnel carrier and ordered the guard to open the gate. The national police vehicle took off along the road at high speed.

Hotman sat in the front seat of the speeding personnel carrier and used a secure phone to call General Agung in Bali.

"Sir, I request you order a speed boat. The buyer lives on Madura. We're finished with the body shop." Hotman referred to the large island to the northeast of Surabaya.

The general replied, "Go to the police dock. Have one of your men drive the boat to Madura. Don't involve the Surabaya police. The VIN matched?"

"Affirmative."

"I'll arrange two Jeeps for you in Madura. They'll be at the dock. Phone me as soon as you find him. Arrest and interrogate everyone there. No mercy."

"Understood, sir."

Two hours later, after the boat ride across the narrow strait that separates Java from Madura, Hotman's two police Jeeps arrived at the van buyer's address in the outskirts of the town of Bangkalan. As one, the six commandos pulled their ski masks back on.

The house was a dilapidated one story affair. The front door was ajar. A rooster and a small flock of chickens scurried around in the dirt yard. An elderly woman, her head covered with a *hijab,* squatted on a stool beside the house and hand-washed garments in a plastic bucket. There were near-identical dwellings on either side of the Rusdiana residence.

The commandos disengaged safeties from their assault rifles

as they spread out and surrounded the house. The terrified washer-woman stood, tripped, fell, got up, and finally ran away. Hotman kicked the front door open and entered the house with two subordinates behind him.

"Show yourself," he shouted.

A reed-thin, barefoot, middle-aged woman adorned with a *hijab* covering her hair and neck and a long, faded batik robe emerged with a slight limp from a bedroom. A skinny, teenage boy with wet hair, wearing a sarong and carrying a bath towel, stepped out of the bathroom. On seeing the armed commandos pointing weapons at them, the two raised their hands in alarm. The woman screamed. Two commandos rushed into the bedrooms and the bathroom and shouted that the rooms were clear.

Hotman swept his weapon at the boy and at the woman. "Jeko Rusdiana! Where is he?"

Neither replied. They stared, petrified, at the menacing weapons and the masked man in black who threatened them. Hotman approached the woman, his mask six inches from her face. "Speak to me," he ordered as he raised his policeman's ID in the space between their faces.

"He is not here," she wailed.

"*Where is he?*" Hotman grabbed the base of the woman's *hijab*. She dropped her hands and held on to it.

"He disappeared. Long ago."

"When?"

"January, sir."

"And you are?" Hotman released the woman's garb.

"I am Jeko's mother. He's gone away. I don't know where. He doesn't call me. What has happened to my son?"

Hotman ordered a commando to take the woman into a bedroom and hold her there. He approached the shaking boy. "Who are you?"

"Abdul, sir," the boy stammered.

"And you know Jeko?"

"My brother."

"Where is he?" Hotman lowered his rifle, pointing it at the floor in front of the boy's bare feet.

"As Mother said. He left the house three months ago. We haven't heard from him. Mother is worried. What has he done, sir?"

"I ask the questions, boy. Where is he?" The colonel lowered his voice.

"Nobody knows. He left the house one morning, early, before we were awake. That was the last we saw him."

Hotman Pardede sensed Jeko's mother, and perhaps the brother, were telling the truth. Nevertheless, he intended to show firmness. An idea came to mind. He went to the open cooking area, searched the drawers, and found a long carving knife.

"Grab the camera. It's in the second Jeep," he ordered one of the men standing guard outside. "Bring it to the woman's bedroom. Move!"

Hotman strode into the bedroom holding the twenty-inch knife before him. "You have a choice, woman. Tell us where Jeko is now! You lie to me and you will lose your fingers, one at a time, until you tell the truth." He motioned toward the commando who was holding the mother to her chair. "Tie her down."

The woman shrieked.

"Gag her."

When the woman was tied to her chair, Hotman stood in front of her and stared into her eyes through the slits in his mask. He removed the gag. "Again, where is he?"

"I beg you, don't hurt me," she cried. "I am telling you all I know. Jeko left the house in January. No one in the village has seen him since."

"Focus on her," Hotman ordered and gestured toward the woman.

Hotman waited a moment until the commando had the camera pointed at the woman. He rushed forward, grabbed the woman's *hijab* in his left hand, and bent her head backward, baring her long, thin neck. He aimed the point of the carving knife in his right hand at her throat. "Now," he ordered the commando with the camera. He heard the camera click four times. The woman screamed and twisted her body. Hotman released her and she fell to the floor.

"I will not hesitate to behead you. Where is your son?"

"Please have pity, sir. My Jeko is not a bad man. What do you want him for? What has he done?" She cried hysterically.

Hotman stared at the woman. He did something unexpected. He knelt, removed his mask and put his face within inches of the woman's tear-stained face. He said in a low voice, "We are taking Abdul. When your mind is clear and you remember where Jeko told you he was going, we will return Abdul to you." He ordered two commandos to grab the boy from his bedroom. He thrust a card at her. There was a number printed on it. "Phone this number when you are ready to talk to me."

Hotman suspected the woman was clueless as to Jeko's whereabouts. He had accomplished what he needed—the photograph of the terrified woman at knifepoint. He was unsure of the younger brother's involvement in the bombing. They would interrogate the boy during the return trip across the water to Surabaya. And scare the shit out of him.

28

ROY HAD TAKEN A SWIM AT THE VILLA AND WAS EATING a spicy lunch poolside beneath a large shade umbrella when he received the text message on the clandestine Indonesian cell phone. It relayed a phone number: 08172546872. The message was sent by Hotman Pardede. This was the cell phone number of the person who last purchased the van, the first step in locating Roy's initial target for interrogation and assassination.

As they did not have secure, fire-walled communications, Jack Chapman and Roy had established a code. The email Roy sent, minutes after receiving the text from Hotman, informed Jack he would buy his club membership for $2,546. That gave him the middle four numbers for the bomber's cell phone. The following day he reminded Jack that he owed $872. On the third day his email stated that he could deduct $55 from the debt, and that spelled $817. They both knew that the first digit for an Indonesian cell phone number was 0. In three days, Jack had the jihadist's phone number. He would pass that number to his brother, Bill.

Locating the jihadist's phone and installing spyware would be child's play for Bill Chapman and his team at the NSA. His unit, the Signals Intelligence Directive, would need to be circumspect in regard to "need-to-know." The few in-the-know would be told by Bill that the phone tracking in Indonesia was part of an ultra-secret mission, and that compartmentalization was vital. In other words, just another day at the office for the SID.

Jack Chapman would surreptitiously relay Bill's discovery to Roy. He would research the location of the phone provided by his brother and devise a plausible business reason for Roy's team to visit the place. If the location grew coffee beans, the team would have a legitimate interest in making contacts in the area. If the place produced something other than coffee, well, Jack knew Roy desired to diversify his business into other areas.

Four days after sending the coded phone number to Jack, Roy received two messages. The first was a text on his burn phone from Hotman. It contained two words: *Jeko Rusdiana*. There was a photo attachment which Roy thumbed open. Again, two words: *His mother*. The photograph was of a terrified woman, wide-eyed and in the throes of a scream. She was being held by an unidentified man in a black uniform. Another man in black held the point of a long kitchen knife against the woman's throat.

The email sent by Jack Chapman said:

Regarding your desire to engage in the teak garden furniture business, suggest you source products in KLATEN in Central Java. (Signed) JC.

So Jeko Rusdiana, the buyer of the van, was hiding in a place called Klaten. Roy found it on the map. The town was to the northeast of Jogjakarta, and near the base of the most active vol-cano in Indonesia, Mount Merapi. It was due east from the famed tourist destination, the Borobudur Temple. He concocted two credible cover stories for his team: tourism and teak. Roy imagined himself joining Marc and Bruno and participating in the interro-gation of Jeko Rusdiana. He would nevertheless remain in the background, in support, and provide the photo of the bomber, his mother, the top secret SID intelligence, and the money for the enterprise.

Roy had decided not to provide meaningful intelligence to General Agung. He did not want to risk having Agung and Hot-man Pardede compromised and subject to prosecution by their own government. Second, he didn't wish to have the bombers arrested, tried in a court of law, and given commuted sentences. In fact, he was not certain Agung didn't have that in mind from the beginning, that he would use Roy as an asset to augment his legitimate intelligence operations. He would keep General Agung at arm's length. Over the years Roy had learned, often the hard way, not to trust anyone outside of the Suryas and his immediate family.

29

LABUAN ISLAND, MALAYSIA

ROY HAD PONDERED OVER THE PAST WEEK ABOUT where to headquarter *Operation Java Sea*. A large city in Asia was out of the question. He needed someplace mid-sized where he could blend in, be inconspicuous. He decided to settle where he was unknown, on Labuan Island. He had the new company, Allegheny Resources Limited, if anyone were to ask why he was hanging around. And he liked the place.

Roy left a sealed letter with Malaysian Airlines addressed to Brewster Levey at the Kuala Lumpur International Airport, listing Levey's flight number and date of arrival on the envelope. He and Bruno were flying first class, and the letter would be delivered to Brewster on arrival. In the letter, Roy told him they would meet in Labuan, and he gave him the name of the hotel. Brewster and Bruno would need to amend their onward bookings with the airline.

The four men arrived on the island the same day, a Sunday, within six hours of each other. Marc and Roy were in the lobby of the Palm Beach Resort when the two wise guys walked in. Bruno appeared to be out of central casting for *Goodfellas*. He was well over six feet tall, built like a brick wall, with an olive complexion. He had an unsmiling, tough-guy visage, and gave the impression that he was casing the joint, searching for cops and the nearest exit. He carried his and Brewster's bags in his large hands—hands to kill with.

Brewster had explained that Bruno spoke just enough English to give orders to the *Tiu Chiu* mobsters he had supervised in their drug trade.

Roy had selected the resort because of the beach, where they could talk with some privacy. After checking in, Brewster and Bruno met Roy and Marc at the seashore.

Brewster spoke a mix of English and Sicilian when he introduced his former soldier. Bruno gave Roy a tight smile and held out his hand for him to shake. Next he turned to Marc and shook hands. A man of few words.

"We'll speak English now, Bruno," Brewster said. The big man shrugged his shoulders. Brewster motioned for Roy to kick off the conversation.

He explained to the big man from Sicily that he and Marc would work together in Indonesia. They'd be a two-man team.

"What about the gun?" Bruno asked. Brewster had briefed him on the mission when they were in Italy.

"Marc will smuggle it in and give it to you after you arrive in Java," Roy replied.

Brewster cut in, "I told Bruno to grow a big black beard. He might have to pass as a European Muslim in order to get inside a mosque."

"That's possible," Roy said, choking back a laugh.

Brewster chuckled. "This guy didn't recognize me when I got to Sicily. My beard and long hair. I said to him, 'Hey, Bruno, this is me, Tony.'"

Bruno lifted his arms in mock surprise.

Roy continued, "I'll operate from here. I feed you the funds and the intelligence. Marc has a prepaid cell phone, the same as I do, that no one can identify. All he needs to do is buy an Indonesian SIM card at a kiosk. They don't ask for an ID. The seller at the kiosk will activate it for you—using his own ID. As soon as you have your new number, text me on my burn phone. Clear?" Marc said he understood.

"Marc, you will open an account at Bank Central Asia. BCA has branches and ATMs throughout the country. I'll wire your operating funds from my ARL account here in Labuan." Roy looked at Brewster. "You and I will settle our account later as we agreed."

Roy looked at his son. "You'll soon have the encrypted laptop that's being sent to Singapore from the U.S. I'll send written, photo and audio intelligence to your computer. Guard it with your life."

"Finally, you're going to need an interpreter in Indonesia. I've decided to involve Wayan for two reasons. You and Bruno need someone who speaks Indonesian when you visit companies in Klaten, and later when you interrogate the bastard. And Wayan will want to be included in this project. He'd be affronted if he weren't."

Roy told the men that the first stage of the mission would be to locate Jeko Rusdiana and keep him under tight surveillance.

Bruno asked in accented English, "What's he look like?"

"I expect to receive an ID photo soon," Roy replied. Hotman said he would text it once he identified the buyer of the van and obtained a copy of his KTP. "You'll have a picture of his face. I'll ask my contact for a description of his height and weight."

Brewster spoke to Bruno in Sicilian.

"I told Bruno he's gotta follow Marc's orders. Marc is the *capo* when they get to Indonesia." Bruno squinted at Roy's son.

Roy continued by detailing their cover stories. "You two will enter Klaten under your true names. No aliases or fake IDs. Too risky. You check into a hotel together, and you hunt for teak garden furniture manufacturers. Wayan will join you at the hotel and act as your translator when you visit the factories. Go ahead and place an order for a container load of lounge chairs and ship them to Italy. We'll pay for it with a letter of credit from the Labuan bank."

"So you're serious about Wayan?" Marc asked.

"Dead serious. I've always had good intuition. Wayan will be a valuable asset. I'll fly to Bali tomorrow to recruit him."

Roy continued, "While you two are scrounging around for teak furniture, my sources will pinpoint the precise location of Jeko Rusdiana. We'll have the latitude and longitude of his phone and that'll give you the street address in Klaten where he sleeps. After that, Marc, the operational details are in your hands. Once you have the smuggled semiautomatic, you and Bruno can do your job. Interrogate him, take his phone, and then kill him."

Roy showed Marc the photograph of Jeko Rusdiana's mother being held at knifepoint. "Use this photo when you question the guy. He should get the message. Make sure before you whack him that you get the *true names* and phone numbers of his accomplices. Go through his call logs with him. The bad guys will be communicating using aliases. After you shoot him, take a photograph of the corpse. I'll need that to get further funding. Any questions?"

"When do we leave? And where do we go from here?" Marc asked.

"You fly to Singapore and meet your girlfriend. The tools have arrived. You still need to recruit her, and explain her role to her." Roy did not mention Ayu's name in front of the others. "Call me on this phone when she agrees to our plan." He indicated one of the prepaid throwaway phones in his pocket. Marc continued looking at the sand as they walked.

"Bruno will fly to Jogjakarta after you collect the gun. The two of you meet at a hotel there. It's a short drive from Jogja to Klaten."

"And if my girlfriend doesn't agree to take the risk?" Marc asked and stopped walking.

Roy paused, gave a tight smile, and raised Bruno's huge right hand. "Our friend here will use this weapon instead." The Sicilian laughed for the first time since they'd met.

Marc said, "I'll phone her when we get back to the hotel and ask for her Singapore flight schedules. Find out when she has a layover."

Brewster had been silent for the most part as they walked barefoot along the hard, wet sand, listening intently. "I wanna join you guys in Java. But at seventy, I'm getting a little too long in the tooth to operate like I did back in the day. I'll return this week to my wives, my Viagra, and life on Apo. I get horny thinking about it. Okay with you, chief?" He looked at Roy. "We can sort out the money when it's over."

3 0

BALI

ROY'S FIRST-CLASS FLIGHTS FROM LABUAN TO DEN-
pasar via Singapore were unremarkable, and the time in
the sky gave him time to plan. Before landing in Bali he
decided to include Wayan and his sister Kadek in *Operation Java
Sea*. He was unsure what role twenty-four year old Kadek might
play. He was uncertain whether they would wish to involve themselves in the project. At any rate, he'd make them an offer. If Roy
were a betting man, he'd wager they would choose to avenge the
murder of their parents.

He surprised them by arriving unannounced at the Bali Sea
Resort in Amed. As Roy walked through the lobby he spotted
Kadek standing behind the reception desk. She was as beautiful
now as she had been in her carefree college life at Berkeley.

Kadek had inherited the natural beauty of her mother. She
was tall, about five-foot-seven, and had a stunning, athletic figure.
Her long ebony hair fell to her waist. She got her tan complexion
from her father. This day she wore a simple embroidered white
blouse and a blue and gold batik sarong. She had a yellow flower
tucked into her thick hair above her ear. Like her mother, she re-

quired no cosmetics to enhance her good looks. Roy had hoped in vain that either Marc or Lorenzo would catch her eye.

She smiled when she saw him walk in. "Mr. Mancini, what a nice surprise. You should have phoned." She walked around the desk and they embraced.

"Do you have a room, Kadek?"

"Oh yes. Business everywhere in Bali is slow since . . ." She paused. "Let me call Wayan." She spoke on the phone in Balinese.

Roy looked out at the blue-green sea, at an underway cargo ship and at a cloudless sky. Lombok Island was in the far distance. Life here—nature—continued uninterrupted, placid, and heedless of those who had been lost.

A poignant moment. He was standing on Putu and Komang's ground. The last time he'd been here, they had gone snorkeling off this beach. As they swam underwater, he'd glanced over at the couple and noticed them holding hands, surrounded by tropical fish of various colors and stripes. They had gone deep and touched bottom before shooting back to the surface together.

"Mr. Mancini, welcome," Wayan Surya broke into Roy's reverie, speaking Indonesian.

"Hello, Wayan. I was remembering the last time all of us were together," he said as they shook hands.

"I met Marc a couple of weeks ago," Wayan said.

"Yes. I remember. You and I spoke on the phone that day. I wanted to see you and Kadek and to tell you how profoundly I've been affected by the loss of your parents, my best friends."

"Thank you, sir. Let me ask Kadek to join us."

"Sure. Perhaps the three of us could walk along the beach and chat."

Kadek joined the men. They removed their shoes and stepped onto the clean, white sand in front of the hotel. Nothing was said for a minute as they walked along the shore.

At last Roy spoke, "I see you still have the fleet of fishing boats." He pointed to the twenty or so outriggers at the far end of the beach.

Wayan looked at Roy. "Thanks to you, Mr. Mancini. You provided the seed money for it."

"Wayan . . . Kadek, I don't know how much your parents told you about the work your father and I did together. It was a couple of years before you were born."

Wayan replied, "Father told me something about helping you prevent a terrorist attack in the Middle East. He never discussed the details with us. I know he used to work on a cargo ship."

"Yes. We met each other in the Panama Canal aboard his ship. He was the radio operator. The ship was chartered to the government of North Korea. One day he saw the Koreans load a lethal surface-to-air missile onto his ship in the port of Wonsan, and he reported that to me. Later, Komang's radio transmissions played a vital role, helping the U.S. Navy locate his vessel and thwart a catastrophic terrorist plot. The sum of money we sent him was our way of saying thanks."

"You were an American intelligence agent?" Kadek asked.

"I was an intelligence officer. Your father was my agent. We worked together for two years." They walked on in silence as Roy allowed the siblings to digest this information.

"Wayan, you told Marc that you would like us to find the killers."

"Yes, I did. I do not believe our government will do all it can to prosecute the Islamist terrorists. There have been several bombings in Indonesia over the past three years. We know who is responsible for them: Abu Najib. He preaches in Surakarta in Central Java. He's the ringleader. And he gets away with murder."

"And you reckoned I could assist you?"

Wayan hesitated before replying. "You are a prominent

American businessman, Mr. Mancini. I thought you might have contacts. We need outside help."

"Would you be willing to join me in that effort, Wayan?" Roy looked at his sister. "And you, Kadek?"

"Finding the murderers?" Kadek asked.

"Yes."

"Absolutely," Wayan answered. Kadek nodded.

"Let me explain my plan to you. When I'm finished, you can opt in. Or not." They continued to stroll in the hard, wet sand along the shore in the direction of the beached fishing boats.

Roy described his private mission of locating and assassinating four Indonesian terrorists, including Abu Najib. He explained that Marc would coordinate the plan on the ground in Java and that he would provide the money and intelligence from outside Indonesia. He wanted Wayan to accompany Marc together with the Sicilian accomplice and to act as their interpreter. His role would be important when it came time to interrogate the first terrorist they captured and to translate intercepted phone calls.

"I'm in," Wayan said after Roy had finished. "Though the jihadis might speak Javanese with each other. Balinese and Javanese are similar. It won't be difficult for us to grasp some of it."

"Would we have to pass ourselves off as Muslims?" Kadek asked.

"Can you do that?" Roy asked.

The two of them looked at each other. Kadek replied, "No. We would have to learn the rituals. We've never been inside a mosque. As you know, we're Hindus."

To Roy's surprise, the two of them were a step ahead of him. He had not considered the probability that the terrorists, led by Abu Najib in Central Java, would speak the Javanese dialect with each other. And the prospect of Kadek and Wayan going undercover as Muslims added a new dimension to the plan.

"What do you suggest?" Roy asked.

Kadek replied. "We would have to go to Java and persuade an imam that we wished to convert to Islam, and that we needed to undergo training."

They walked in silence until they arrived at the boats. Roy leaned against the hull of one and faced them both. At last he made a decision. "Wayan, I would like you to join Marc and Bruno in Java as soon as possible. We know where one bomber is staying, and we can't let him escape. You'll interrogate him in the Indonesian language.

"Kadek, you will travel to Surakarta and execute your plan of feigning to convert to Islam, and train in the religious rituals. Beyond that, we will let it play out. Perhaps you will be the first to make personal contact with the bomber. We'll see. His name is Jeko."

"Jeko?" they both asked.

"Yes. We know his name and his whereabouts. He's in a town called Klaten in Central Java, not far from Jogjakarta."

"I know Klaten. We bought our teak furniture from a factory there," Wayan said. "A coincidence. What's the first step?"

"You both fly to Jogja. Kadek heads from there to Surakarta, contacts an imam, and converts to Islam. Wayan, you go to Klaten, check into a hotel, and wait there for Marc and Bruno. Let me know where you're staying. I'll give you my number after we return to the resort."

Wayan and Kadek discussed in their Balinese dialect how they would arrange the management of the resort with a cousin during their absence from Amed.

Roy continued, "Kadek, after you convert to Islam, you will go to Klaten and meet Wayan. You brief him on what it takes to feign being a good Muslim." The siblings looked at each other. "As you probably know, women and girls are not allowed to pray in the same room with the men. You won't be allowed to pray together. So Wayan has to be prepared to go undercover inside a mosque and pray alone."

"I've always wondered why they prohibit that," Kadek commented.

"A Malaysian taxi driver, an Indian named Sammy, once told me the reason. He said it was because they all get on their knees, drop their heads to the floor, and thus their bottoms are raised. A man praying right behind a woman in this position, and viewing her rear end, might experience immoral images of lust. It could be distracting."

3 1

SINGAPORE

MARC HAD CHECKED INTO THE RAFFLES HOTEL IN Singapore in the late morning to wait for Ayu. She arrived in the afternoon on a flight from Tokyo. Her layover was twenty hours. She told the other crew members that she was staying with friends and that she would meet them at Changi Airport for the flight home to Denpasar.

Ayu asked the front desk clerk for Marc's room number and phoned him. They met in the lobby and he escorted her to the room. As soon as they entered, they embraced and kissed passionately. "I've missed you," she said at last, leaning back and looking into his eyes.

"My God, you're beautiful." Marc caressed her hair and kissed her neck.

Marc removed Ayu's blouse and unfastened her bra, dropping both to the floor. He bent and kissed the firm brown nipples on her uplifted breasts, one and then the other. They kicked off their shoes, stripped off each other's clothing and fell onto the bed together. The oral foreplay continued until they were both near their peak of release. Marc entered her from behind, a position that drove them wild. When Marc sensed himself about to climax, he withdrew and turned Ayu onto her back, her bottom raised on a pillow. He entered her again and launched the final journey home.

"Now, Marc," she wailed.

He drove faster, deeper, calling her, "Ayu, Ayu . . ."

Moments later Marc whispered, "Talk about perfect timing."

After making love unhurriedly a second time, napping, and showering together, the couple walked downstairs to the hotel's outdoor Palm Court. Marc had reserved a secluded table for two at the edge of the lawn, beside the swimming pool. He ordered a bottle of premium Bordeaux with the beef stroganoff.

After a dessert of chocolate mousse, a white-suited waiter served the liqueurs. Marc raised his glass to Ayu. "To us. Happily ever after." She smiled and pantomimed a kiss across the table.

"I'm working on a special project with my father, Ayu. We'd like you to join us. Dad and I need your help." He sat back in his chair, sipped his Armagnac, and looked Ayu in the eye. She cocked her head to one side, curious, and raised her eyebrows. "What is it?" she asked.

"We're going to bring the Bali bombers to justice. Your government in Jakarta is unlikely to do the job. So we will." She listened without comment.

"We don't believe they will prosecute the murderers as they should. Hartono seems ambivalent."

She nodded. "I would agree. Hartono hasn't shown much compassion. She never visited Bali. We're offended. She's supposed to be the president of all Indonesians, not only the Muslims. What's your plan?"

"First let me ask. You once mentioned you have a contact on the airport customs team who allows you to smuggle luxuries into Bali. I recall his name is Gusti. You said you pay him every month so he'll let you pass without an inspection. Remember you showed me your suitcase loaded with cosmetics and jewelry after a trip to Hong Kong."

Ayu smiled. "You don't forget anything, do you Marc? Can you keep a secret?"

"Sure."

"My suitcase is now packed with expensive ladies' garments from Tokyo. I'll double my money."

"And your contact, Gusti, will be at the airport tomorrow?"

"He'd better be." She gave a nervous laugh. "It's what I pay him for. He has my flight schedule." She turned serious. "Why do you ask?"

"I want you to bring in some necessary tools. I'll collect them here in the morning. They're vital for our mission. We'll use them to avenge the murder and maiming of those Americans and Indonesians at Nusa Dua."

There was a long silence. Ayu frowned and stared at her empty glass. The quiet was broken by a waiter who appeared at the table and asked if they would like something else. Marc ordered two more liqueurs.

"Want to tell me about it?" she finally asked.

Marc didn't hesitate. It was now or never. "We will locate and assassinate the bombers—the ring leader and his confederates. The ones who are still walking around free."

"*You* will do that?" she asked sotto voice and wide eyed.

"We have hired a hitman, a professional, to kill each of them. My job is to smuggle in the weapon. That's where I need your help." He raised a hand as she opened her mouth to speak. "I would *never* ask you to risk this, Ayu, if we had any doubt about Gusti being at the airport tomorrow when you arrive."

She hesitated for several seconds before saying, "He's never failed me. What is it you need me to bring in?"

"A semiautomatic pistol, ammunition, and a silencer. Are you comfortable with this?"

"No. Would you be?" she answered, looking him in the eye.

Marc folded his arms and cocked his head to one side. "I've been in tight spots. I believed in my mission. I do now."

Ayu frowned and continued to look at her lover for several moments. "All right. I believe in this too. It's the right thing. We call it *hukum mati* in Indonesian."

"Translation?"

"It means justice by the death penalty." Ayu swallowed her entire drink, Cointreau, in one swallow, grimaced, and closed her eyes. "Let's go upstairs and make love, darling. Explain it to me later."

32

BALI

AYU'S FLIGHT FROM SINGAPORE HAD TOUCHED DOWN five minutes early at 8:10 in the evening. She and the crew remained aboard the Boeing 777 until the passengers disembarked and the cleaning staff entered the plane. Her colleague, Sari, whispered to her as they walked along the Jetway, "Did you bring anything in?"

Ayu continued looking straight ahead. "Yes. I bought some dresses in Tokyo. Designer stuff."

"I've got perfume and cosmetics," Sari said. "I should have a profit of five million rupiah. Nice, huh?"

Ayu was distracted. She was envisioning the contents of the unopened package Marc had brought to the hotel room that morning and how they had wrapped it deep inside the Japanese garments that filled her suitcase. He'd carried the encrypted laptop computer with him on an earlier flight.

She saw the plane's pilot and co-pilot walking ahead. There was no reason for her to be nervous, she told herself. Gusti had never failed her. Nevertheless, her stomach was acting up.

Ayu walked slowly beside Sari. She was determined to be the last crewmember to pass through the baggage claim area.

"You seem nervous, Ayu. What is it, you forgot to pay your man this month?" Sari giggled and looked askance at her friend. Ayu shook her head. She was not used to this sudden taste of acid in her throat.

They placed their hand-carry luggage on a conveyor belt prior to entering the baggage claim lobby. The flight attendants knew better than to smuggle their products in their carry-on luggage because of this initial scan. Here a lackadaisical customs officer motioned them through. As soon as she entered the main lobby Ayu spotted the suitcase on her flight's luggage carousel just before it disappeared back inside the loading area.

"See you next week, Sari," she said to her companion. "We fly to Bangkok on Tuesday."

"Yes, Bangkok." Sari lowered her voice. "Jade, rubies, and emerald jewelry. I always make a fortune on that trip, Ayu. You must meet my Thai dealer. I'll introduce you to her next week."

"That would be nice. *Ciao.*" Ayu walked away, to the area of the conveyor belt where luggage would first appear from the loading area. Her suitcase had already made one round on the belt and had disappeared back, behind the partition again. She expected it to emerge in a minute or two. She glanced in the direction of the customs examiners. And her heart stopped.

Gusti was not at his table. She dropped her hand-carry bag onto the floor and stood on her toes so she could see above the throng of passengers blocking her view. No, Gusti was not one of the three examiners on duty. She could see each of the uniformed officials. There were two men and one unfamiliar woman. The woman was manning the table where Gusti usually stood. At that moment, she was ordering a passenger to open his suitcase for inspection. Ayu looked beyond the customs inspection area, at the glass exit doors. According to plan, Marc would be waiting for her outside the building. She felt nauseated and there was sweat on her hands and in her armpits. Her stomach felt as though the floor had dropped out from under her.

The suitcase appeared again, in front of her, having passed through the opening that separated the loading area from the lobby. She could not leave it on the carousel and run. The luggage had her name and address attached to it. Leaving it there would raise suspicion. It might be scanned and pried open. She would be identified, and prosecuted, and jailed, as a gun smuggler. She staggered once as her knees were about to buckle.

Ayu looked at the case without lifting it. She had not taken a baggage cart because her suitcase had wheels. Typically she would pull it across the room to Gusti's table where he would motion for her to continue on, and she would exit the building.

At last she followed the suitcase, lifted it off the conveyor, and pulled it away. She glanced at her watch and noted all of the crew members from her flight had left the building. Again she tasted acid. If she was going to throw up she had to get to the restroom, fast.

Ayu moved quickly pulling the suitcase to the opposite end of the lobby and entered the women's lavatory. She found a vacant wash basin, filled her cupped hands with cold water, and brought them to her face. She looked in the mirror and saw an image of utter fear on her wet visage. Finally, she dried her hands and face with paper towels and left the restroom.

She headed back through the crowd of passengers to the baggage carousel, pretending that she had forgotten to collect something. No one appeared to notice. She did an about face and glanced at the customs inspection area. The same severe woman was in charge of Gusti's table. She was rifling through a passenger's baggage, removing one item at a time, and placing them on the table for closer examination. Ayu knew the game the woman was playing.

She would inform the passenger that he would have to pay a two hundred percent tax on an item from his luggage. The passenger would realize the examiner was looking for a bribe, and he would cautiously remove several thousand rupiah from his wallet and drop them into his open bag. The inspector would remove the cash, pocket it, and motion for the passenger to repack and move on.

At that moment, Ayu spotted Gusti as he appeared behind the woman. He was walking fast, aware that he had arrived late. He scanned the passengers in the hall until he noticed Ayu. He nodded in her direction and gave a thin smile. Gusti turned and spoke to the female customs examiner. She abruptly marched out of the room, evidently annoyed by Gusti's tardiness.

MARC HAD BEEN KILLING TIME IN AN AIRPORT COFFEE SHOP during the two hours since his Singapore Airlines flight had landed. Twice he'd wandered in and out of the café as he waited for Ayu's flight to arrive. At last he noted on the large arrivals board that her plane landed at 8:10. By 8:25 he'd paid his bill, grabbed his backpack and small suitcase, and walked the one hundred meters along a sidewalk to the main terminal.

Marc sat on a concrete bench and kept his eye on the glass door. At nine o'clock he was anxiously watching the activity around the exit area. At nine-thirty he was a nervous wreck. He now stood in front of the door and watched as each passenger, crewmember, and uniformed official departed the building. At that instant, 9:36, he saw Ayu push through the door and walk out, hauling her suitcase behind her. He saw the anguished expression on her face, a look he had not seen on a woman since a day in Kandahar where a mother had reported that her young son had been kidnapped by a policeman. Ayu rushed toward him a moment later.

"Get a taxi," she commanded without another word. It was obvious to Marc a disaster had been averted inside the terminal

Earlier Marc had purchased a taxi ticket for the drive home to the villa. The airport taxis were parked in a lot across the street. "Follow me."

They crossed the street and walked as fast as they could into the dark parking lot until they found an available cab. The driver got out of the car, took the voucher, and placed the luggage inside the trunk. Marc kept his bag containing the encrypted laptop with him in the back seat. He gave the driver the villa's address and reached for Ayu's cold hand. No word was spoken during the forty-minute ride home.

The next day, Marc traveled to Klaten in Central Java in a series of taxies and buses. His backpack containing the weapons and laptop was never examined. Bruno Cazadero had already checked into the Jayapura Hotel when Marc arrived.

33

KLATEN, CENTRAL JAVA, INDONESIA

WAYAN SURYA FLEW FROM DENPASAR TO JOGJAKARTA early in the morning and drove a rental car north to Klaten. He too checked into the Jayapura Hotel. As soon as he was alone in his room, he used his secure phone and called Roy Mancini in Labuan.

"I'm checked in," he said after Roy answered.

"They've arrived in Klaten. Good luck," Roy replied. They disconnected.

Wayan took the stairs to the lobby and dialed Marc's room from there. "Sir, I am Wayan. I'm your guide. I've checked into the hotel."

"Okay Wayan. We'll meet you downstairs in fifteen minutes."

"Yes, sir. I am wearing a batik short-sleeved shirt."

Marc Mancini and Bruno Cazadero entered the large lobby from an elevator. Marc made a show of searching for someone. They approached the man in the batik shirt.

"Are you our guide?" Marc asked.

"Yes, sir. I am Wayan." They shook hands.

Marc made the introduction. "Bruno, this is Wayan. He's the

interpreter and guide we've hired to lead us around Klaten." Wayan bowed and offered his hand. Bruno, expressionless, shook it.

"I have hired a car," Wayan said. "I'll drive you to your first appointment if you're ready?"

"Yes, let's go," Marc replied. "As I believe you know, we are going to purchase garden furniture and ship it to Italy. Bruno is the importer. I hope to find a market for those same products in the United States."

The three men walked outside the hotel.

"Bruno, do you have a business card for Wayan?"

Bruno withdrew his wallet and removed one of the cards he'd had printed and handed it to the Balinese. The card identified him as Bruno Cazadero of Allegheny Resources Limited, with a business address on Labuan Island and a branch office in Palermo, Sicily.

"Bruno doesn't speak much English, Wayan. His company in Palermo has informed me of its needs. You and I will transact the business with the factory owners. The letters of credit and all our communications will be through Labuan. And in case the factory owners wish to launder money there, we will accommodate them. I'll leave that negotiation to you, on the sidelines . . . the under-invoicing for their shipments. Any questions?"

"No, sir. That's clear. If you're ready, I'll bring the car around. Wait here."

Marc had decided not to discuss the trio's true purpose around the hotel or inside the automobile. He'd wait until they found a space where they could walk and talk. They spent the morning inspecting premium-grade teak furniture at a large factory on the outskirts of Klaten. The cover story aside, Marc concluded teak garden furniture might be a business to explore with his father.

Marc placed a trial order with the factory for a twenty-foot container load of lounge chairs for shipment to Genoa. The factory owner did request, through Wayan, that some of his money be stashed in Labuan. He would invoice each two hundred-dollar chair at $165. The thirty-five dollars owed per chair would remain briefly in Allegheny's Labuan account. Later the Indonesian businessman would have this money transferred from the bank in Labuan to his personal account in Singapore.

Marc asked Wayan to drive to Borobudur after the meeting at the factory. He knew about the world's largest Buddhist temple, built in the ninth century, and that it had areas where they could appear as tourists and talk. The ancient temple was fifty miles west of Klaten. Not a word was spoken about *Operation Java Sea* during the drive.

The parking lot was a distance from the temple. The trio strolled west on the pedestrian walk that wound through a large park with lush foliage.

"Our target is Jeko Rusdiana. He's hiding in Klaten. Soon we'll have his precise location. We now have a lock on his cell phone. After we find him, we'll keep him under surveillance and determine if he's using a computer for email." Marc said as he walked between the two men.

"When do I kill him?" Bruno asked. He lit a cigarette and flicked the match onto the path.

"Not until we interrogate him and drain him of information about his accomplices."

Wayan asked, "Do you know how to interrogate a prisoner, Marc?"

"There's one method I used in Afghanistan. We referred to it as speech therapy. It induced the terrorist to talk. We had some deadly snakes there. I've read the same holds for Java. The Russell's viper. We'll need to capture one."

Marc continued, "Where's Kadek?"

Wayan answered, "She arrived in Surakarta today. This week

she'll inform a Muslim priest that she wishes to convert to Islam. It's a simple process. She only needs to recite a kind of declaration of faith. She'll spend a while there praying five times a day and studying the other four pillars of the religion. Afterward, she'll join us in Klaten."

Marc stopped walking when they arrived beneath the shade of a pine tree. He pulled his clandestine cell phone from his front pants pocket and looked behind him to be sure no one was near. Bruno dropped the butt of the cigarette onto the ground and stamped it out.

"This is a photo ID of Jeko Rusdiana." He passed the phone to Bruno who stared at the picture before handing it to Wayan. "He is five-foot-seven and weighs 145 pounds according to his driver's license. He's twenty-seven years old." The picture showed a long-haired Asian man with a smirk on his thin face.

After a while, Bruno said, "This will be a pleasure. I don't like him."

Marc continued, "I agree. He's arrogant. We'll wipe that grin off. Meanwhile, we must be deliberate in our methods. I'm planning to use Kadek as bait. Jeko looks like he might be a Don Juan."

"What about the snake?" Wayan asked.

"One of the deadliest snakes in the world, the Russell's viper, resides here in Central Java. I want you to find a farmer tomorrow who agrees to capture a large one for us. Offer him ten million rupiah. He's to keep the snake in a box with wire on top, so we can view it. We pay the farmer a three-million rupiah bonus for a viper that is at least four feet long."

"That's a lot of money," Wayan said.

"We don't have a lot of time. The farmer needs to be motivated. Tell him we need the snake by the end of the week. Pay him an advance of two million rupiah. Earnest money. Tell him you work for the zoo in Jakarta.

"Bruno and I will wait for you in Klaten. After you find the farmer and the snake, and pay him, I need you to find a location for the interrogation, a secluded, forested area. Drive north to Magelang and search for a remote spot at the base of the mountain. We can't risk being seen or heard. The interview might get noisy.

"Leave the snake in its crate wherever you decide to interrogate Jeko. Be sure it has enough food. By the time you return to Klaten, I should have a clearer idea on where Jeko is staying. You'll call Kadek and ask her to join you."

It wasn't clear how much of this Bruno understood, given his rudimentary English. He barely spoke.

Wayan smiled inwardly at the prospect of working with his sister on a plot that was now becoming more and more involved, and cleverly planned by Marc Mancini.

At last the trio arrived at the massive temple. There appeared to be nine stacked platforms before them—six square and three circular. At the top was a central dome. Hundreds of Buddha statues surrounded the structure.

Wayan explained, "This temple was abandoned six hundred years ago following the conversion of Java to Islam. My ancestors, the Hindus, fled from Java to Bali."

"So your ancestors were from Java?" Marc asked.

"Originally, yes. That's why the Balinese and Javanese languages are similar. It would not be difficult for Kadek and me to learn Javanese."

"Wasn't there a terrorist bombing here?"

"Yes, in 1985. Nine bombs damaged several statues. The mastermind, a Muslim preacher, received a prison sentence."

"Will it ever end?" Marc asked.

Wayan shook his head.

34

_____

CENTRAL JAVA

WAYAN HAD LEFT THE CRATE CONTAINING THE four-foot-long viper in a hiding place: a ravine in a forested and unpopulated area along the foothills of an active volcano, Mount Sumbing.

He spent two days exploring the roads west and north of the city of Magelang while Marc and Bruno inspected teak furniture at the factory where they'd placed the order for lounge chairs. He returned to the hotel in Klaten three days after their journey to Borobudur. The next day, the trio drove to Wayan's spot at the base of the mountain. They parked the car at the dead end of a dirt road and walked on an animal trail for another two hundred meters. Wayan pointed to a white chalk mark he'd left on a tree trunk.

"The snake is under the tree," Wayan said. "There's a small clearing behind it. I chose this spot for the interview." Marc smiled at the use of that term.

"We call that a euphemism, Bruno," Marc explained to the bemused Italian.

"Is this where we kill the asshole?" the Sicilian asked.

"It's possible. First we have some fun with Jeko and the snake. When Russell is pissed off, he becomes aggressive" Marc pointed to the cage. "We'll need to cut a hole through the screen. One large enough to fit a man's arm. Let's take a look."

The three men walked toward the rectangular hardwood crate. The top was covered with a screen mesh. They peered in and saw the coiled dark-brown-and-yellow reptile, its flattened, triangle-shaped head and the agitated tongue flicking in and out of its blunt snout and between its fangs. There was the carcass of a rat in a corner.

Wayan explained, "The farmer trapped the viper in a bushy area outside his farm. He told me the snake's favorite dishes are lizards and rodents—mice and rats. We fed him the rat before I left for Klaten yesterday."

Marc walked to the clearing on the other side of the tree. "We'll bring a chair and place it here, beneath the tree. Haul the box in front of the chair. At that point we cut open the hole on top." Bruno finally caught on that Russell was the name of the snake. The big Sicilian grinned.

"How dangerous is it?" he asked, blowing cigarette smoke at the angry reptile.

"He's the deadliest in Southeast Asia. It's the fourth most poisonous snake in the world. More people die from a Russell's bite than from any other snake. The bite is excruciatingly painful. Wayan can remind Jeko of that once we have him tied down."

When they returned to the hotel, Marc went to his room to check for email on his encrypted laptop. There was a message from Roy. He decoded it and learned the location of Jeko Rusdiana's cell phone in Klaten. The SID had zeroed in on the latitude and longitude of the phone at night when Jeko was asleep. Bill Chapman's NSA unit had hacked into the phone's memory. The email listed the contacts chain—each of the phone numbers Jeko had called before and after the bombing. Marc called Bruno and Wayan to meet him in the lobby.

"Let's take a walk," he said when they met.

The trio strolled along the dusty streets of downtown Klaten for five minutes before Marc spoke. "We've pinpointed Jeko's location. It's beside the Al Fatah Mosque. I assume he's renting a room. Perhaps a boardinghouse that's connected to the mosque. They track the phone when he moves around during the day. He doesn't go far."

Bruno asked, "What's the plan?"

"The mosque is located near a street called Jalan Raya Kalikebo. Nearby streets are Jalan Nuri and Jalan Rajawali. Wayan, take the car and drive around that area until you spot the mosque. You and I, Bruno, can't go anywhere near the place. We'd stick out. Surveillance of the area will be a job for Wayan and Kadek."

"I've told Kadek to join us," Wayan said. "She'll check into a boardinghouse tomorrow. I'll join her there after she gets a room."

The surveillance plan was settled. Kadek and Wayan would each have photographs of Jeko Rusdiana downloaded to their secure cell phones. After determining if there was a boardinghouse behind the Al Fatah Mosque, they would alternate watches in the neighborhood. When Jeko was identified, they would inform Marc and would tighten the surveillance, never letting him out of their sight whenever he ventured outside his room. Marc would decide on the timing for the next act.

35

KLATEN

KADEK ARRIVED IN KLATEN IN THE MORNING. SHE took a room in a boardinghouse on Jalan Nuri, two hundred meters from the Al Fatah Mosque. Later the same day Wayan moved into a room in the men's section of that same house.

Kadek was the first to visit the mosque, where she introduced herself to the imam, explaining that she was a recent Muslim convert from Bali. Thirty minutes later, Wayan arrived in the neighborhood. He spotted a shop beside the mosque that rented motorbikes.

Wayan inspected several used Hondas, selected one, and befriended the owner. He said he was a Balinese tour guide and that he was new to Klaten. He explained he was waiting for clients to arrive from Jakarta, that he would take them to Borobudur and that he had a couple of days to kill. He asked if there was a boardinghouse nearby. The owner told him that indeed there was, behind the mosque.

"Can I get a room there?" Wayan asked the man.

"Perhaps not. The rooms are reserved for Muslims who pray at the mosque. You are Balinese? A Hindu?"

"Alas, yes I am. Though I have been planning to convert to Islam. Is there an imam in the mosque who can guide me in that quest?"

The shop owner smiled at this news. "I can speak to him. His name is Mahatmah. Come back tomorrow morning after prayers. I will introduce you. You will have made a wise decision if you convert to our religion."

"How much do I owe you for the motorbike?"

"You can pay me fifty thousand rupiah per day. Do you agree?"

"That's fair." Wayan removed his wallet and withdrew cash. "Here's two hundred thousand for four days. Do you mind if I sit here and relax with you for a while? I have nowhere else I need to be today. You can tell me about places we should see in Central Java."

"Be my guest, brother."

"Hold on," Wayan said. "I'll buy some drinks for us." The Balinese walked to a kiosk next door and purchased two ice cold coconut drinks.

And so Wayan Surya spent the afternoon positioned beside the mosque and thirty meters from the boardinghouse where Jeko Rusdiana was staying. The owner of the motorbike shop, a Klaten native, had a gift of gab, and was pleased to tell stories of local lore to the friendly tour guide from Bali. Wayan stayed until after sunset when the shop closed. Jeko never appeared.

Kadek had elected not to wear a *hijab* to cover her hair. This was not uncommon for the women of Indonesia. The country's brand of Islam was the most moderate in the world. The majority of Muslim women in Java did not wear traditional Islamic attire.

Kadek found a hair salon one block from the Al Fatah Mosque at 7:15 in the evening. And there she got the full treatment of a shampoo followed by a pedicure and manicure and a thorough massage. The entire process took one and a half hours. All the while she kept her eyes on the street in the direction of the mosque and the boardinghouse. The target never showed.

The following morning Wayan returned to the motorbike shop where he greeted the owner. The man informed him that he had spoken with the mosque's imam and that Mahatmah was looking forward to meeting the Balinese and guiding him in his conversion to Islam.

"I would like to live somewhere nearby," Wayan explained. "So I can concentrate on my training and pray five times a day at the mosque."

The shop owner hesitated for several moments before speaking.

"I have a spare room upstairs. It is small. There is a bathroom with a bucket of water for bathing. I suppose I could rent it to you for a short while. How long do you believe you'll need it?"

Wayan replied, "Only for a week. I am expecting my Jakarta clients to arrive soon. I could pay you in advance for the week. This way I can devote myself to my lessons."

They agreed on a price for the week, and Wayan told the owner that he would move in that same day.

"Now let me introduce you to Mahatmah. He lives in a house behind the mosque. Wait here."

Wayan took a seat inside the shop's small office and waited for the owner to fetch the imam. The two men entered the shop together fifteen minutes later. Wayan stood and shook hands with the Muslim priest.

"Greetings, Mr. Wayan. May peace be with you," Mahatmah said. "My brother tells me you wish to become a Muslim. Is that true?"

"Yes, Imam Mahatmah. I have been planning this for several months. Now that I am in Java, I believe it is time. It would have been awkward for me to convert in Bali. My family would not approve. I am prepared to move to Java and live a new life."

The two Javanese men smiled.

"That is a coincidence, Mr. Wayan. There was a lovely Balinese woman, a Muslim, who stopped by our mosque yesterday. Do you know her? I recall her name was Kadek."

"I doubt it, Imam. I have not met any Balinese here. It is indeed a coincidence."

"Well, perhaps you will have the chance to meet her if she returns. She is beautiful," the imam said with a suggestive grin. "I would like nothing more than to introduce our religion to more of your friends in Bali."

"God willing, Imam Mahatmah. We will succeed."

Wayan explained to the two Javanese men that he needed to collect his personal effects before he moved into the room atop the motorbike shop. He thanked them for their hospitality and bid them farewell before climbing onto his motorbike and roaring off down the road. At the corner he stopped and looked over his shoulder. He was not being followed. Nevertheless, he rode in a circuitous route before arriving at the boardinghouse on Jalan Nuri. He parked the motorbike out of sight before climbing the stairs to his room.

He waited in his room for ten minutes before sending Kadek the signal. He dialed her number and let it ring three times before disconnecting. He dialed again and let it ring once. A moment later he opened his door and caught sight of her leaving through the front. Wayan waited five minutes before walking downstairs and exiting the building through a back door. He carried with him a small valise containing a couple of shirts and some toiletries. They met fifteen minutes later beyond the dead end of Jalan Nuri and inside a forested area adjacent to the river that ran through the center of Klaten.

"I'm moving into a room today across the street from Al Fatah," Wayan explained motioning with his bag. "The imam mentioned you to me earlier. It's best you not visit again. The coincidence of two Balinese hanging around would cause suspicion. Wait in the boardinghouse until I spot Jeko."

"Got it," she replied.

Kadek turned and walked back to the street and to the board-inghouse. Wayan waited in the forest for ten minutes before going back to the spot where he had left his rented motorbike.

36

KLATEN

W AYAN UNDERSTOOD THAT MUSLIMS PRAYED FIVE times a day. This was one of those five pillars of Islam. Throughout the first day, he positioned himself at his upstairs window, behind the curtain, at each of the specified times for prayer, beginning before sunrise and finishing late at night before going to bed. From there he had a bird's-eye view of the Al Fatah Mosque entrance and of the men who entered and departed the small building. Jeko Rusdiana was never one of them. And unless he was praying in his room, this suggested to Wayan that the terrorist was not a religious man.

In the morning, two days after Wayan moved into his room above the shop, there was a knock on his door. He opened it and was greeted there by the imam, Mahatmah.

"*Salaam alaykum,*" the imam said. *Peace be with you.*

"*Salaam alaykum,*" Wayan replied.

"Are you prepared at this time to convert to Islam, brother?" Mahatmah asked.

Wayan replied, "I am. Please come in."

The imam entered the tiny room and Wayan closed the door. Kadek had explained to him what was to follow.

"Please repeat after me . . . are you ready?"

Wayan nodded his head.

"Say, 'I bear witness that there is no deity except Allah.'"

Wayan repeated the words.

"Now say, 'I bear witness that Muhammad is the messenger of Allah.'"

Wayan again complied.

"Now you must bathe, brother Wayan. You will be cleansing yourself of your past life. I will wait here." The imam pointed toward the door.

Wayan grabbed a towel, his phone, and a bar of soap and left the room. He had not left any compromising items behind. Five minutes later, he returned. The imam was standing in the same spot where Wayan had left him.

Wayan said, "Imam Mahatmah, I wish to learn to pray five times every day. It would be easier for me if you would allow me to live in your boardinghouse, behind the mosque, and join our brothers there. Would you have a room available for me? I don't mind sharing."

"Yes, we have a bed. You would have to share the room. Your roommate will be Sayed. He is devout and can help you learn to pray and to be a good Muslim. Perhaps you can move into the room today after *Dhuhr*, the time for prayer around noon. I will introduce you to Sayed at that time. Pack your things and bring them to the house behind the mosque. You can park your motorbike in the lot at the back."

Mahatmah introduced Wayan to Sayed after prayer. He moved into the boardinghouse following *Dhuhr*, sharing a second-floor room with the pious, middle-aged Javanese man. After parking his motorbike at the rear of the house, it was apparent why he might have missed Jeko. There was a back door to the boarding-house that led to the parking lot. Four bikes were parked there when he pulled in. A boarder would have been able to exit through the back door and ride his bike along an alley to and from the lot without being observed from the front of the mosque.

The ground floor bathroom and shower were communal and shared by each of the eight men who stayed in the house. There were two bedrooms on the second floor and two bedrooms on the ground floor.

The day after he moved in, and soon after *Maghrib* prayers at sunset, Wayan came face to face with Jeko Rusdiana as the latter exited the bathroom. There was no mistaking the pockmarked face of the man who had murdered Wayan's parents. He appeared the same as in the photograph downloaded onto the cell phone. The men stared at one another as they passed in the hallway. Wayan entered the room with the toilet, locked it, and kept his ear to the door. He heard the faint sound of a door opening and closing at the end of the hall. Jeko's room, the one beside the rear exit door.

37

BOROBUDUR, CENTRAL JAVA

MARC CALLED THE TEAM TOGETHER AFTER WAYAN reported his encounter with Jeko inside the boardinghouse. Marc and Bruno drove the rented car from Klaten to the Borobudur parking lot. Kadek rode with Wayan on the back of his motorbike, and they arrived at the temple's lot ten minutes later. The four walked together along a deserted pedestrian walkway that led to the temple. Marc asked Wayan to explain the situation at the boardinghouse.

"Jeko stays in a room on the ground floor near the back door. I don't know if he has a roommate or not. The back door leads to the parking area behind the house. I suspect he always enters and exits the house using that door. The imam told me the doors are locked from ten o'clock at night until five in the morning. So far I haven't seen Jeko enter the mosque. Perhaps he prays in his room in order to stay out of sight. Perhaps he is not religious. There is a window on the second floor where I can observe anyone leaving or entering through the back door."

"Wayan and Kadek, you'll have to continue to work as a

team. Kadek, you need to return to the mosque. Ask the imam if you can volunteer to help—housekeeping, running errands, doing the boarders' laundry. Are you willing?"

Kadek replied, "Of course."

"You need to make contact with Jeko. That's why I suggested the laundry bit."

Kadek nodded her understanding.

"Wayan, without being too conspicuous, you should stand watch at the window overlooking the parking lot. Possible?"

"The other boarders on the second floor go off to work in the morning. So after about eight o'clock I could position myself there without arousing suspicion," Wayan explained.

"We need to learn where Jeko sends and receives email. Wayan?"

"I should be able to follow him at a distance on my bike. I suspect he uses an internet cafe. Can you find where the cafes are located in Klaten?"

Marc replied. "I'll do that and send you a list by text message."

Bruno broke his silence. "How soon do I interrogate and shoot the guy?"

Marc replied, "The urgent thing is to capture his email. We need to do that before we confront him. All we have now are phone numbers from his contacts, before and after the bombing. They must be emailing messages to each other. We need more information on the terrorists' whereabouts and plans. I've been told they're no longer using cell phones. They've gone silent. Our guess is they're using email. We've got to find his computer."

The following day, Kadek returned to the Al Fatah Mosque and offered her services to Imam Mahatmah. She explained that she was willing to wash clothes. The imam suggested she assist the old woman who was taking care of the boarders' laundry. The woman also cleaned the boarders' rooms twice a week. Mean-while he said she could help him with chores around the mosque—sweeping and polishing.

Wayan watched the parking lot from the second floor window. He saw the men depart on their motorbikes. By eight-thirty all three of the other boarders on the second floor had left. Patience. At last Jeko emerged from the building at ten minutes past ten o'clock in the morning. Wayan saw him put on his helmet and straddle and start a black Yamaha motorbike. He took off along the back alley. Wayan made a mental note of the license plate number

Wayan rushed downstairs and out the rear of the building. He rode his Honda at high speed down the alley in the same direction as Jeko. When he arrived at the intersection of Jalan Raya Ka-likebo, he looked both ways. The street was full of motorbikes, cars and smoke-belching trucks passing in both directions. Jeko was long gone. Wayan made a right turn and sped past the other bikes and vehicles, hunting for the man on the black Yamaha in the blue windbreaker, wearing a red and silver helmet. After twenty minutes, he abandoned the search and returned to the boardinghouse and his perch on the second floor. An hour later, he saw Jeko return to the lot.

That same morning Kadek located the elderly washer woman behind the boardinghouse. Kadek introduced herself and ex-plained that the imam had asked her to help with the laundry. She made it clear to the old woman that she would not have to share her meager income. She was volunteering to help out. The gray-haired woman smiled wide, displaying her red, sirih leaf-stained gums and teeth. She was grateful for the offer.

"Where do the boarders leave their dirty clothes, *ibu*?" Kadek asked, calling the old woman "mother" to show respect.

The woman replied, "Outside their door."

"How do we keep the clothes separate?"

"The men place their dirty clothes in laundry bags and leave them there before seven o'clock in the morning. Each bag has the boarder's name on it. Every morning at that time, I go through the house and collect them."

"There are two men living in each room?" Kadek asked.

"All except for one. There is a boarder on the ground floor who lives alone. The imam told me he pays more money so he doesn't have to share the room."

"Oh?" Kadek frowned. "Why is that?"

"I guess this brother isn't friendly," the old woman replied, shaking her head.

"What's his name, *ibu?*"

"I don't know. He's been here about two weeks. Keeps to himself. I see him go out the back door and ride off somewhere on his motorbike and return an hour later. Mostly he stays in his room. Doesn't even bother to pray in the mosque. The laundry bag has his initials, JR, printed on it. And he doesn't want us to clean his room."

"I will remember not to disturb him. Which room is he in?"

"The one close to the back door. He has never spoken to me. He leaves his laundry twice a week. The rest of the men here are nice to me. Not him. He is always scowling when he walks outside."

"Where is he from? Do you know?"

"The imam told me he is from Surabaya. Says you can tell by his accent."

Kadek paused for a moment before speaking. "*Ibu,* why don't you allow me to collect the laundry bags each morning? That way you don't have to climb the stairs. I can arrive before seven in the morning."

"That is kind of you, daughter. So the laundry bags will be here when I arrive at seven-thirty? What is your name?"

"My name is Kadek. I have recently converted to Islam."

"Praise be to God. You are from Bali? Your accent?"

"Yes, *ibu*."

So it was agreed. The next day, Kadek would collect the laundry from outside each boarder's room, and she would place the bags behind the house before seven-thirty in the morning.

3 8

KLATEN

KADEK SET HER WRISTWATCH TEN MINUTES FAST.
She'd make it appear to be an accident. She wore a tight,
form-fitting Balinese batik sarong, a *baju kebaya*, and a loose
white blouse that buttoned down the front. She'd applied a light
floral perfume behind her ears and between her breasts and a
subtle pink shade of lip gloss.

At 6:50 in the morning, seven o'clock by her watch, she entered the boardinghouse through the back door. She knocked on
the door nearest to the exit. There was no answer. She knocked
again. Kadek glanced down the hall to her left. She saw a man
come out of a room. He wore a sarong wrapped around his waist
and had a towel draped over his shoulders. His long hair was wet
and hung in his eyes and below his ears. She assumed it was the
shower room that the man had exited. When the man saw the
woman standing at his door, he walked hastily in her direction.

"What are you doing there?" he demanded in the Javanese
dialect.

Kadek replied in the Indonesian language. "Sir, I am collecting laundry. I wanted to know if you have anything for us to wash today."

He replied in Indonesian as he approached Kadek. "If I did, it would be in the hall. You are early. It is not yet seven o'clock. Who are you?"

"I am Kadek, sir. I am helping the imam with chores. I will collect the laundry every morning and clean your room twice a week." She glanced at her wristwatch. "It is five minutes past seven. I . . ."

"Your watch is fast. It is not seven o'clock yet. And no one cleans my room. Ever."

Kadek bowed her head. "I apologize, sir."

"You are Balinese? A Hindu? What are you doing here?"

"Sir, I have converted to Islam. I am from Bali, but I plan to settle now in Java where I can practice my faith without prejudice."

Jeko Rusdiana stared at the woman's face. He gave a tight grin as he inhaled her scent.

"You do not appear to be a virtuous Muslim woman wearing your tight Balinese *baju kebaya*." His eyes took in her body, from her uplifted breasts past her slim waist and wide hips to her bare feet. "You should dress more conservatively in Klaten. This isn't Kuta. And cover your head with a *hijab*. You might provoke lustful cravings among the men here." He smirked as he continued to stare at her.

"You do not approve of my *baju* sir?" She glanced down at her sarong.

"Oh, I like it. I mean the other men around here, they, you know . . . might get the wrong impression," he stammered. "Let me enter my room now. You can collect my laundry in a few minutes, after I put on some clothes."

"I'll return later."

"Come back in fifteen minutes." Jeko entered his room and closed the door.

Kadek walked along the hall and gathered two laundry bags that had been left at another door. She carried them both outside and dropped them beside the wash tub. The old woman had not yet arrived.

She returned through the rear entrance twenty minutes later and knocked on Jeko's door.

"Who is it?" he shouted.

"It is Kadek, sir. May I collect your clothes now?"

He opened the door. She stood outside, bowing her head.

"You had better set your watch to the correct time," he said. "It is about 7:25."

Kadek removed her wristwatch and reset it. "You are kind. Again, I am sorry for disturbing you earlier. May I know your name, sir?"

"Call me Jeko," he replied with a lewd grin. "So how is Bali? I have never been there. Perhaps you can show me around."

"I would like that, Mr. Jeko."

"Make it Jeko. Drop the mister. I'm not an old man." He snickered.

"I only wish to show respect."

"You are polite. I like that," he said. "Do you have a motorbike, Kadek?"

"No I don't, mister . . . ah, Jeko. I take public transportation. I must find a job in Klaten so I can buy a motorbike. On credit. I left Bali with next to nothing. My family is not pleased with me. They know I have converted." Kadek again bowed her head, looking at the floor.

"I may be able to help you until you get yourself together. I could loan you some money. Could you use five hundred thousand rupiah?" Jeko asked as he made eye contact with a wry grin. "You do not appear to be a washer woman, Kadek. More like a celebrity."

"Oh, Jeko. You flatter me."

"Perhaps you suspect I am flirting with you."

"Are you?" she asked coyly.

He paused. "No. I'm testing you."

"Testing me?"

"Sorry. It's second nature. I didn't mean to offend. What time do you take your lunch, Kadek?"

"I don't know yet. I suppose whenever my work is finished for the morning. Why do you ask?"

"No reason you should spend your own money for lunch. Let me take you out to eat."

"That would be nice, Jeko. I don't know my way around Klaten. I often eat in my room."

"So it's settled. I'll meet you in the back after noon prayers. We'll ride on my bike. I know a couple of places where we can eat."

"Do you pray in the mosque?"

Jeko answered, "Not often. I pray in my room."

"Same with me."

"Do you have a prayer rug?" he asked.

"I have not been able to buy one yet. I don't have the money."

"We will find you a nice one after lunch. There are various designs, imported from Afghanistan and Turkey. We cannot have you praying on the floor and soiling your beautiful *baju*." Jeko cocked his head to one side and lifted his thick eyebrows as he looked into her eyes.

Kadek doubted he prayed five times a day. She was tempted to ask him for the direction to Mecca. She decided not to.

39

KLATEN

KADEK RETURNED TO THE BOARDINGHOUSE THROUGH the rear entry twenty minutes after midday prayers were finished in the mosque. She knocked on Jeko's door. Ten minutes earlier she had slipped inside the restroom at the salon across the street. There she had applied a dash more perfume between her breasts. The top button on her white, short-sleeved blouse remained unfastened. Anticipating the ride on the back seat of a motorbike, she had changed into jeans.

"Who is there?" Jeko called from inside his room.

"It is Kadek, Mr. Jeko"

A moment later he opened the door and glared. "It is Jeko, remember. Drop the 'mister.'."

"Did you go to prayers, Jeko?" she asked.

He smirked. "I am not religious. Don't tell the imam. He expects us all to be pious, you know."

"I asked because you might be able to coach me. Perhaps the imam can recommend someone." Kadek gave a demure smile.

"Ah, I can do that; coach you how to pray. Let's go. We'll have lunch and find you a prayer rug."

Jeko led Kadek out the back door and mounted his motor-bike. "Hop on," he said.

Kadek straddled the back seat of the Yamaha and wrapped her bare arms around Jeko's waist, her hands pressed tight against his stomach above his belt buckle. He switched on the engine and took off down the alley. When he arrived at the main road, Jeko was perhaps too distracted by her hands and the firm breasts pressed against his back to notice the man with the visor and black helmet following them.

Wayan had waited in the lot behind the boardinghouse and he now followed them at a steady distance of fifty meters.

Ten minutes later, the couple entered a small open-air *warung* in downtown Klaten. They moved along the buffet-style line and heaped food on their platters. Kadek noted the large scoops of red hot chili peppers Jeko plunked onto his plate. They found a table for two in the crowded room. As they sat she glanced out at the road and saw Wayan astride his parked motorbike. He switched on the engine after they made eye contact and took off down the street.

"So tell me about yourself, Kadek," Jeko said. "I'm curious why a Balinese would convert to our religion. Isn't that unusual?"

"I grew up and studied in Denpasar. My best friend at school was a Muslim girl. She persuaded me that there is one God. The Hindus, you know, believe in several gods. She prayed often, five times every day. I respected her for that. And she explained that the Quran was a book of peace and harmony. I am looking for that in my life, Jeko." Kadek gazed into his eyes as she spoke. "Last year I made the decision to become a Muslim. I could not reveal this to my parents. I would have been disinherited. My only recourse was to flee to Java, where I could convert to Islam without ridicule."

"I suppose your friend in Bali explained to you how we Muslims have been persecuted and attacked by crusaders and infidels throughout our history. Did she not?"

"No Jeko. I don't recall her ever mentioning conflict among the religions. She is a girl who wants to live her life in peace. The same as I do."

Jeko scoffed. "How naïve! Our lives are a struggle. And we Muslims are in the first stage of a great reawakening where we cut off the head of the snake."

"The snake?"

"America."

"I do not wish to talk of war and conflict, Jeko. Please don't speak like that."

"All right. Tell me about Bali, Kadek."

She related the story she had concocted about a simple life growing up in Denpasar and how this was the first time she had left the island. She confided that she had had a Balinese boyfriend who wanted to marry her. She broke off the relationship at the time she committed to becoming a Muslim. She left it to Jeko's imagination as to whether or not she was a virgin. After forty-five minutes, they had finished eating.

Before standing Kadek looked at Jeko and said, "You know, you would be more handsome if you trimmed your hair. It's a little long. I used to cut my brother's hair. Perhaps I can repay you for this delicious lunch by offering you a haircut when we return to the boardinghouse."

He looked at her, open-mouthed, before saying, "You would?"

She smiled seductively.

"Let's look for your prayer rug," Jeko said as he stood. "There is a shop not far from here. I pass by it often."

As they left the restaurant, Kadek noticed Wayan seated side-saddle on his parked Honda one block away.

Again Kadek climbed onto the back seat of Jeko's motorbike

and wrapped her arms around his waist as he started the engine and shifted into low gear.

"Hold on. We make a U-turn here." Jeko swung the bike into a circle that brought them to the other side of the street, heading back in the direction from which they had come. He gunned the engine and sped past motorbikes and cars in front of them.

"Slow down, Jeko. You frighten me."

He laughed and turned his head to the side so she could hear him. "Like I'm making a getaway? Don't worry. I've had a lot of practice."

"Like a bank robber?"

"Yeah, right. How did you know?" He laughed.

They made turns on three different streets until Jeko pulled over in front of a shop that displayed carpets in a window. As Kadek swung her leg off the seat and dismounted, she glanced back and saw Wayan driving slowly behind and then past them.

Inside the shop, Jeko lifted a prayer rug off the pile.

"This one is nice. I'll buy it for you."

"It looks expensive."

"Nothing too good for our new Balinese convert." Jeko grinned.

Kadek turned around and feigned that she was looking into the display window behind her. She saw an internet cafe across the street.

She turned to Jeko. "By the way, Jeko, do you know where I can send an email? I want to contact my classmate in Bali and tell her I have converted to Islam."

Jeko replied, "Why don't you ask the imam if you can use his PC?"

"Oh. I'd be ashamed to ask. I would not presume such a thing."

He hesitated for a moment. "No, Kadek, I don't use email. I can't help you."

Kadek noted the address of the café. She figured Jeko was not terribly bright if he had selected a carpet store across the street from his internet café. She trusted Wayan had also identified it.

Jeko paid for the prayer rug and instructed the cashier to have it delivered to the boardinghouse. He wrote down the address of the mosque. "Leave it with the imam and tell him it is for Jeko Rusdiana."

He and Kadek left the shop and returned to the boarding-house. Wayan followed them at a distance.

As Kadek thanked Jeko for lunch, she asked him if he would like her to trim his hair. "It would enhance your appearance. Not that there is anything wrong."

Jeko answered, "We are not allowed to have women inside our rooms."

"Of course."

"On second thought, I need to train you to pray. Perhaps we get together at *Isha.*" He referred to the time of prayer before a Muslim retires for the night. "They lock the door at ten o'clock. If you can arrive here tomorrow night before ten o'clock, perhaps we can kill two birds with one stone—you clip my hair and we pray together." He stared into Kadek's face for an uncomfortable moment.

She replied. "But if they lock the door . . ."

He grinned at her. "You can slip out of my room before ten o'clock. Would you agree?"

"Are you not afraid of being caught by the imam, Jeko?"

"I'm not if you're not. Anyway, he's harmless. If I have to move out of here, so be it. Are you game?"

She paused and looked into his eyes. "I guess I'm game if you are."

"The prayer rug will be delivered tomorrow. You bring the scissors. Tomorrow night?"

She bowed her head bashfully before speaking. "Oh, Jeko. I'm afraid. This is new to me. If we are caught . . . I would be punished. What would the imam do to me? It would be so humiliating."

"I have money. I would make a contribution to Al Fatah and tell him to forget about it. I can be persuasive. Trust me. So tomorrow night, Kadek? Around nine-thirty?"

She looked into his eyes and smiled.

"Good. Knock on my door three times like this." He knocked, waited three seconds before knocking again, then repeated it a third time. "When I hear it, I will know it is you and I will open the door. Make sure no one is in the hall. Enter my room, and I will close the door behind you."

40

CENTRAL JAVA

WAYAN DROVE THE CAR. HE STOPPED FOR KADEK two blocks from her boardinghouse on Jalan Nuri. Next he parked in the lot behind the hotel and picked up Marc and Bruno. Marc asked Wayan to drive north toward Mount Merapi, Fire Mountain, the most active volcano in Indonesia. At the outskirts of Klaten they saw smoke billowing from the mountain top.

As they approached the foothills, Kadek said, "I wouldn't get too close. This mountain can erupt at any time. It happens often."

Marc said at last, "Turn left here. This road looks secluded."

They drove south for five minutes. Marc turned and looked behind them. There were no vehicles following.

"Wayan, pull over to the left, beside the field."

Wayan parked and they got out of the car, strolling toward a plot of scrub land.

As they walked, Marc asked Kadek to explain the latest developments. She related the events of her day with Jeko Rusdiana.

She turned toward Wayan. "Did you see the internet café across from the carpet store?"

"I did."

"He mentioned to me that he passes by the rug store often."

Marc replied, "Follow him, Wayan, and observe which computer he uses."

Wayan said, "He leaves the boardinghouse in the late morning. I lost him last time. Tomorrow I'll see if I can tail him to that café."

Kadek continued, "I'm to meet him tomorrow night in his room to learn how to pray and to give him a haircut. He wants me there at nine-thirty. They lock the doors at ten. What do you want me to do, Marc?"

"We can't snatch him until he uses a computer to send his email. Either he uses the internet café, or he has one in his room.

"Go ahead, Kadek, make your meeting with him tomorrow night. Do what you need to do. And be sure you leave his room before they lock the back door. Suggest to him that you wish to meet again another night at the same time for more coaching."

Kadek grimaced. "He's looking at me for more than praying."

"String him along. Flirt with him a little longer. Can you do that?" Marc asked.

"This is difficult, Marc. He killed our parents. It makes me sick being near him, not to mention having to smile at him."

Marc placed a gentle hand on Kadek's shoulder. "It's nearly over. Soon you'll see the fruits of your efforts."

The four of them walked in silence. They knew the final stage of the operation against Jeko Rusdiana was imminent.

Marc looked at Bruno, who appeared to be brooding. "Soon you'll see action. Patience, my friend. This is still Kadek and Wayan's game."

The big Sicilian replied, "Yeah. We let it play out."

Marc said. "He's stopped using his cell phone. It's got to be email."

The next morning, Wayan sat at the window on the second floor of the boardinghouse. He looked below and observed Kadek chatting with the washer woman as she assisted with the laundry. At 9:45 Jeko emerged from the house. Wayan saw him stare at Kadek before he hopped onto his motorbike and took off down the alley.

Kadek glanced at the second floor window. Wayan had already left and was on his way downstairs.

41

KLATEN

W HEN WAYAN ARRIVED AT THE INTERSECTION OF the alley and the main road, Jeko had already disappeared into heavy traffic. Wayan made a left turn. His route would take him to the internet café across the street from the carpet shop. He traveled at a moderate speed. If that was Jeko's destination, he wanted to arrive when the terrorist was settled at a computer. Ten minutes later, he approached the café and spotted what he believed to be Jeko's Yamaha parked at the curb. As he passed he noted the plate number and confirmed that it was Jeko's bike.

Wayan parked, removed his helmet, and placed a baseball cap on his head, pulling it low over his eyes. He wore dark glasses. He entered the internet café and walked up to the cashier. In his peripheral vision, he spotted Jeko sitting at a computer. Jeko was typing furiously, oblivious to his surroundings. Wayan made an inquiry regarding the hourly rate before he exited the café, crossed the street, and entered the carpet store.

He inspected several prayer rugs, at the same time keeping an eye on the entrance to the internet café. The sales girl asked if he needed assistance. He replied that he was searching for a carpet as a gift.

At 10:25 Jeko left the internet café, mounted his motorbike, and sped off in the direction of the boardinghouse. Wayan dropped the rug he was inspecting onto a pile, thanked the sales girl, and left the shop. He jogged across the street, entered the café, and approached the cashier. As he entered, he noted that Jeko's computer was vacant.

"I need to use the internet for thirty minutes." He motioned to the computer Jeko had used. "Is that available?"

"Yes. That will be ten thousand rupiah. Good for an hour."

Wayan removed the bills from his wallet and handed them to the young woman. He walked to the computer station and sat.

He withdrew a slip of paper from inside his wallet. He'd memorized the email address that Marc passed to him the day before. Nevertheless, he read it again. His instructions were to send an email from the computer Jeko had used to the address listed on the paper. Roy Mancini's colleague in the U.S. would receive Wayan's email, and thus be able to identify the IP address and server Jeko used. The body of Wayan's email would state the approximate local time of ten o'clock to ten-twenty a.m. that Jeko had been using that computer. The contact would take it from there, hacking into the café's server. The terrorist's internet activity for that twenty-minute period would be revealed. Jeko's communications with his team of terrorists would be an open book.

Wayan logged into his own Hotmail account. He addressed his email to: info@instatel.net and listed the time that Jeko had been using the computer. He hit '*Send*'.

As Wayan was leaving the café, he heard his cell phone ping. The text message from Marc said: '*Urgent. Need to meet. Usual place 30 minutes. Bring car.*' The time was 10:45.

Wayan rode his Honda to Jalan Nuri where he'd parked the rental car behind Kadek's boardinghouse. He drove through the streets of Klaten at random until 11:10, arriving at the lot behind Marc's hotel at 11:15. At the same time Marc exited the rear of the hotel carrying his laptop case. He climbed into the passenger seat.

"Go," he said as Wayan put the car in gear.

"Where to?" Wayan asked.

"I've got something you need to hear. Find an out-of-the-way spot where you can park. You'll need to listen to this inside the car." Marc patted the case.

"We'll take the road to Magelang."

Twenty minutes later, they pulled into a cul-de-sac off the main road.

Wayan said, "This is about as quiet a spot as we're going to find. I'll stop at the end of the road."

Marc removed the laptop from its case.

"There's an audio file. I received it this morning. Jeko made a call. We need you to translate."

Marc booted the computer, went to his encrypted email account, and clicked on a link. He played the audio.

Wayan bent his head toward the laptop and listened. Right away he said, "They're speaking Javanese. Not my language but close enough. You'll have to play it back a few times so I can get the gist of it."

Wayan removed a pen and paper from the glove compartment and scribbled notes as he listened.

"Play it one more time," he said.

The conversation on the recording was animated and lasted a mere forty-five seconds. At last Wayan motioned for Marc to shut it off.

"All right. I got a sense of their conversation. Jeko phoned someone he calls Ghazali. Jeko is impatient . . . angry . . . wants to know how much longer he needs to remain in Klaten. Ghazali sounds like he's Jeko's superior. He orders Jeko never to use a cell phone again. He's pissed at Jeko for making that call. And he disconnects in the middle of whatever Jeko was trying to say next. Jeko had started to say something about Abu Najib."

"So we now have a cell phone number linked to a name— Ghazali. Dad's contact in the U.S. informed us that the phone was traced to Medan, North Sumatra. They are zeroing in on the exact location."

Wayan said, "I followed Jeko to the internet café this morning and sent an email to the address you gave me."

"Good work. We'll know soon if we can connect the dots between Jeko, Ghazali, Abu Najib and whomever else. I'll hear from Roy after they hack into Jeko's email. You and Kadek continue your surveillance. Let Kadek know he's getting impatient. She needs to be careful."

"She'll meet him in his room tonight as planned."

"Right. You loiter nearby, Wayan."

"I intend to."

42

ARC RECEIVED THE ENCRYPTED EMAIL FROM HIS father later that afternoon. The SID had hacked into the computer at the internet café, and Jeko Rusdiana's usage for eighteen minutes had been revealed. He had logged on to a Yahoo email account. The username was *awakening*. The password was *mati2003#*.

Jeko had drafted an email that he had not sent. In fact, there were dozens of emails in draft form on the account. The bombers were communicating with each other by way of email drafts. Each member of the cell knew the username and password for the Yahoo account. They would compose drafts and leave them unsent on the server. Clever.

Roy informed Marc that they wouldn't have time to translate the scores of emails from Indonesian to English. Each email had been signed off with what appeared to be an alias. Jeko used the name *Roger*. There were ten different aliases in use—ten members of the cell.

Roy Mancini had translated the email Jeko sent that morning. Jeko told the members of the group that he was getting tired of hanging out in Klaten and felt he needed to make a move as soon as his false passport and KTP card were ready. The complaint appeared to be addressed to an alias: Edgar. Roger told Edgar that if he couldn't give him an answer within a week, he would go directly to *Gunung*. The same day, Edgar replied that they were working on Jeko's counterfeit passport and KTP card, and he would get back to him. He mentioned that *Hitam* received his fake passport in Surabaya that week, and that Roger's documents were next in line. Edgar's computer had been traced to an internet café in Medan. Edgar was Ghazali.

Roy commented that he suspected the drafts were all written in Indonesian, and not in Javanese, because some of the terrorists were not from Central or East Java. Perhaps *Hitam* and others were from different parts of Indonesia, and Indonesian was the one language they all had in common.

43

KLATEN

K ADEK ARRIVED AT THE REAR OF THE HOUSE AT 9:20 that night. Wayan followed her and parked his Honda in the lot. He stood in a shadow and watched her enter through the back door.

Kadek knocked three times in the code Jeko had told her to use. There was no response. She looked down the hallway, and seeing no one, knocked again. He opened his door, and motioned for her to enter his room without uttering a word. She stepped inside and Jeko closed the door.

"So you've come to learn how to pray, Kadek," he said. He gave her a wry smile. "I had my doubts."

Kadek glanced around the room, taking it all in. There was no computer.

"I have a lot to learn, Jeko," she replied, with a bowed head.

"They delivered the prayer rug this morning." He pointed to a carpet on the floor. "Here, let me show you how we do it."

Jeko went to his knees on the rug and dropped his head to the ground.

"Some men have permanent marks here because of the many times they perform like this, knocking their heads on the floor. As you see, I don't." He pointed with an index finger to his forehead.

He continued, "Now, why don't you try your new carpet, Kadek. Come and get on your knees like I did and bend over. I will stand behind you."

Kadek hesitated, aware that he was telling her to do something out of the ordinary. She recalled Marc's final instruction: *'String him along. Flirt with him a little longer.'*

"Are you allowed to watch me, Jeko?"

"Why not?" He placed his hands on his hips and grinned at her.

She dropped to her hands and knees. Jeko positioned himself behind her.

"Like this?" she asked.

"No. Drop your forehead to the ground and spread your legs. There, to the northwest, in the direction of Mecca."

Kadek obeyed. She was wearing tight-fitting jeans, and she knew that her raised ass was now prominent. She glanced back, through her spread legs, and saw Jeko staring at her, wide-eyed, his mouth open. She saw him take a deep breath. She stood.

"I'm not ready for this yet," she said. "Perhaps tomorrow night, Jeko. Give me time. Please."

He was speechless, and seemed to be making an effort to regain his composure.

"And tomorrow night I will trim your hair as I promised."

He didn't move away.

"Will you allow me to return tomorrow night?" She smiled, making direct eye contact with him.

At last he spoke. "Oh, yes, Kadek. You must return tomorrow night for further training. And if you wish to cut my hair, you are welcome to it."

She looked at her watch. "It is nearly ten o'clock. I'd better leave."

"Come earlier tomorrow night. We have more to accomplish, don't we?"

"What time would you like me to knock?"

"At 9:15. Be sure no one is in the hallway. This time I'll let you in right away."

Kadek's eyes moved along his body. She noted the hard ridge up along the crotch of his jeans. She shifted her gaze into his eyes.

"I'll go now." She walked to the door, unlocked it, and pulled it open. "Good night, Jeko."

He remained speechless as she closed the door behind her.

44

KLATEN

THE NEXT DAY, MARC LOOKED FIRST AT BRUNO AND then at the two Balinese. "You'll meet him tonight, Kadek?"

"Yes, at 9:15. He wants me back," Kadek replied. "Marc, make this the last time I need to do this. Please!"

"This is the night we snatch him, Kadek. We have what we need. We've hacked into their email correspondence and we have the aliases of ten of them. One of them is in Medan. Jeko will tell us the rest of what we need to know. Guaranteed."

It was late afternoon. The four continued to walk along the side of the grass field at the end of the isolated cul-de-sac, off the main road to Magelang. There was now a spring in Bruno's step. The big Sicilian may have been rehearsing in his mind the forthcoming event at the base of Mount Sumbing.

Kadek's expression was one of relief. Her earlier tense look had disappeared. Wayan's face was impassive.

Marc continued, "Wayan will bring the car to the rear of the parking lot five minutes before Kadek enters the room. That will be at 9:10. Bruno and I will lay low in the back seat." He looked at Wayan. "One minute before Kadek knocks on his door, at 9:14, you park as close to the back door as you can, pop the trunk, and keep the engine running. Kadek will knock on his door at 9:15. Bruno and I will take it from there. Let's synchronize our watches now. It is 4:25."

The three others adjusted their timepieces.

"What if there is someone in the hallway?" Wayan asked.

"Bruno and I will be wearing Indonesian Special Forces attire and ski masks. I acquired the uniforms last week. Indonesians have been conditioned over the years to respect military authority. Bruno's semi-automatic will be visible. It's most important to stick to the timeframe."

"Do I need to enter his room?" Kadek asked.

"No. You knock three times in accordance with the code. And if he asks who's there, you reply that it's Kadek. At that point, you get out of our way and stand at the back door. I'll collect whatever evidence I can inside the room. You ride in the front. Bruno and I will sit in the back. Jeko goes inside the trunk. Any questions?"

The three shook their heads and continued walking. After a minute's silence, Marc stopped and turned around. "Let's go to the car and drive to Mount Sumbing. I want to be sure the setting there hasn't been disturbed. Russell ought to be hungry by now. We'll leave the chair, wire cutters, and flashlight there beside his cage."

Wayan and Kadek glanced at each other and smiled for the first time that afternoon. Bruno, never one to display much sentiment, laid a hand on both Wayan and Kadek's shoulders. "Soon, kids, soon," he said.

When they returned to Klaten after dark, Bruno and Marc got out of the car downtown and took a taxi to their hotel. Wayan dropped Kadek off three blocks from her boardinghouse. He drove on to her boardinghouse and parked the car behind it. He rode his motorbike to the downtown area, where he killed time until 8:45. He returned to the boardinghouse on Jalan Nuri where he got into the parked car and waited.

Kadek exited the house at nine o'clock and climbed into the passenger seat beside Wayan. They drove to the back of the Jayapura hotel where Marc and Bruno were waiting, holding kit bags. As soon as they got into the back seat, the men stripped to shorts and T-shirts and donned the Indonesian Special Forces attire they'd packed.

Wayan turned off the car's headlights as they arrived at the parking lot behind the Al Fatah boardinghouse at 9:10. Kadek had gotten out of the car one minute earlier, two blocks north of the mosque. She would walk to the boardinghouse.

Marc and Bruno were out of sight in the back seat. At 9:14 they pulled on their masks and Wayan drove from where they had been parked to a spot three meters from the back of the building. As he stopped the car, the two masked men emerged and stood at the door while Kadek arrived in the parking lot on foot. The three of them entered the building together. There was no one in the hallway.

At 9:15 Kadek knocked on the door three times, using the coded intervals. A moment later the door was opened inward. Jeko made an unsuccessful effort to slam it shut the instant he saw the two men dressed as Special Forces operatives. The muscular Bruno applied a long strip of duct tape across his mouth and wound it several times around his head and then inserted plugs in Jeko's ears so that the prisoner would not be able to hear in the event one of them inadvertently spoke English. Satisfied, Marc dropped a black hood over the Indonesian's head and tied it around his throat. Bruno tied the man's hands behind his back with plastic strips. Marc spotted a cell phone on a bedside table.

He pocketed it, and then collected all the papers on the desktop and inside the drawers. Bruno and Marc marched Jeko Rusdiana out the back door as Kadek held it open. After she closed the door she opened the trunk of the car. Bruno lifted the man off his feet and tossed him hard into the back. Marc hogtied his ankles together and closed the trunk. The time was 9:18. Throughout the ordeal, Jeko had not been able to make a sound.

Wayan drove the car along the alley with Kadek in the front seat. Marc and Bruno sat in the back. When he got to the intersection, he turned on the headlights and merged into the thin nighttime traffic, heading northwest toward Mount Sumbing.

45

CENTRAL JAVA

"HERE'S THE PLAN," MARC SAID AS THEY TURNED OFF Highway 14 forty minutes later and drove west toward the small town of Windusari. "Bruno and I will continue to wear these Special Forces outfits and ski masks during the first stage of the interrogation. He's likely to be intimidated by the presence of two elite military types. We'll continue for a while with that charade. We remain silent, of course, and stare at him. Wayan, you soften him up. Later on you translate for me. You guys want to flip a coin and decide who shoots him?"

Wayan looked over at Kadek and replied, "Later."

"Okay with me," Bruno exclaimed.

They drove in silence until they arrived at the end of the dirt road, at the base of Mount Sumbing. Wayan had turned off the headlights soon after leaving Windusari.

"We're clear. No one following us," he whispered as he parked the car.

"Open the trunk, Wayan. Bruno, you and I will march him along the path. Kadek guide us with the flashlight. Remember Bruno, not a word," Marc whispered. He put his index finger to his lips, signaling silence. He and Bruno pulled on their ski masks.

Bruno raised the trunk door and untied the plastic strips from the prisoner's ankles, hauling him out of the car. The man, sightless because of the hood over his head, twisted on the ground and made a futile attempt to scoot away. The Sicilian kicked his feet out from under him.

"Stand up, Jeko," Wayan ordered, speaking Indonesian.

Bruno and Marc grabbed the man's arms, hoisted him to his feet, and guided him forward. Kadek held the flashlight and led them to the narrow path and into the forest. They arrived at the tree ten minutes later.

Marc opened the metal folding chair on the near side of the tree. Bruno placed Jeko on the chair, removed his hood, and held him down. Marc untied his hands and used the strips to retie his ankles together. Kadek pointed the flashlight at Jeko's face, blinding him. Wayan pulled the duct tape from around the captive's head, removed the earplugs, and stood in front of him. Kadek moved the light from the man's face and aimed it at his wet crotch. She stared into his eyes with a blank expression.

"Good evening, Jeko." Wayan spoke Indonesian. "Or is it Roger? Seems you've pissed in your pants."

Marc and Bruno stood three meters behind Wayan. Bruno raised the semi-automatic pistol in full view of the prisoner.

"Answer the question, asshole," Wayan ordered. "Is it Jeko or Roger?"

There was a long silence. At last the prisoner spoke. "How did you find me?" He stared menacingly at Kadek.

Wayan continued, "The Mitsubishi van. What else did you buy, Jeko? The chemicals for the bomb?"

He was startled. "How did you know that?"

"You left the receipts inside your home in Madura. That was stupid, Jeko. You purchased the chemicals in Surabaya."

"You know nothing," Jeko shouted. He spat on the ground in front of him. Bruno took a step forward. Marc took the Sicilian's arm and held him back.

"We know enough," Wayan said in a calm voice. "We can make this interview painless. Or . . . here, let me show you a recent picture. Someone you know?"

The Balinese removed the cell phone from his pocket. He opened it and selected a photograph, the one showing Jeko's mother with the carving knife at her throat.

"Your mama, Jeko?" he asked as he placed the picture in front of the prisoner's face. "She's still being held. And we will kill her tonight if you fuck with us. Your mother and brother will pay with their lives because of you. Now about the chemicals? Tell us about the bomb."

Jeko's mouth opened and closed. Yet he was speechless. He made a high-pitched cry.

"The bomb materials, Jeko."

"Yes, I bought them." Panic in his voice.

"Tell us all about it. From the beginning."

Jeko hesitated. He swallowed. "Can you untie my legs?"

"Later. After you talk to us. The bomb?"

"I bought the chemicals in Surabaya at different stores. We made the bomb at a warehouse outside the city."

"Go on."

Jeko took a deep breath before speaking. "The explosive was made of potassium chlorate, aluminum powder and sulfate. We packed the van with twelve plastic filing cabinets, filled with the explosives. The weight of the bomb was one thousand kilograms."

Wayan spoke when Jeko fell silent. "Continue."

"The booster was TNT, connected to one hundred and fifty meters of detonating cord. I packed the cabinets in the van and drove from Surabaya to Bali. I trained the driver and turned the van over to him on the night of the bombing. It was huge. None of us knew how big the explosion would be."

"And the bomb-maker? Who put it together? Give me a name—the man's alias and true name."

"I don't know. Our cells were compartmented. I was involved in purchasing. The car and the chemicals." Jeko raised his hands in surrender and shook his head.

"Where did you get the money?"

"I can't say."

"Can't or won't?"

Wayan and Jeko stared at each other for several moments. The bomber shifted his gaze to Kadek and gave a wry smile.

"You're a good actress," he said to her.

She stared back at him in silence.

"Let's get on with it," Wayan said. "Who was the bomb-maker? You are not going to leave until you tell us."

"I told you. I had my job. I never knew the others."

"Roger . . . right? The email account. We don't believe you. You've communicated with all of them. Shall we go through the names, the aliases? You're going to tell us in the end, Jeko. Make it painless for yourself. Tell us now, and we'll set you free. We want the bomb-maker and the mastermind. You're a small fry, as a matter of fact, and you don't mean shit to us."

Jeko shook his head and folded his arms. At that point, Wayan turned and looked at Marc.

46

MARC AND BRUNO WALKED BEHIND THE TREE. THEY lifted the crate and placed it in front of Jeko. Marc grasped the wire cutters and snipped a round hole into the wire mesh at the top of the cage. As he did so, the four-foot-long snake became agitated. It issued a loud hiss that startled everyone. Marc quickly stepped away from the crate. Jeko gasped at the sound and cried out when he looked down at the viper making its rapid S-loops at the bottom of the cage.

"Recognize him, Jeko?" Wayan asked.

Jeko opened his mouth, eyes wide.

"I know that one," he uttered.

Wayan asked Jeko, "And you know his bite causes excruciating pain? You're aware certain death comes within an hour? And that you'll be in agony during that time?"

The terrified prisoner nodded his head. Marc and Bruno stood in front of him, having kept on their black ski masks. Marc grabbed Jeko's right wrist and held it above the hole at the top of the cage.

He spoke to Wayan in English. "Tell him I'll thrust his arm

196

inside the cage in five seconds if he doesn't start talking." Wayan translated to Indonesian. The irritated snake was now coiled and hissing.

The terrorized captive shouted rapidly in Indonesian.

Wayan translated. "He says the bomb-maker's name is Omar, and he is preparing to leave Indonesia using a forged passport."

"What's the name on the passport, and where is he going?"

Wayan and Jeko spoke to each other.

"He doesn't know the name on the bomb-maker's passport. It was prepared by an accomplice in Surabaya. Jeko is supposed to receive his own false documents soon. Omar will go to the Philippines to train Abu Sayyaf on how to make large bombs."

Marc demanded, "Give me the address of the passport forger."

Jeko hesitated for a moment too long. Marc gripped his wrist and thrust his hand into the hole at the top of the cage.

"No!" Jeko screamed in English. "I have it." Marc pulled his hand out of the opening an instant before the snake struck.

Jeko removed his wallet from his pocket and pulled out a piece of paper and handed it to Marc.

"Where is Omar now?" Marc asked.

Wayan and Jeko conversed.

"He's in North Sulawesi arranging the boat that will take him to Mindanao."

"Where in Mindanao?"

"Zamboanga."

"Ask him from which port in Sulawesi he's departing."

Marc held the prisoner's hand against the top of the cage. The four-foot-long snake continued to coil and lunge at the sides and top of the cage. Kadek pointed the beam of the flashlight at the head of the angry reptile.

"The port is Bitung. Near Manado."

Marc asked, "What is Omar's alias on the email account?"

Wayan said, "Jeko says they call him Hitam because of his dark complexion. Hitam means black in Indonesian."

At that point, the petrified Jeko bent forward and vomited on top of the cage. The snake hissed louder than ever and struck at the wire above him, snapping an inch from Jeko's hand. Jeko choked on his vomit as he attempted to scream and pull away.

"Let's move on," Marc said. "Who is Edgar?"

Wayan translated.

"He is Ghazali, Jeko's superior. Jeko takes his instructions from him. He says Ghazali was the operational commander for the bombing."

"Where is he?"

"Jeko says he's in Jakarta."

Marc knew better because of the intercepted phone call. He held onto Jeko's wrist with both hands and forced his fingers back into the hole at the top of the cage.

Jeko spit bile out of his mouth and spoke again.

"He says Ghazali is in Medan and is preparing to leave Indonesia under an alias."

"Where to?"

"He says he'll take a boat from Sumatra to Penang, Malaysia. He'll meet a senior Al Qaeda operative in Penang."

"Who will he meet?"

"Hambali," Jeko whimpered.

"Holy shit! That's Osama bin Laden's chief lieutenant for Southeast Asia. Ask him how Hambali was involved with the Bali bombing."

Wayan and Jeko now spoke at length as Marc pressed the latter's hand firmly onto the crate's wire mesh.

"Hambali coordinated the bombing with Abu Najib in Surakarta. The joint venture, as he calls it, was planned by Al

Qaeda. Abu Najib commands Jamaah Islamiyah. Osama bin Laden passed funds to JI through Hambali. Ghazali reports to Abu Najib. Jeko calls Abu Najib their spiritual leader."

Marc turned his head and said to Bruno and Kadek, "Seems Russell is having the desired effect. We have our four: Jeko Rusdiana, Ghazali, Omar, the bomb-maker, and Abu Najib at the top. We're going to have to move fast to make martyrs of them all."

Marc continued, "I'm curious. How much money did Osama bin Laden send to Indonesia through Hambali?"

Wayan replied, "He heard from Ghazali that Hambali delivered thirty thousand dollars. Jeko received money to buy the Mitsubishi van and the bomb-making materials. He's living in Klaten with the leftover cash."

Now that the prisoner was singing, Marc figured it was time to go over the cell phone's contacts chain. He now knew each of the terrorists' true names, and needed to link them to phone numbers so that their locations could be pinpointed by the SID. Marc had the list of numbers in a pocket of his uniform.

"Bruno, hold his hand to the cage," Marc instructed.

He pulled out the list and at the same time held the cell phone in front of the terrorist's face.

"We have every number on your phone," Marc announced, forgetting for a moment that Jeko did not speak English. He glanced at Wayan. "I will give you a date and a phone number. I want the *true* name that matches the number. Hesitate for an instant and we feed your arm to the snake." Wayan translated.

Wayan spoke the phone numbers from Marc's list and the dates that the calls were made during the week prior to the bombing. Jeko identified from memory the phone numbers of Ghazali, Omar, and three other accomplices. There were calls to minor confederates and one call to the suicide bomber who had driven the van along the road to the hotel in Nusa Dua. There were no calls to Abu Najib. Jeko insisted that Ghazali was the only member of their team who communicated with the Jamaah Islamiyah commander in Surakarta. And with the Arab.

"What Arab?" Marc asked.

"He says he never met him. The members of the cell only refer to him as the 'Arab'."

Marc turned his back on his captive and looked at Wayan and Kadek. "It's time," he announced.

Bruno turned and handed his weapon to Kadek.

Marc stared into Kadek's eyes before speaking. "You up to it?"

She grimaced and replied, "*Hukum mati.*"

Wayan translated. "It means justice-by-execution."

Bruno and Marc each took an arm, lifted Jeko to his feet, pulled him away from the cage, and turned him around so that his back was to the Balinese siblings. He protested in a hoarse voice. Marc gagged him with duct tape which he clipped to size with the wire cutters.

Kadek stood in place for a moment, straining to control her emotion, as Wayan stepped in front of Jeko, stared into his face, and noted the fear in his eyes. He then glanced at his sister and moved away. She stood behind the murderer of her parents, and raised the pistol to the nape of his scrawny neck. "I should have given you that haircut," she muttered in his ear before she squeezed the trigger.

The bullet cleaved his spinal cord and entered the base of his skull, traversed his brain, and exited his temple above the right eye. He fell forward against the cage causing the viper to emit an extraordinary hiss. The cage continued to rock as the snake struck hard at the wire ceiling.

Kadek lowered the weapon to her side. She knew another bullet would not be necessary. Jeko's blood flowed from his head like dark oil.

Marc took a photograph of the corpse with his cell phone and asked of no one in particular, "Should we give him a proper burial?" He would delete the photo as soon as he had copied it onto his laptop and transmitted it to his father.

Wayan replied, "He doesn't deserve it. Let him provide a proper meal instead for the wild animals in the forest."

They agreed to leave the snake in its cage rather than risk being bitten themselves. Bruno stared at the agitated Russell's viper, flipped his cigarette in its direction, and joined the other three as they strolled along the path leading back to the car.

47

KLATEN, CENTRAL JAVA,
AND MEDAN, SUMATRA

At 1:45 A.M. in Klaten, Marc emailed his father the list of cell phone numbers and the corresponding true names extracted from Jeko. The email continued: "(A) One dead: JR. Photo attached. (B) Most urgent need is tracking of Ghazali and Omar. Both departing Indonesia. Using forged passports. (C) No cause for remaining targets to be aware of JR death. Request you draft emails appearing to be written by JR alias Roger." Marc ended the email by listing the address of the passport forger in Surabaya.

The reply from Roy Mancini arrived in the morning the next day. "(A) Ghazali confirmed in Medan per cell phone tracking. Overnight location No. 15 Jalan Panjaitan north of intersection Jalan Seri Bahorok. KTP photo attached. (B) Omar confirmed in Bitung, North Sulawesi. Overnight location corner Jalan Dumais and Jalan Tangkudung. Photo not yet available. (C) Hambali drafts identified. Alias: *Sultan*. (D) Police to raid passport forger's address. Expect to have passport names used by Ghazali and Omar soonest. Will revert."

Marc called the team together at noon. They met in the forested area near the river beyond Kadek's boardinghouse on Jalan Nuri.

"The three of you need to fly to Medan tomorrow morning," Marc said. "I've forwarded Ghazali's ID photo to Wayan's cell phone."

"Got it," said Wayan.

"We know where he stays at night."

Bruno asked, "What's our cover?"

"There's a lumber export business in that area. The logs come from forests in North Sumatra and Aceh, and the sawmills are around Medan. You'll pose as lumber buyers for the Italian market. Kadek, you'll be Bruno's local guide and interpreter. Wayan, you keep Ghazali under surveillance.

"I doubt you can invent a plausible reason to catch him in his room like you did Jeko. You might have to force an entry late at night. Bruno will make the hit. I'll fly to Penang tomorrow. We could have a target of opportunity in Malaysia: Hambali. An unexpected bonus."

The following day, Bruno, Wayan, and Kadek took Garuda Airlines flights from Jogjakarta to Medan. Marc flew to Jakarta and connected on a Malaysian Airlines flight to Penang, Malaysia.

Bruno and Kadek traveled from the Medan airport together and took rooms at the Novotel Hotel in the downtown area. Wayan arrived on a separate flight and checked into the budget Kesawan Hotel. He rented a motorbike nearby and traveled to the address of Ghazali's boardinghouse at No. 15 Jalan Panjaitan. After lurking in the area for two hours without seeing the target, he entered the boardinghouse and inquired about room and board. The owner of the house informed him that there were no vacant rooms, but one guest had given notice that he was going to leave that day. Wayan paid in advance to secure the room for himself. The owner was unsure at what time the current boarder would depart. Wayan asked him to call his cell phone as soon as the person was preparing to leave. Finally Wayan inquired about the location of the nearest mosque.

At 3:45 in the afternoon, Wayan rode his motorbike to the nearby Al-Jihad Mosque. Posing as a Muslim, he entered the building, dropped to his knees, and observed the twenty men who were performing late afternoon prayers. There were three young men in the group who, from a distance at the back of the room, resembled his photo of Ghazali. Wayan decided to extend his prayers, keeping his forehead to the floor, until most of the others had filed out. He knew the first two men weren't his target once he saw their faces up close. The third man was Ghazali. Wayan recognized him even though he was now clean-shaven, unlike the man with the unkempt beard depicted in Wayan's cell phone gallery.

Wayan followed Ghazali's motorbike, at a discreet distance, back to the boardinghouse on Jalan Panjaitan. He lingered at a spot a hundred meters away, where he could keep an eye on the entrance to the house.

At the same time Wayan was watching the boardinghouse, Bruno and Kadek were inspecting dark red Meranti lumber at a saw mill in the nearby town of Binjai, west of Medan. At the end of the visit, Bruno placed a verbal order for a container-load of premium-grade lumber for shipment to Genoa. After negotiating the order and promising that a written contract and letter of credit would be forthcoming, Kadek felt her cell phone vibrate in her jeans pocket. The message was from Wayan. The text said: *Ghazali spotted and currently inside boardinghouse. I plan to check into a room there later today.*

Bruno and Kadek returned to the Novotel in the hired car and told the driver to stand by. They huddled in the hotel's lobby, where Kadek fired off a text message from her cell phone to Wayan's: "*Back in hotel. Advise.*"

Wayan replied five minutes later. *"Received call advising my room available at five p.m. Will update you later."*

Wayan entered the house at 4:45 and took a seat in the reception area, waiting for his room's current tenant to check out. Thirty minutes later, Ghazali came down the stairs lugging a large backpack. He walked to the reception desk without glancing at Wayan. Wayan continued sitting and remained poker-faced during this unexpected twist of fate. Through the corner of his eye, he watched Ghazali settle his bill and exit the house. The receptionist looked at Wayan, and raised a finger, indicating he could now check in.

Wayan removed his cell phone from his pocket and typed a message to Kadek: *"Ghazali checked out. Prepare to move."*

Kadek responded: *"We're checking out."*

Wayan walked to the desk and apologized to the receptionist, explaining that something had come up, and that he would not be checking into a room after all. He loitered in the hallway for a few seconds before leaving the house. As he exited he saw Ghazali across the street climb into the backseat of a red taxi and give the driver instructions. Wayan had parked his motorbike at the curb in front of the house. He allowed the taxi to take off before starting his bike, making a U-turn, and following the taxi at a distance of a hundred meters.

The taxi headed north on Jalan Panjaitan before turning left. The driver did not appear to be practicing counter-surveillance, but was driving a direct route on major streets going west through the city. He continued for a couple of miles. All of a sudden, the taxi made a right turn across the traffic without signaling and pulled into the parking lot for the Pinang Baris bus terminal. Wayan was unable to cross in front of oncoming traffic and continued past the terminal until he was able to make a U-turn and return. When he entered the parking lot he noted the red taxi exit the station. Ghazali was no longer inside the cab. Wayan parked his motorbike among the others outside the terminal.

Wayan feared Ghazali might recognize him from the board-inghouse, so he sauntered into the terminal with his head bowed. He had removed his helmet and put on a cap, which he pulled low. Moments later he spotted Ghazali standing at one of the counters, evidently purchasing a ticket.

Wayan bought a newspaper at a kiosk and took a seat at the far end of the terminal among several passengers. As he pretended to read the paper, he focused on Ghazali, who sat staring straight ahead at the opposite side of the large room. At last Wayan typed a text message to Kadek: *"Ghazali at Pinang Baris bus terminal. Purchased ticket. Destination not known. Keep your hired car and driver. Wait at hotel lobby for further information."*

At 7:45 Wayan saw Ghazali stand, lift his backpack onto his shoulders and saunter outside. He appeared to look along the corridor for a particular bus. Finally he found it. Wayan walked past several buses until he got to the one Ghazali had boarded. He continued walking and glanced at the bus as he passed it. The sign above the windshield displayed BANDA ACEH. Wayan knew that was a seaport at the north tip of Aceh province where Ghazali might make his exit from Indonesia.

48

WAYAN WALKED THROUGH THE CROWDED TERMINAL and out to the lot where he had parked. Before starting the motorbike he sent a text to Kadek: "*Leave hotel now. Meet me with car and driver outside Tip Top Restaurant at nine. We drive to Aceh tonight.*"

The funky, Dutch-era Tip Top Restaurant was across the street from Wayan's hotel, the Kesawan. Wayan checked out of his room and left his motorbike with the hotel manager, requesting that it be returned to the nearby shop the next day. He trotted across the street to the Tip Top at 8:45 and sat alone at a table in the restaurant's street-side patio. He ordered a tall marquiza juice. At 9:05 the green Toyota pulled in front of the restaurant. Wayan grabbed his backpack, left a tip on the table, stepped onto the sidewalk, and dashed to the car. Bruno opened the rear door and Wayan slipped in. He announced to the driver, "We're going to Banda Aceh."

"Very far. And too dangerous," the middle-aged driver replied.

"How much do you need?" Wayan asked.

"Mister, I won't get a return fare from there. None of us go to Aceh. Too much trouble."

"So how much are you going to charge us?"

"Three million rupiah." The driver turned and looked back at Wayan.

Wayan hesitated for a second. There was no time to haggle. "All right. Get us there before sunrise and we'll pay you three million. Now go."

Wayan turned to Kadek. "You'll have to wear your *hijab* while we're in Aceh, you know. And change out of your jeans into a loose-fitting *kebaya*. It's the only province in Indonesia where they practice sharia law. They're ultra-conservative, as bad as the Saudis."

"So I've heard. Maybe we can stop someplace so I can change before we get to the border," she replied.

Wayan asked the driver to pull into a gas station and fill the tank before they got to Aceh. Kadek got the message. She'd change her clothes and cover her head with the *hijab* in a restroom when they stopped for gas.

They drove through the night and small hours of the morning north along National Highway 25. Bruno, Kadek and Wayan took turns sleeping. One of them remained on watch in the front passenger seat, awake and alert. At three-thirty in the morning, the driver complained that he couldn't drive any further, he needed to sleep. Wayan told him to pull over to the side of the road, where they exchanged places. The Balinese drove on. Bruno road shotgun.

As they approached Sigli City on the coast of the Malacca Straits at four in the morning, Wayan saw the taillights far ahead. He accelerated and, in five minutes, caught up to the fast-moving bus. The bus slowed as it arrived at the outskirts of the city. Wayan pulled close behind. It was too dark to distinguish the colors of the vehicle. But he figured the odds were that this was the Medan-to-Banda Aceh bus that had departed the Medan terminal after eight o'clock the night before.

"Kadek, wake up," Wayan whispered.

She sat upright. Wayan glanced at the rearview mirror and saw that the driver was asleep, breathing through his open mouth.

"That's the bus." He pointed. "I'm going to follow it into Banda Aceh."

Wayan put a hand on Bruno's forearm as the Sicilian reached into his bag and felt for the Beretta and silencer. "Patience, Bruno. I'll follow at a distance until we arrive in the city. There could be soldiers riding in the bus. This is a hazardous place. People in Aceh are in rebellion against the government in Jakarta. The rebels want independence. There are army forces on patrol throughout the province. We're lucky we haven't met any check-points."

49

ACEH PROVINCE, SUMATRA

"BRUNO, HIDE THE GUN AND SILENCER UNDER YOUR SEAT. Quick!" Wayan ordered. The Sicilian saw the flashing red light ahead of them at the same instant. He removed the weapon from his bag and shoved it beneath his seat. Wayan glanced into the rearview mirror at the sleeping driver.

"A military checkpoint. Remember your cover story: lumber buyer. I'll handle this," Wayan whispered. "Trouble ahead, Kadek." She was wide awake.

Wayan slowed the car, stopped at the lighted barricade, and rolled down his window. The checkpoint was manned by ten soldiers, each attired in full combat gear, with automatic weapons at the ready and trained on the car. Two of them walked to the driver's side.

"Good morning," a soldier said in Indonesian. "Show me your KTP, driver's license, and registration."

"Good morning, officer," Wayan replied as he reached for his wallet. He removed his national ID card and driver's license. "We're renting this car. The driver is asleep behind me."

"Wake him."

Kadek nudged the man in the ribs twice until he opened his eyes.

"You're from Bali. What are you doing in Aceh?" the soldier asked Wayan as he studied the ID card.

"Our Italian client is traveling in Sumatra, searching for sawn timber exporters." Wayan nodded toward Bruno. "My sister and I are his guides. We're going to Banda Aceh."

"Everyone out of the car," the officer ordered. "Slowly."

The four of them stepped onto the road.

The soldier ordered Kadek and the driver to present their IDs, and for Bruno to hand over his passport.

"Why are you dressed like a Muslim? You are Balinese according to your KTP."

"Sir, I have converted to Islam. I did so in Java earlier this month," Kadek replied.

"You need to amend your KTP. It still identifies you as a Hindu."

"I will do that, sir, as soon as I return to Bali. I can change it when I get home, after the job is finished with this Italian client." She motioned toward Bruno.

"All right. Be sure." The soldier returned the cards to the Indonesians and the passport to Bruno. "And be careful. Don't stop for anyone unless it is a military or police checkpoint. The rebels are dangerous. Your foreign client needs to buy his wood in some other province. You may proceed."

Wayan nodded and climbed back into the car. The others followed. The soldiers lowered their weapons, opened the barricade, and stood back, allowing Wayan to move forward.

Forty-five minutes later, an hour before sunrise, they arrived at the outskirts of Banda Aceh, the largest city and capital of the province. The earlier delay at the checkpoint had prevented

Wayan from following close behind the speeding Medan-to-Banda Aceh bus. It was now lost to them.

They needed to locate the bus terminal. But first Wayan would pay off the driver and return the car to him. They arrived in the center of town, and Wayan drove along the main street.

"Let's find a place to stay," he said.

He pulled over in front of a small two-story hotel. Bruno removed their bags from the car as Wayan paid the driver three million Rupiah. They stood on the sidewalk until the car was out of sight.

"We'll wait here for a taxi," Wayan said.

They stood for ten minutes. At last a cab stopped in front of them.

"Take us to the bus terminal," Wayan said. "The one for the Medan bus."

They arrived at the station ten minutes later. As they climbed out of the cab they noticed a bus leave and pull onto the road. The sign over the windshield read BANDA ACEH-MEDAN.

"That looks like the one I saw him board in Medan. Same company," Wayan exclaimed. "Kadek, go inside. You memorized the face on his photo ID, right? He's clean-shaven now."

Kadek rushed inside the terminal as though she were late. She went to a ticket window to ask if she could still board the bus to Medan. She was told that the bus had left. As Kadek turned away, feigning a look of frustration, she scanned the men sitting and standing in the waiting room. None matched the picture of Ghazali. She returned to the street. The sky was turning from grey to dark blue in the east.

"He's not there," she said as she joined the other two. "We're too late."

"All right. Let's find a hotel and live our cover," Wayan replied. "I'll contact Marc and give him an update."

They flagged a passing taxi and Wayan asked the driver to

take them to one of the better hotels in town, the Hotel Permata Hati. As soon as Wayan checked in to his room, he sent a text message from his secure phone to Marc's: *"Ghazali arrived Banda Aceh this morning. We've lost him. Request you pinpoint his location."*

5 0

SURABAYA, EAST JAVA

WHEN GENERAL AGUNG AND HOTMAN PARDEDE had confidential matters to discuss they took a drive. Typically they would head to the general's home-town, Ubud. And that is what they did the day the colonel received the latest news from Roy Mancini. The American had sent Hotman the name and address of the forger in Surabaya, with an urgent request to provide the aliases that were being used for the targets' false passports.

After a long silence, General Agung spoke. "Colonel, it occurs to me that you will have to take on this mission in Surabaya by yourself. We cannot risk that a member of your team will talk. If this went up the chain of command, the commanders would be suspicious. They would wonder why we are not following through with an arrest."

"Yes, General. It would appear odd to the members of my group if we do not apprehend the forger, interrogate him, and charge him as an accomplice. It is better I take care of the case myself."

"Yes. Text me the aliases that match the true names. I presume the forged passports will be Indonesian. But you confirm that."

"I will fly to Surabaya in the morning."

Hotman Pardede arrived in Surabaya on the earliest flight from Denpasar at 6:20 the next morning. He had studied a map of the city and determined where he would position himself to keep the forger's residence under surveillance.

He wore civilian attire and carried a small overnight bag and a briefcase. Before boarding his flight in Bali, he had shown his police ID to the authorities at the airport and was thus permitted to carry his Glock 9mm semi-automatic pistol and hunting knife aboard the plane. The silencer was concealed inside a secret compartment of the briefcase.

The forger's address was in the center of a densely populated residential area. Hotman Pardede sat inside a *warung* across the street, ordered breakfast, and observed a two-story building that appeared to be a men's boardinghouse. Several men of various ages, leaving for work or school, exited the building before eight o'clock a.m. The colonel counted eleven of them.

Hotman surmised that the forger was performing his counterfeiting in his room. What was not evident was whether or not he had accomplices living in the same house. The *Batak* colonel made a mental note to order a raid on the building after his mission was completed.

By eight-thirty there was no further activity at the house, no one entering or leaving. Hotman had not recognized any of the men who left the boardinghouse as being the one in the photograph on the copy of the national ID card that he held in his hand. The forger's name was Idris Mohammad. The KTP card indicated that he was twenty-five-years old and that he was from Bandung in West Java.

Hotman paid his bill, left the restaurant, and jogged across the street to the house. He had planned to make his move against the target late at night. But seeing now that several of the boarders had left the building, it occurred to the colonel that catching the forger alone would be opportune.

The front door of the building was unlocked. Hotman entered and walked down a musty hallway, past a series of six doors, three on either side. There were no sounds from any of the rooms. When he arrived at the end of the passage, he climbed the stairs to the second floor and strolled back along the hallway. Near the third door on his left, he heard the sound of a man coughing twice. Hotman turned his head and looked behind him. There was no one else in the hall. He knocked on the door. A man inside the room asked who was there in the Indonesian language—not in Javanese, which was the dialect of Surabaya. The colonel had, over many years of interrogating suspects, become expert at recognizing accents. The voice inside the room had the accent of West Java.

Hotman answered the man. "I am looking for Idris Mohammad. Can you help me?"

"Wait a moment," came the reply. "What is it you need?"

"I have a package for Mr. Idris, sent from Bandung."

"Who are you?"

"Special delivery from the post office, sir. Can you tell me which room belongs to Mr. Idris?"

"Leave the package outside my door. I'll collect it later."

"Sir, I require Mr. Idris to show a photo ID and to sign a receipt. I cannot leave this package outside, unattended."

"Who is the sender in Bandung?" the man inside asked, annoyance in his tone.

"It appears to be from a lady, sir. It says "Miss." The name is not clear. If you cannot sign for it, I will have to go. I am not allowed to leave special delivery packages in a hallway."

Footsteps approached from inside. "All right," the voice in the room said. "I'm Idris Mohammad. Hold on."

The colonel heard the sound of a chain being unlatched. He reached inside his bag and withdrew the Glock and the silencer. The man inside twisted the door's deadbolt. As Hotman saw the door handle turn, he kicked it hard with his booted foot. The man inside fell backward onto the floor and made a grunt. Hotman entered fast, shutting and locking the door behind him. He planted a foot onto the man's mouth to keep him quiet. He attached the silencer and pointed the gun at the man's head; and with his left hand, he flashed his police ID card.

"You are a dead man, Idris, if you make a sound."

The man's eyes were wide open. He made an effort to move his head despite the weight of the policeman's boot on his face.

"I am going to release you. You are going to stand and get me the passports. Clear?"

The man made no movement. Hotman applied all of his weight onto the man's face. His prisoner slapped the floor with both hands in agony.

"Clear?" Hotman asked again, taking some of the weight off the man's head. Idris Mohammad attempted to nod in the affirmative.

The colonel kept the Glock trained on the man's head and removed his boot from his face. "Now stand. Slowly. I will shoot if you make a quick move."

Idris got to his feet and stood before Hotman Pardede.

"The bombers' passports. Hand them to me. I'll give you five seconds." The policeman glanced at the watch on his left wrist. The man turned and moved to the desk. He removed a key from his pants pocket, unlocked the second drawer, and withdrew four Indonesian passports. Trembling, he handed them to Hotman.

Hotman ordered the man to sit and put his hands on top of the desk, then walked over to the open drawer and rummaged through it and pulled out several documents.

"Open all the drawers," Hotman ordered.

After Idris complied, Hotman removed the contents of each drawer. There was an assortment of blank Indonesian and foreign passports, photographs of men and *hijab*-covered women, and forged and blank KTP cards.

"Where is your equipment?"

The man replied, "What do you mean?"

Hotman pointed the Glock at the man's face. "Your counterfeiting equipment, asshole. Where you make all this stuff."

Idris dropped his eyes to the floor, then turned and pointed at a blanket in a far corner of the room. "Beneath that cover."

"Remove the blanket," Hotman ordered.

Idris did so. There was another desk, much larger, which appeared to be covered with artist's supplies.

"Now, Idris, which of these passports did you prepare for Jeko Rusdiana?" Hotman held the four forged passports out to the man. Idris took them, opened one, and handed it back to the policeman. Hotman recognized the passport photograph of Jeko Rusdiana from his KTP card. So far, so good.

"Which one is for Omar in Manado?"

The forger appeared in shock. "Who are you? How did you know about . . .?"

He got no further. Hotman kicked him hard in the gut, and the man fell across the table, scattering his forging equipment onto the floor.

"I ask the questions. Omar in Manado. Which passport?"

The man held his stomach and rolled over the table top as he tried to catch his breath. At last he spoke in a hoarse voice, "He picked it up a week ago. He's leaving Manado by boat."

"What name is he using and where is he going?"

"The passport identifies him as Salim Habib. He's going to Zamboanga in the Philippines."

"And Ghazali?"

"He took his passport a week ago." The man was shaking.

"His alias is . . .?" Hotman's face was three inches from Idris's.

"Parto Abdullah."

"Where is he going?"

"He's on a boat to Penang. He doesn't need a visa to enter Malaysia because Indonesia and Malaysia are ASEAN countries. Same with the Philippines."

Under normal circumstances, Hotman Pardede would have allowed Idris Mohammad to live another day. He was, after all, second-tier. He wasn't a bomb-maker, nor was he directly involved in the actual bombing. The problem was that Idris would contact his superior, Ghazali, and inform him that they had been compromised. The American's mission would unravel. They would forfeit the all-important element of surprise.

"Sorry, Idris." The colonel aimed his silenced weapon at the forger's left temple and pulled the trigger. He'd only required the one shot from the semiautomatic.

51

BANDA ACEH, SUMATRA

W AYAN RECEIVED THE TEXT MESSAGE FROM MARC in the late afternoon. He read it aloud to Kadek and Bruno as they walked along the shoreline at the old port in search of a ferry that was large enough to make the voyage across the Malacca Straits to Malaysia.

> *"Ghazali located in Banda Aceh and travelling with a fake pass-port and KTP under the alias Parto Abdullah. Spent last night at the Hotel Prapat. Email intercept indicates target departing this week. Ferry boat to Penang sails every Friday at 6:00 p.m., ETA Penang 11:00 a.m. Saturday. Tickets for the boat purchased at the Indonesia Ferry Company office on Jalan Rama Setia. In view of short time period until departure, I request you follow target onto ferry boat and seek opportunity there to confront. Purchase tickets and board ferry separately."*

"Let's think this over," Wayan said after reciting the message to the other two. "Marc is right. We need to board separately. We can't be seen traveling together."

Kadek pointed out that it would be foolhardy to try to bring a gun and silencer onto the passenger ferry. There would be a security inspection upon boarding. Wayan asked her what she had in mind.

"I can hide a knife in my clothing. They are not going to frisk me. Not in this culture. I will dress the part of a conservative Muslim woman. I need to find a shop where I can buy the garments. You find a seller and purchase a sharp knife. We'll meet back at the hotel."

"And you pass me the knife after we board the ferry?" Wayan asked.

Kadek gave him a stern look before replying. "Right. I took Jeko. This one is yours."

Wayan pointed out that as Bruno had the semi-automatic pistol and silencer, he would remain ashore. It was best that he leave Aceh by bus and return to Medan, where he should take a room at the Novotel. He would wait there for further instructions from Marc.

"You guys have all the fun," the big Sicilian said with a scowl after he checked out of the hotel. He left them in the lobby.

Wayan's concern was that Ghazali, alias Parto, would recognize him from the boardinghouse in Medan. He found a shop that sold eye glasses and he bought a pair with outlandish, black horn-rimmed frames. He purchased a wide-brimmed rain hat, a size too large. Finally Wayan bought the knife in an alley behind the public market: an expensive, fifteen-inch-long Muslim *Kris* dagger with a sharp point and edges, and a decorative handle. He would pass it to his sister in her hotel room before they checked out.

Meanwhile, Kadek located a women's dress shop. She bought the most conservative black *hijab* she could find which covered her head, ears, and neck. The billowing shoulder-to-ankle *kebaya* gown disguised her full figure. Her face and hands were the only skin that showed on her body. The effect caused her to look ten years older than she was.

After she left the apparel shop, she walked past a pharmacy. And stopped. She turned back and entered the store. Later she would recall that she didn't know why exactly she went inside the pharmacy other than a sense that it related to their mission. She strolled along each aisle in the shop, observing various products from toothpaste to aspirin. Then she saw it. An assortment of laxatives. She selected one after another and read the labels. There were two brands that required an enema. And there was a selection of saline laxatives administered orally. Kadek grinned. As much as she would relish driving the drug into the terrorist's rectum, the practical method would be oral. She selected a bottle of magnesium citrate and brought it to the pharmacist.

"How long will it take this brand to have the desired effect? I'm in a hurry," she asked the woman behind the counter.

The pharmacist replied, "This one could take anywhere from thirty minutes to over an hour. It is fast-acting. Be warned, you should not take more than one dose per day. It is potent, and an overdose could cause dangerous side effects."

Kadek took the drug to the cashier, paid for it, and left. She hailed a taxi and returned to the hotel. Wayan was waiting in the lobby when she arrived.

The two of them checked out of the hotel thirty minutes apart. By four-thirty in the afternoon, they had purchased tickets for the six o'clock ferry to Penang. Kadek arrived in a taxi at the Banda Aceh pier departure lounge after five o'clock. Wayan's taxi arrived at the ferry dock at 5:45. He spotted his sister sitting inside the building, huddled with a group of conservatively dressed Acehnese women. When asked, she had told the women that she was going to Malaysia to work as a housemaid for a family in Kuala Lumpur.

Kadek and Wayan made eye contact. She scratched her right ear; the signal that she had spotted Ghazali inside the lounge. Five minutes later the passengers boarded the ferry, *Sumatra Princess*.

52

MALACCA STRAIGHTS

THE BOAT GOT UNDERWAY THIRTY MINUTES LATE AS the sun set, and sailed north toward We Island. The sea was rough in the strait between Banda Aceh and the island causing the ferry to pitch and yaw from side to side. Kadek took a seat among the frightened women she had met in the lounge. They had all heard stories of capsized passenger ferries sinking in heavy seas. Kadek attempted to soothe the two women sitting beside her.

Wayan walked to the stern of the boat where a group of men sat apart from the women. Ghazali was not among them. He wore his large hat and the new black-framed, non-prescription glasses. He took the last remaining seat between an elderly Acehnese and a teenage boy.

Within an hour of casting off, several men, women, and children became sea sick, vomiting into the drains that ran along either side of the compartment. The luckier ones made it in time to the two restrooms at the forward end of the boat. After two hours at sea, the stench became overpowering. As heavy rain lashed against the portholes, Wayan heard the solemn murmur of prayer from the terrified old man beside him.

The ferry turned southeast and entered the middle of the

Malacca Straits, the world's busiest seaway. Wayan remained seated and searched the faces of the men in the compartment. Kadek did the same from her position farther forward. Passengers continued to stumble to the sides of the boat to throw up. Wayan observed each man that got to his feet, searching for Ghazali.

By midnight the waves were pushing the ferry boat from the stern as it made its way through the night.

Kadek finally stood, holding on to whatever structure she could, and staggered to the stairs that led to the boat's small dining area. As she reached the top of the stairway she spotted an empty seat at one of the four tables in the room. A wave hit the boat hard from the rear, causing her to lurch toward the seat. She grabbed the side of the table and fell onto a seat, brushing against a woman beside her. The sullen and sick men and women in the room stared at her. The woman beside her was wiping spittle from her lips with the loose ends of her *hijab*. Kadek apologized to her. The woman stared back and uttered, "When will this end?"

Kadek replied, "Another twelve hours."

She spotted him across the room. Ghazali sat hunched over, staring into a cup. The collar of his jacket was pulled over his ears, and he wore a baseball cap down over his eyes. To anyone else, he would have been well disguised. He appeared to be traveling alone. Kadek looked away from him. A waiter asked if she wanted to order. She asked for a bottle of mineral water.

After thirty minutes, Kadek returned to the main deck. Her seat had been taken by another woman, so she wandered aft until she spotted Wayan. The two made brief eye contact. A moment later, Wayan stood and headed toward the line of passengers waiting to use the restroom. Kadek fell in line behind him. He turned to his sister and saw her look up at the ceiling and scratch her right ear. The signal. She glanced at Wayan's carry bag. He gave an imperceptible nod.

Kadek needed to meet with Wayan somewhere with more privacy, and plan the next stage. There she would pass the *Kris* dagger to her brother. The strong laxative was inside her handbag. She would attempt to beguile the terrorist as she had done with Jeko Rusdiana in Klaten. She had to return to the dining room to keep an eye on Ghazali, and this time allow him to observe her. She would first change into more casual attire. The ploy of appearing as a conservative Muslim boarding the ferry in Aceh with the secreted knife had served its purpose.

Kadek entered the restroom, changed her clothes, and applied a trace of lip gloss. When she exited, she was wearing jeans and a form-fitting long-sleeved white blouse. She had removed the *hijab*. Her black hair fell in a long ponytail. Wayan waited for her at a secluded area along the starboard bulkhead.

"I will spike his tea with an overdose of a strong laxative," she whispered to her brother. "Look for him to rush down the stairs between three and three-thirty. Most of the passengers should be asleep or too sick to care. Stand near the toilets." She slipped him the dagger which he hid inside his pants beneath his untucked shirt.

"Good thinking," he said out of earshot in the Balinese dialect. "Do we have a Plan B?"

"No. This is it. Wish me luck," she replied.

Wayan walked unsteadily back to his seat as the boat continued to roll before the large waves in the middle of the Malacca Straits. Kadek stood for a moment and took a deep breath before turning and climbing the stairs to the dining room.

53

The Malacca Straits

G HAZALI WAS SITTING AT THE SAME TABLE AS HE HAD been earlier. Kadek suspected he wished to remain in the one area with the least passengers to avoid being recognized or disturbed. There were five people at the four tables. Each one appeared to be sleeping and had his or her head resting on a table. The only sound was of the rain and men snoring. A crewmember appeared half-awake behind a beverage counter and barely acknowledged the arrival of the pretty young woman. The waiter was off duty.

Kadek squeezed herself onto a chair beside her sleeping target. She noted the man's padlocked backpack beneath the table between his feet. She would remember to retrieve it later. Kadek glanced at her wristwatch. The time was 2:15 in the morning. Ten minutes later, a wave hit the ferry broadside, causing the boat to shudder and roll ten degrees. Ghazali groaned. A second later, she brushed into him, feigning that she had been flung toward him in her sleep.

"Oh, pardon me, sir," she gasped. "I didn't mean to wake you. The waves are so big."

Ghazali raised his head from his folded arms, squinted, and looked for a few seconds at the woman beside him. "No problem," he mumbled.

Kadek yawned and stretched her arms over her head. "The rough weather never ends. It's so hard to sleep. I'm fortunate I brought medicine for seasickness with me. At least I'm not running to the toilet to throw up like all the others."

The man continued to stare at her. At last he spoke. "Have we met somewhere?"

She replied, "Not that I know of. I'm not from Aceh."

"Neither am I," he said. "Your accent—Balinese?"

"You have good ears. Yes, I am from Bali. I am working in Medan. Where are you from?"

He ignored the question. He stared at her face and said, "Perhaps we met in Bali. Could that be?"

"No, sir. I don't think so. You have been to Bali?"

"Many years ago," he replied with a straight face. "How is it there these days?"

"It has gotten so touristy. Not the paradise-on-earth like when I was young." She registered his lie about not having been in Bali for some time.

Ghazali dropped his head and placed a hand over his face. There was a silence for several moments. The boat continued to pitch.

"Are you not well, sir?" she asked, concern on her face.

He shook his head. She noted his body odor and the sweat on his forehead.

"So many passengers are sick. Thank goodness for my medicine," Kadek commented. "Have you eaten anything?"

Ghazali replied without looking at her. "I can't keep anything down."

Kadek made a gesture of looking through her handbag. "Listen.

I have something here that can help. It works wonders. I haven't been ill the entire trip. Would you care to try it with me? I'm about to take some now so I can eat breakfast later."

Ghazali looked at her with a tortured expression. "Shit. I'll try anything. This is miserable. Does it really work?"

"Trust me. The medicine is formulated especially for your condition." She stood. "I've been taking it with tea. And I've eaten meals without any problem." She looked at him with an expression of sympathy.

He dropped his head after wiping sweat from his brow.

Kadek walked to the drinks counter behind them and roused the attendant. She glanced backward at Ghazali. He remained still, staring at the table. The others in the room were sleeping with their heads on folded arms and jackets.

She ordered a pot of tea and two cups. When it was served to her, she paid and waited for the attendant to return to his seat. When his back was turned she removed a packet from her bag and poured the powder into one of the cups. She withdrew another pack and poured half of its contents into the same cup. There were now one and a half doses of the saline laxative at the bottom of the one cup. She poured hot tea into both cups and spooned and stirred sugar into them.

She placed the cups on the table. "Here you are. This will fix you up. You'll be able to eat a full breakfast when it is served in a few hours." She handed the cup containing the purgative to Ghazali and glanced at her wrist watch. The time was two-thirty a.m. "I hope you take sugar. I added two teaspoons." He continued to stare at the table. She suspected that the sizable amount of sugar would disguise the taste of the laxative.

Ghazali grimaced before lifting the cup to his lips. He consumed the entire cupful of tea within two minutes. "Thanks," he said, looking at her now. "What's your name?"

"My name is Kadek Surya," she replied before she finished her own tea.

He attempted a thin smile and said, "I feel better."

"That's good. Give it about an hour and you will be good as new. And as they say, *bon appetite*. I must go now and try to get some sleep below. *Ciao*."

Kadek stood, and without a further glance at the man responsible for organizing the murder of her parents, she slipped away from the table and walked to the stairs. Wayan was standing beside the small alcove where she had left him. She scratched her right ear and walked to the port side of the compartment, where she found a place to sit among the scores of sleeping passengers.

54

T 3:40 A.M. A MAN WITH A TORTURED EXPRESSION ON his face, holding his stomach with both hands, rushed from the dining room and down the stairs to the main deck. He turned to his left into the narrow three-meter long alcove and groaned as he lurched and threw open the restroom door on the right side of the passageway.

Wayan had been on the lookout for thirty minutes. Now he heard the man on the stairs before he saw him, and he made his move. As Ghazali threw open the door to the toilet. Wayan slipped past him, turned, and hauled the terrorist inside the small cubicle. He stuffed an oily rag deep into the man's mouth, gagging him.

Wayan locked the door's deadbolt with his left hand as he gripped the shaken man by his neck with his right. He had seen Kadek walk toward the alcove, and he knew she would be blocking the entranceway, as though waiting her turn to use the restroom. He'd noted that all the passengers were still either asleep or in the doldrums. The activity around the restroom hadn't caused any particular alarm. All was quiet in the lavatory.

Inside Wayan stared into the face of the gagged Ghazali and

held him around the neck with both his hands. He squeezed his thumbs at the man's throat for several moments and watched his eyes bulge. Then he turned him around and forced his head into the filthy toilet bowl, submerging him beneath the water.

Ghazali thrashed his arms and kicked backward with both feet at his attacker. Wayan smiled, adrenaline working at a high level, and held the terrorist's head underwater for thirty seconds, until the man was still. He pulled him upright by the collar and grimaced as he saw the combination of feces and vomit drip from Ghazali's hair and lifeless face. The man's eyes were wide open. Wayan decided to make sure the man was indeed dead.

"Drowning in shit isn't good enough for you, Ghazali," Wayan whispered in his ear as he removed the sheathed *Kris* from inside his pants.

He sat the terrorist on the open toilet bowl, unsheathed the dagger, and slit the man's throat from ear-to-ear, stepping backward to avoid the flow of blood. "Now when they identify you, you bastard, they'll know who you are and why."

Wayan slipped the Kris back inside the sheath and knocked three times on the door. Kadek replied with four knocks. Her brother unlocked the door and the two of them hauled the dead man out, dragging him to the closet at the forward end of the alcove. The locker was filled with life jackets. On Wayan's whispered count of three, they heaved Ghazali's body inside.

"Wait," Kadek whispered. She reached inside the dead man's pants pocket and removed a key.

Wayan took his cell phone from his front pocket and snapped a picture of the dead man before Kadek closed and latched the steel door. The removal of the body from the toilet and its placement inside the life vest locker had taken twenty seconds.

"I need to go to the dining area and grab his backpack. It's under the table where he was sitting," Kadek said, *sotto voce,* as she raised the key. "Roy and Marc may be able to use it. If I have to, I'll tell the guy at the counter I'm getting it for my companion who has decided to sit out the trip below."

"You had better put your *hijab* back on, and cover part of your face. There will be an investigation."

"Right."

Kadek turned and walked out of the alcove, back to where she had been sitting. All of the women nearby were asleep. She removed the black *hijab* from her bag and wrapped it around her head. She walked to the stairway and up to the dining room.

Wayan had found a signboard hours earlier and at three-thirty had placed it on the floor against the alcove's bulkhead: *Toilet Temporarily Closed for Cleaning.*

He lifted the sign and attached it to the starboard restroom's door handle. That would give at least a couple of hours for the blood to dissipate before the cleaning crew checked on the toilet.

Wayan walked back through the passenger compartment and returned to his seat between the old man and the boy. Like everyone else, they were asleep. He glanced at his watch. It was three-fifty-six. He looked forward and saw his sister come down the stairs carrying a dark blue backpack over her shoulders.

55

PENANG, MALAYSIA

THE FERRY PULLED INTO PENANG AT TWELVE NOON ON Saturday. Kadek and Wayan spotted Marc across the room when they entered the crowded terminal. The American caught their eye and exited the building. The two ambled across the lobby and went outside. Marc was standing beside a car parked in the lot across the street. He gave a brief wave, got in the car, and started it when he saw Wayan raise his hand. They waited at the curb for him to pull up.

"Hop in," he said. Without a word, the two Balinese loaded their hand-carry luggage into the back. Kadek climbed into the passenger seat and Wayan sat behind.

"We have rooms at the E&O Hotel. The two of you deserve some luxury from the looks on your faces," Marc said as he drove off in the direction of Georgetown. "How did it go?"

"Messier than Jeko's final minutes. Same result," Kadek replied. "We haven't slept for thirty hours. Wayan has the photograph you asked for."

"Send it to me after we get to the hotel."

Marc described how the Eastern & Oriental Hotel, known around the world as the E&O, had served as a residence for travelers like Somerset Maugham, Rudyard Kipling, Noel Coward and Charlie Chaplin. The elegant hotel faced the narrow shipping channel that ran between the island of Penang and the Malaysian mainland.

"I arranged rooms with a sea view," Marc said as he parked at the hotel's entrance and handed the keys to a valet. "Why don't you take a *siesta* this afternoon? We'll meet later for a swim in the pool and have drinks and dinner."

"Perfect," replied Wayan as he hauled his and Kadek's bags out of the car. "Give us a ring before sunset. I'll send you the photograph I took on the boat."

"I look forward to that. Roy needs it to secure future funding."

"You'll have it as soon as I settle into the room."

Marc waited while Kadek and Wayan purchased bathing suits at the gift shop. The three of them were led through the vast lobby by two bellmen. "Ring us, Marc, in about four hours," Kadek said as they walked together. "And here, take this backpack and key with you. They were his."

Marc unlocked Ghazali's backpack as soon as he returned to his room. Inside he found an Acer laptop computer, a Nokia cell phone, a worn notebook, an assortment of toiletries, and a change of clothes. He powered on the laptop and, as expected, was faced with the need to enter a password. He would not waste time attempting to break into the computer. Likewise, the Nokia was password protected. He would leave it to his father's friends to crack the encryption.

The notebook contained entries written in Indonesian. Wayan or Kadek would translate. Odds were the jottings would be in code.

As he was replacing the items into the backpack, Marc heard the ping on his secure cell phone. He noted a message from Wayan had been received and that it required downloading. A moment later he saw the photograph of a dead Ghazali laid out on a stack of orange life jackets. His throat had been slit open, blood staining the front of his shirt and trousers. His hair and face appeared to be soaking wet, his eyes wide open. Marc forwarded the photo to his own laptop computer. He sent the encrypted email to his father in Labuan.

Marc phoned Wayan in his room at five p.m. The Balinese answered on the second ring.

"Ready?" Marc asked.

"Yeah. I couldn't sleep. I suppose my adrenaline is still running high. I'll call Kadek and see if she's ready for a swim. I see the pool below my balcony. Great view."

"Meet you there," Marc replied.

Thirty minutes later Kadek, wearing her new Malaysian batik two-piece, and Wayan strolled to the side of the pool together. Marc was swimming laps and didn't notice them. They sat beneath an umbrella and waited. When he made a turn at their end of the pool, Wayan called out, "Looking good, Marc."

"Join me," Marc replied.

The three of them swam together for another ten minutes without speaking. At last they hoisted themselves out of the water, and after toweling themselves dry, sat at the table. Palm trees lined the walkway between the sea and the pool area. A waiter arrived and took their drinks order.

When they were alone again, Marc complimented them on a mission well done. "Two down and two to go."

"Marc, we need to return to Amed, if that's all right," Kadek declared. "We left our businesses in the care of our cousin. Give us a few days to check on things."

"By all means. In fact, I'll handle the next mission myself. The bomb-maker, Omar, left North Sulawesi in a fishing boat and is en route to Mindanao. I wanted to meet and debrief you first.

After you fill me in on what occurred on the boat from Aceh to Penang, and translate the notes I found in Ghazali's backpack, you're free to take off."

Wayan and Kadek described their activities during the rough voyage across the Malacca Straits. Marc listened in rapt silence. He expressed amusement when Wayan described how Ghazali raced down the stairs an hour after consuming the fast-acting laxative. When the story was finished, he remarked, "You two pulled it off like pros. Well done."

Kadek said, "Now let's shower and take a look at those notes."

The three went to their separate rooms to shower and change. Afterword, Kadek and Wayan went to Marc's room. He removed the notebook from his briefcase and handed it to Wayan.

Wayan studied it for ten minutes and handed it to his sister. Kadek skimmed through it and motioned for Wayan to translate.

"It's a kind of things-to-do journal and diary. The notes go back for more than a year. He mixes Javanese and Indonesian. And much of it seems to be in code. He's using aliases, ones I've never heard of," Wayan explained. "And there are financial accounts. Money received and spent. The final entry lists the amounts he paid for the hotel in Banda Aceh and the ferry boat ticket."

Kadek interrupted. "There is something here on the last page. It appears he is referring to someone in Penang named *Sultan*. An alias."

"Hambali!" Marc exclaimed. "He was supposed to meet him on arrival."

"This part is written in Javanese. I can't translate all of it," she replied, shaking her head and pointing to the page. "There doesn't seem to be any information about a meeting place. Perhaps he was at the terminal when the ferry arrived, and when this *Sultan* didn't see Ghazali disembark, he might have taken off."

Two days later, and one day after Wayan and Kadek had left Penang, Bill Chapman opened the terrorist group's Yahoo email and discovered a draft written by Hambali to the group's Indonesian spiritual leader, Abu Najib. In it, Hambali, the Al Qaeda operative and financier, reported that he had waited for Ghazali outside the Penang ferry terminal. When he didn't appear, Hambali left the island and returned to Thailand with his Malaysian wife.

56

DUMAGUETE CITY, PHILIPPINES

Three weeks after September 11, 2001, the Pentagon sent a Special Forces team to the southern Philippines at the request of the host government. Their mission was to assist and train the Filipino Marines' counterterrorism task force and help them defeat the violent militant group, Abu Sayyaf. Marine Corps Lieutenant Marc Mancini had been a member of that elite contingent of 320 American advisors in Zamboanga.

AT THE TIME THE SURYAS WERE BOARDING THEIR flight back to Bali, Omar the bomb-maker was entering the Celebes Sea in a fishing boat he had chartered in the northern Sulawesi port of Bitung. His destination: the island of Basilan off the southwestern tip of Mindanao in the Philippines.

The dense jungles and tropical hardwood forests on Basilan provided the headquarters and training camps for the blood-thirsty Filipino terrorist group, Abu Sayyaf. Omar was now the most notorious bomb-maker in Southeast Asia. His reputation had been enhanced in the underground world of jihad with the Bali massacre. Ghazali had recommended him to Hambali, who in turn had referred him to Abu Sayyaf's commander. A deal was made. Omar would train Abu Sayyaf's bomb-makers at a location deep in Basilan Island's wilderness.

239

Omar's role in the Bali bombing and his future plans had been discovered when Bill Chapman's SID team at the NSA hacked into the group's email account and cell phones. The terrorists were referred to now as the Bali Five: Hambali, Abu Najib, Ghazali, Omar and Jeko.

Before he checked out of the E&O, Marc used his encrypted laptop to email his father. He requested Roy meet him in Dumaguete, as Marc would travel from there to Zamboanga City. Roy replied that he would fly from Labuan to Cebu the next day, and catch a ferry to Dumaguete City. They would meet each other at the hotel-by-the-sea two days later.

Roy phoned Marc in his hotel room at the Bethel Hotel. "Hey, partner. You must have arrived on the earlier boat from Cebu."

"Right. Let's meet downstairs and take a stroll along the Boulevard."

"I'll be there in ten minutes."

When they met, the first thing Marc said was, "I've got some things to pass to you when we get back to our rooms. A laptop and cell phone. They belonged to Ghazali."

The two men walked along the Dumaguete seaside in the late afternoon for five minutes before Marc revealed his plan. The sun was low in the west and would disappear behind the mountains of Negros Oriental in another ten minutes. Lights were being switched on in the mansions that lined the opposite side of the road.

"Dad, you've told me your NSA contact discovered that Omar is sailing on a fishing boat to Basilan Island. I plan to meet some former colleagues in Zamboanga and surprise the bomb-maker when his boat arrives," Marc said.

Roy turned and looked at his son. "I remember now. Your first overseas assignment in the Marines was in the Philippines. Special operations. I never knew what you were doing over here."

Marc explained how he had deployed to Mindanao following 9/11, after he had undergone training at a military intelligence school and been assigned to a Marine Corps' Humint Exploitation Team. He operated with a Philippine Marines intelligence unit in southwestern Mindanao. Their target: the Abu Sayyaf terrorist group, which had free reign throughout the islands in the Sulu Sea.

Marc had befriended several of the Filipino Marines he'd worked with. In particular he and a Major Alfonso Reyes hit it off, and even double-dated two virginal Spanish *mestiza* sisters, Amalia and Dolores Villagracias, from a prominent local family. The girls' parents were delighted to have their daughters courted by the clean-cut Marine officers. The father, a powerful local politician and well-known *haciendero*, had hinted to Marc Mancini that there was a thriving export business waiting for him in Zamboanga should he decide to stay in the Philippines and tie the knot with his twenty-year-old daughter, Amalia.

"When we return to the hotel I'm going to call Al Reyes. He's a Filipino Marine officer I worked and partied with in Zamboanga. We became good friends," Marc explained. "He may still be in Mindanao. He'll have the connections I need down there."

"What's the plan?" Roy asked as they took a seat on a bench at the seashore. "Your email was vague."

"Depends. We'll have to see how much cooperation I get from the Filipinos in the south. I'll leave tomorrow to be sure I arrive in Basilan before Omar's boat pulls in. A lot will hinge on Reyes and how much influence he still has there. He was head of their intelligence unit at the time. It's been two years since I've seen him."

Roy told his son he would go to Apo Island the next day and hang out with Brewster Levey at the Rusty Pecker and do some sailing on *Jambalaya*. He would wait there until he heard from Marc.

"By the way, Marc, there was an online news article I read this morning in the Singapore *Straits Times*. Something about the discovery of a homicide victim on a passenger ferry that had made a trip from Sumatra to Penang. And thanks for the photograph. I'll forward it to the general in Bali. He'll relay it to my contact in the U.S."

Marc replied, "Kadek and Wayan did good work."

He stood and continued, "We'd better get back to the hotel. I need to call Al and ask if he can meet me in Zamboanga. I've got his number in my unsecured phone," Marc said as they strolled north along the sidewalk beside the sea. "I'll fill you in after I talk with him."

Roy replied, "And pass me the items you mentioned, the ones the Suryas retrieved from Ghazali. There will be people back home who'll wanna crack into them. They'll be interested in snatching Hambali. He fled to Thailand."

Marc phoned Roy two hours later. "The news is good. My friend has rotated back to Mindanao after a tour at Marine HQ in Manila. When we spoke it was like old times."

"Great. And Marc, I've got something to tell you. Meet me outside in fifteen minutes. I'll find you."

They met at a bench in front of the hotel. The night was dark, there was no moon. The only lights along the Boulevard came from the street lamps and nearby Spanish mansions.

Roy told his son that he had received an email from Jack Chapman. The attached audio gave the name of the fishing boat that Omar, alias Salim Habib, had chartered. The information had been gathered from an intercepted phone call from Omar to an unknown phone number in the Philippines.

"The name of the boat is *Wanita Indah.* Omar was told where to meet his contact in Isabela City, complete with recognition signals and code words. They spoke Indonesian, which I translated. This indicates that there is at least one other Indonesian terrorist operating on Basilan Island."

Roy continued, "It is no secret that the Indonesian group responsible for the Bali bombing, Jamaah Islamiyah, is in cahoots with Abu Sayyaf. Omar isn't the first JI operative to slip into the Philippines. I suspect Hambali, with instructions from Osama bin Laden, is coordinating their joint operations in the region."

Marc replied, "Good. I'll have something to offer Al Reyes in return for his help. They can arrest Omar's JI contact on Basilan. Give me the location of their meeting site. I suspect the Filipinos will want to keep him under surveillance before they grab him."

Roy said, "The boat has an ETA in Isabela City three days from now. The Indonesians plan to meet the same day at the Maligaya Inn on the outskirts of town."

Marc replied, "We'll provide Omar with a reception party in Isabela he won't forget for as long as he lives."

57

ZAMBOANGA CITY, PHILIPPINES

A DOZEN LOCAL MUSLIM SEA-GYPSIES HAD GUIDED THEIR outrigger boats to the Lantaka Hotel bar while Marc waited there for Al Reyes. The cheerful hawkers beckoned to him to inspect their products: colorful and rare seashells, exotic *Kris* daggers, and batik sarongs. These peaceful nomads roamed the Sulu Sea and Moro Gulf between Mindanao, Jolo and north Borneo. Marc nursed a San Miguel and inspected an array of multi-colored sea shells. After some jocular bargaining he bought a shiny cowrie and a brightly patterned cone.

"There you are, *amigo*," a voice behind him called out. Marc turned when he heard the familiar baritone. The tall, fit-looking Filipino walked up to the bar.

"Hey, Alfonso." Marc reached out and shook hands. "Couldn't stay away from the fun and games in Zamboanga, could you, old friend?"

"Yeah, Marc. If it weren't for all the ASG crap, this would still be the finest spot in the Philippines. What brings you here?" Alfonso Reyes had referred to the Abu Sayyaf Group.

Marc replied, "I'll explain to you later. Have a San Mig." He motioned to the bartender for two beers. "I was happy to catch you here in Zambo, Al. What's your job?"

The Filipino took a large drink from his bottle. "I'm the senior liaison officer, working with your guys."

The Filipino officer glanced at Marc. "Someone told me you left the Corps. That surprised me. I was sure you were a lifer. What happened?"

"Long story, short, I had some trouble in Afghanistan. I'll tell you about it later. How are the lovely Villagracias daughters?"

Reyes smirked. "You mean your beloved Amalia? She married a U.S. Marine earlier this year. They'll move to the states in a couple of months."

"And Dolores? Her parents still insist on a chaperone when you take her out?"

"Ha! You remember. Yeah, Amalia chaperoned Dolores who chaperoned Amalia on our double-dates back in the day. If their uptight parents only knew what the four of us got into, right?"

"I'll never tell," Marc replied with a broad smile.

The American continued, "Al, we need to talk someplace in private. I'm here on a mission, and I need your help. I'm working on something with my father."

"Oh, yeah. The coffee merchant, right? Did you join the business?" Reyes finished his beer and ordered two more.

"Yeah, I did. And I flew here to discuss a special project with you."

"I'm all ears, Marc. We can take my car to a spot where we can talk. Let's finish here." Reyes lifted his bottle in another toast.

The sky was near dark. The sea-gypsies had packed their wares, raised the sails on their outriggers, and sailed away like ghosts to their homes out at sea.

Al Reyes suggested to Marc that they discuss his project as they drove west on the national road that passed along the seashore. After some small talk as they navigated through the city's nighttime traffic, Reyes asked Marc what his mission was all about.

The American explained. "It's about payback for the bombing in Bali last month. My father and I have made it our goal to bring the bombers to justice. I've been carrying out his plan on the ground in Indonesia, one terrorist at a time."

There was silence for several seconds before the Filipino spoke. "Fill me in here, friend. This sounds like it should be a mission for the Indos. I don't get it."

Marc continued. "Reliable sources within Indonesian law enforcement informed my father that President Hartono is unlikely to pursue the investigation with much enthusiasm. My dad lost two of his best friends in the bombing. They were Balinese. And around one hundred and fifty Americans were killed that night. Many more injured terribly. It's personal."

"And the American intelligence community and Special Forces? Why aren't they involved?"

Marc hesitated before replying. "Good question, Al. They should be. But the Indonesians have warned us off, telling our government that they'll handle it on their own. And that brings us back to square one, where we've learned they won't pursue the investigation with much vigor. The president in Jakarta can't afford to offend the Islamists in her midst. There's resentment there about the Iraq invasion."

"I still don't get it. Why are you here in Zamboanga?"

"Take a wild guess, Al."

Now there was a long silence as they drove along a dark coastline. The car windows were rolled down, and the men could hear the small waves lapping along the shore to their left.

"They're here in Mindanao? The Bali bombers? Don't tell me!" Al exclaimed.

Marc looked at his friend. "One of them, the Indonesian bomb-maker, arrives on Basilan Island in two days. His mission is to train the Abu Sayyaf bomb-makers."

The Filipino braked, pulled across the road and parked, with the car facing the sea.

Marc continued. "That's right. We monitor the jihadis' cell phones and email. Omar, he's the bomb-maker, chartered a fishing boat in North Sulawesi several days ago. He'll dock in Basilan day after tomorrow. The ASG has hired him. He plans to meet a compatriot, a member of Jamaah Islamiyah, here on your turf. I'll give you all the information you need to spot the local JI guy and do whatever you need to do with him."

"And in return, Marc, you want my people to apprehend the bomb-maker when he reaches Basilan?"

"In a word, yes." Marc paused for several seconds before explaining. "But you won't turn him over to the authorities here—neither Filipino nor American. They'll throw him in jail, and that's not good enough for us. Do you follow me?"

Marc could see the Filipino raise his eyebrows. "You intend to terminate him with extreme prejudice, as you American spooks put it. Am I right?"

"You're fast on the uptake. We're assassinating each of the principal bombers, one-by-one. Our team in Indonesia has killed two of them. This one will be the third if you and I can figure a way. Are you with me?"

Reyes suggested they get out of the car and walk along the narrow beach. As they strolled together, Marc overheard his friend say, "Guantanamo."

Marc frowned and glanced at Al. "What about it? We have no intention of . . ."

"I'm thinking out loud, Marc," Reyes answered. "We'd need to pretend when we capture him that our objective is to transport him to Guantanamo. It's the only way to keep your plan covert. I have two Marines working for me whom I can trust."

"Go on," Marc said.

Reyes hesitated for several moments. "All right. Nothing I like more than a good challenge. But if this caper goes south, my career is finished, *amigo*."

"Tell me what's on your mind."

"We keep it private, with the exception of the two Marine sergeants who will make the arrest in Isabela when the boat pulls in. I'll swear those two to secrecy and give them the cover story. Tell them we need to move the bad guy to Manila where he'll be put on a special flight to Guantanamo.

"We'll need a private helicopter standing by in Basilan."

Marc interrupted, "We have the funds for that. Go on."

"Armando Villagracias owns one, which he keeps at his *hacienda*. I've flown it a couple of times recently for sport." Reyes grinned.

"So you're still involved with Dolores?" Marc asked, stopping in his tracks.

"Yeah. And that's another secret that could doom me if it were discovered."

"Your wife in Manila?"

"Let's not digress, Mancini," Al Reyes snapped.

"Okay. Back to Villagracias's helicopter. I'm listening."

"I'll need the ETA of the fishing boat. What's its name?"

"The *Wanita Indah*. We don't have a lot of time. Two days."

"I'll phone Villagracias as soon as we're through here. He relishes being involved in hush-hush stuff. I won't give him any details. I'll tell him we need his chopper for a secret mission. Trust me, he'll go along with it. There's a small airfield in Basilan, outside Isabela City, where we can park it."

"We take off with the bomb-maker, Omar," Marc said. "You're flying the helicopter?"

"Right. And my crew will lash him to a seat before we take off. They won't fly with us. Beyond that, Marc, you call the shots, where you want me to land and so forth. It'll be just the two of us plus Omar in the chopper when we're in the air."

Marc explained how Omar was using an alias, Salim Habib, and that he was carrying a forged Indonesian passport.

Al Reyes's team would board *Wanita Indah* before the crew was allowed to disembark in Isabela City. The Marine sergeants would detain Omar on the basis of a suspicious passport. They would keep him below deck, where they would handcuff him, gag him, put a hood over his head, bring him ashore, and place him inside a windowless van at the dock beside the boat. Al Reyes would drive the van to the airfield, where the sergeants would lift Omar into the helicopter. Marc would be inside the aircraft. The two sergeants would remain behind and drive the van back to Isabela.

Marc spoke. "Now let me tell you what I know of Omar's accomplice in Basilan. They plan to meet at the Maligaya Inn at four in the afternoon the day of Omar's arrival. We don't know his name. We do know the recognition signals. The JI guy in Basilan will wear a baseball cap with an L.A. Dodgers logo. Ironic huh?"

"I know the hotel. It's a small two-star," Reyes said. "This Omar, or Salim Habib, what's he look like?"

"The photo and information has him of slight build. He's a skinny little fucker. Short hair, very dark complexion. Height five-foot-seven. Your men only need to grab the guy with the Salim Habib passport. Match the photo to his face."

"That makes two calls I need to make as soon as we return to the city—the one to Villagracias, and one to my men to pick up the Indonesian at the hotel."

Marc asked, "How large is the chopper? Can it hold the three of us?"

"Oh, yeah, it's a Bell 205. The old man bought it second-hand to haul his friends and family around. And he's got a full-time pilot on his payroll. Of course, we'll dispense with the pilot."

The two men turned around and walked back to the parked car.

"One last thing, Al. Can you get me a map of the Philippines? I'd like to work on a flight plan, one you can file with ground control prior to takeoff."

"Sure. What do you have in mind?"

"Oh, we'll head north. I'll study the map and let you know."

58

BASILAN ISLAND, PHILIPPINES

THE *WANITA INDAH*, FLYING AN INDONESIAN FLAG AT
its stern, pulled into the port of Isabela City on the island
of Basilan two days later, and tied up to a pier. Two Filipino Marine sergeants stood on the wharf cradling their M-16s.
They had been alerted that their target might be armed and dangerous. They were prepared to shoot first.

A gangplank was tossed ashore, and the Marines walked
aboard the thirty-five-foot vessel. In English, they ordered the
crew members to hand over their passports and national identity
cards. The skipper of the boat spoke to each of his three crew in
Indonesian. Before the men could go below to fetch their documents, the Marines rushed inside the cabin and leapt to the lower
deck. There they found the man they were expecting.

"Your passport and ID card," one of the Marines ordered.

The well-dressed, slim Indonesian smirked and reached inside
his tote bag. He was obviously not one of the crew. The Marines
trained their M-16s on him. He withdrew a passport and handed
it to a sergeant.

"And your national ID card?" the other sergeant demanded.

The Indonesian replied in halting English, "I left at home. I need a passport only to enter your country."

The Filipino made as if to study the passport that identified the Indonesian as Salim Habib. He stared at the photograph and matched it to the Indonesian's face before passing it to the other Marine. After a minute the first Marine said, "You will come with us. Stand up."

The smug smile left the Indonesian's face. "What do you mean? Passport is good."

The second Marine scowled and replied, "No, it's not good."

The Filipinos moved fast. One grabbed the Indonesian and held his arms behind his back. The other removed a bandana from his pocket and wrapped it around the captive's head and mouth as a gag. The first Marine handcuffed him with plastic strips and threw him back onto a seat. The other took a black hood and placed it over the man's head, securing it at the neck. One of them grabbed the prisoner's tote bag, opened it for inspection, and placed it over his own shoulder.

"You're coming with us," a Marine ordered.

They guided the Indonesian bomb-maker up the ladder, along the main deck, and across the gangplank.

Before leaving, one of the Marines ordered the boat's skipper to remain on board with his crew so they could be cleared by immigration and customs officers. Should they leave before then, the boat would be confiscated.

Someone unseen slid the side door of the van open. Within less than one minute of disembarking from the boat, the Marine sergeants tossed the Indonesian inside, and the door was slammed shut. The van took off at high speed. Life on the dock went back to normal.

The Basilan airport, several miles from the town of Isabela and in the middle of nowhere, was surrounded by forest. There was one runway and little air traffic to and from the remote area. At the far end of the runway, Armando Villagracias's Bell 205 helicopter was parked. Twenty minutes after leaving the port, the brown van arrived beside the nine-passenger chopper. The sergeants hauled the hooded captive out of the vehicle. Marc Mancini opened the helicopter's door from inside. If anyone at the other end of the runway noticed, they would have seen two Filipino Marines escorting a hooded prisoner from a vehicle and hoisting him into a helicopter. Just another day in the violent southern Philippines.

Inside the Bell, the two sergeants bound the Indonesian securely to one of the plush leather seats. At the same time a tall, muscular Filipino in civilian clothes, Major Alfonso Reyes, climbed into the helicopter and took the pilot's seat. Marc sat in a leather seat facing forward, where he could stare into the face of Omar once he removed the bomb-maker's hood.

"Will there be anything else, sir?" a Marine asked the pilot, his commanding officer.

"Thank you, sergeant. That is all. Drive the van back to town and return it to the shop where you rented it."

The Marines saluted and hopped to the ground. Al Reyes switched on the aircraft's engine and the rotors turned slowly.

Marc reached for his burn phone and hit speed dial #1.

"Yeah, Marc," Roy Mancini answered after two rings.

Jambalaya was at anchor one hundred meters off Apo Island. Roy Mancini was standing on deck when he answered the phone.

"Get underway in an hour," Marc said. "Sail to a spot between Apo and Siquijor. Be sure you have a camera. We're in a helicopter. Look for us in about two hours."

"Got it." They disconnected.

The Bell 205 lifted off at 2:10 in the afternoon. As the same time, Marc removed the hood from the bomb-maker's head. He untied the gag and dropped the bandana onto his own lap.

"Speak English, Omar?" Marc asked, staring at the prisoner.

The Indonesian's eyes narrowed. He spat in the face of the American in front of him. Saliva spattered on Marc's jaw. The American took the bandana from his lap and wiped off the spittle. Marc sat for a moment, staring at his captive. Then, in one split second, he balled his right fist and smashed it with all of his might into the terrorist's face, breaking his nose. Blood poured over the man's mouth and onto his polo shirt.

"Hold that pose, asshole. I want to take a picture of that face of yours," Marc ordered. He reached into his backpack and removed his Nikon SLR camera.

"Say cheese," he said as he clicked off four photos of the man. "This is to prove we've captured you, Omar. Now, tell me— who are you working for? Abu Najib?"

The Indonesian closed his eyes, held his bloody face in his hands, and dropped his head.

"Ghazali is dead. We slit his throat as he was traveling to Penang. And so is Jeko. Do you want to live? Or should I kill you too, here and now? It's all the same to me." Marc wrapped the bandana around the Indonesian's neck and held it in both hands. "If you speak English, nod your head. I have some questions for you to answer." Omar stared back at the American.

"How much money did you receive from Hambali?" Marc stood and tightened the cloth around his captive's neck until his tongue protruded and his eyes bulged. "Talk to me."

"Stop," the man gasped. Marc released the pressure.

"Speak!" he ordered.

"I only hear. Hambali give thirty-thousand dollars to Imam. Ghazali tell me that. He pass to Jeko. I don't see it. The money."

"And Jeko?" Marc asked. "What did he do with all that money?"

"He buy all the material. The explosives. And the car."

"You made the bomb?"

The Indonesian appeared to smile. "*Ya*. Big bomb."

"Who trained you, Omar? You wouldn't have known how to make a bomb that big." Marc and the Indonesian glared at each other for several seconds.

"Who helped you? Answer me."

The Indonesian answered in a whisper. "The Arab."

"Name?" Marc spat.

"He calls himself Al-Saudi. Not his real name. He speaks Indonesian and lives in Java." Omar hesitated. There was silence for several moments. "He helped me outside Surabaya."

"Why did you do it, Omar? Make that bomb and kill so many innocent people?"

"Abu Najib ordered it. He says Bali is sinful place. Tourists are worms and snakes. Americans are infidels and crusaders. They must die for the crimes they commit against us believers."

"And Abu Najib takes orders from Osama bin Laden?" Marc leaned forward inches from Omar's face as he tightened the slip knot. The Indonesian nodded his head once.

Marc Mancini had heard enough. He placed the black hood back over the bomb-maker's head and tied it.

He called forward, "Hey, Al. Where are we?"

The pilot replied, "We're above Zamboanga Del Norte. We'll be over the Bohol Sea in twenty-five minutes. How high do you want me to fly?"

"Take us to the limit."

"All right. We're at ten thousand feet. We can continue at this level without worrying about lack of oxygen."

"I wanna give him a nice ride. And when you get out over the sea, west of Siquijor, look for a sailboat. One with two sails. Steer toward it."

Marc sat back in his seat and looked at the hooded man three feet in front of him.

"I'm curious, Omar. Do you believe all that nonsense about meeting seventy-two virgins in paradise when you die for your cause?" Silence. "Maybe not, huh?"

Marc continued, "What *do* you believe in?" There was no reply.

The only sound for the next twenty minutes was of the helicopter's engine and the whirling rotors.

"We're over the Bohol Sea, Marc. You want me to maintain ten thousand feet?" Al Reyes asked.

"Yeah. And keep your eyes peeled for the sailboat. It should be cruising somewhere between Apo and Siquijor."

Reyes remarked, "We're headed due north now. We'll fly between those islands in approximately . . . twenty minutes. What's the plan?"

"I want my dad to observe the fate of this asshole. Number three."

There was silence from the cockpit for several seconds. At last Al remarked, "I take it your prisoner will no longer be a passenger when we land on Mactan."

Marc looked closely at the hooded man in front of him to discern if he had understood what was in store for him. After a moment, he replied, "No. It will only be the two of us. How's the nightlife in Cebu?"

Marc heard a chortle in the cockpit. "Worthy of celebration. And thanks for the information about this guy's associate in Basilan. Right about now our team is making an arrest at the Maligaya Inn."

Marc noticed the hooded man make a sudden move and utter what sounded like an expletive at the mention of the hotel where he was supposed to meet his Indonesian accomplice.

Al turned back toward Marc. "I see a sailboat dead ahead. About ten minutes."

"All right. Try to fly as close as you can to it. Any other boats or ships around?"

"None. They're all alone out there, sailing east toward Siquijor."

Ten minutes later, Al called out, "We'll be forward of the yacht in about one minute."

"All right. I'm going to release him from his seat after I slide the door open."

Marc reached to his left and unlocked the door of the Bell. "Hold it steady," he said.

Marc glanced out the window on the left side of the helicopter and, looking forward, he spotted the sailboat, its sails full, on a fast beam reach.

"Looks like they've got some wind," he remarked.

"I'm adjusting our course now so we're forward of the boat," Al said. "All right, we're there."

"Opening the door," Marc shouted.

He thrust the door open and locked it in place. A moment later, Marc lifted Omar to his feet, turned him toward the door and guided him to the opening. There was a shriek from beneath the hood. "No virgins in hell, Omar."

Roy Mancini and Brewster Levey had spotted the approaching helicopter several minutes earlier as they held their course due east. The aircraft was flying at a high altitude, such that it remained tiny as it approached the boat. Roy had the helm and asked Brewster to go below and get the camera.

As the helicopter flew directly across the boat's course, both men saw an object being tossed out of the aircraft. In seconds it was apparent that a human had been ejected from the chopper. Brewster Levey stared at the sky, laughed, and called out, "Nice work, Marc."

"Take the helm, Brewster. I've gotta get a picture of this."

Roy took the camera and focused on the body as it fell. He clicked off several frames until it splashed into the sea two hundred meters ahead of the boat. "That was close," he said. "Head for the body and luff the main. I need to get another shot of the corpse before the sharks get to it."

The helicopter continued on its course, north to Mactan Island, Cebu.

59

As they sailed *JAMBALAYA* across the Bohol Sea back to Apo Island, Brewster Levey commented that Bruno was getting impatient. "I mean, he's still getting paid per hit, but he wants to be part of the action. Right now he's cooling his heels in Medan, bored and in a foul mood."

Roy replied, "I'll phone Marc and discuss how Bruno can fit in. Can he pass as a European Muslim?"

"He's grown the black beard, and I suppose he can dress the part. If he pretends he doesn't speak any English, who's to know?" Brewster said.

"First, Wayan needs to return to Java and assess the situation in Surakarta and lay the groundwork before Bruno wanders in there clueless."

After they arrived at Apo, Roy sent an encrypted email to his son asking him to summon Wayan back to Java, where he would feign again to be a recent Muslim convert, and settle in Surakarta, the home of Abu Najib.

"Tell me about Abu Najib, Roy," Brewster said later that evening as they sat at the bar of the Rusty Pecker.

"He's a bad actor, the godfather of Jemaah Islamiyah, Al-

Qaeda's offshoot in Indonesia. He ordered the Christmas Eve church bombings three years ago. I'm working with a policeman who lost his family in one of those bombings.

"The man was born in Java, of Arab descent. He's been a militant all his adult life. His violent brand of Wahhabi Islam is derived from the Arab Middle East. Believe me, he does not represent the moderate Islam as it is generally practiced in Indonesia.

"He was arrested during the Suharto dictatorship for espousing sharia law. The regime held him in prison for four years. Soon after he was released in 1985, he plotted the bombing of the Buddhist temple, Borobudur. Before they could arrest him, he fled to Malaysia, where he remained, in exile, for several years."

Brewster ordered two more San Miguels and a plate of calamari. His young, ravishing girlfriends, Veronica and Sissy, sidled to the bar and helped themselves to the calamari. "Jun, give the girls their drinks," he said to his bartender.

"You were saying, Roy. . ."

"Yeah. After Suharto was overthrown in 1998, Abu Najib was allowed to return to Indonesia and settle in Surakarta in Central Java. He runs a *madrassah* there. That's an Islamic boarding school. President Hartono offered him amnesty and a 'welcome home' if he promised to behave himself. Which he hasn't. Instead, he has taken advantage of Indonesia's new freedoms.

"And that brings us to Bali. Abu Najib was the spiritual leader and mastermind for the bombing. Two weeks ago, he claimed to the local press that the CIA was behind it. He's next on our hit list, Brewster. The last."

"Bruno?" Brewster Levey asked.

"Yeah. This one is reserved for Bruno. It'll be more risky than the other three kills. He'll be surrounded by his security detail and his loyal students. You've told me Bruno is good." Roy drank his beer from the bottle.

Brewster replied, "He's better than good."

Roy continued, "I'm formulating a plan. I should be able to give you the go-ahead for Bruno tomorrow or the next day. And I'll email the op plan to Marc."

60

SURAKARTA, CENTRAL JAVA

ARC, WAYAN, AND BRUNO EACH ARRIVED SEPA-
rately in the Central Javanese city, Jogjakarta, over a
weekend in late April. The American and the Italian
hit man checked into different hotels. Wayan took a room in a
cheap downtown boardinghouse. Marc called for a meeting on
Monday.

After picking up Bruno and Wayan in his rental car, Marc
drove northeast to the ninth-century Hindu Prambanan Temple,
eleven miles outside of the city. There the three strolled, as casual
tourists, through the ornate temple's lawns and tree-lined gardens.
Marc described the next step in the mission.

Wayan would travel to the city of Surakarta in the Solo district of Central Java. Abu Najib operated his Islamic boarding
school there, and it was where his disciples paid homage to him.
Wayan's mission would be to infiltrate the jihadist's lair and to set
the stage for the arrival of the Sicilian.

Marc reminded Wayan of Jeko Rusdiana's revelation that
there was an Arab member of the cell who had been involved in
the bombing.

Wayan rode in a local bus to Surakarta the following day. He rented a motorbike at a shop near the terminal and paid in advance for one week. The shop assistant gave him directions to the Hotel Syariah, which Wayan knew was in the general vicinity of Abu Najib's boarding school. Wayan had changed into his disguise, and was wearing the skull-cap and loose-fitting, long white tunic of the pious Muslim.

During the next four days, he prayed at the mosque adjacent to the boarding school, all the while observing the other men who prayed there the required five times a day, from pre-dawn until late at night. He identified a man who had the bearded, hawk-nosed appearance common for men from the Middle East. Wayan approached the man outside the mosque following the afternoon prayer on the fourth day.

Wayan spoke to him in Indonesian. "Pardon me, brother, are you from Surakarta?"

The man stopped walking, turned, and stared into the face of the stranger. Finally he replied in the same language, "No, I am not of this place." Wayan noted the man's foreign accent.

"Nor am I," the Balinese exclaimed. "I have recently arrived, and only this year have I become a believer."

"Yes. I noticed you this week and that you join us in prayer throughout the day as you should. You are to be commended."

Wayan continued, "I have much to learn, and I seek guidance. I was hoping you could direct me to an imam who can educate me in the ways of the Prophet, peace be upon him. I must learn to speak Arabic so I can read the Quran. I wish to devote myself to language lessons."

The man continued to speak passable Indonesian. "My name is Ibn Al-Saudi. I am from Saudi Arabia. I am in Surakarta on holiday and to practice speaking your language. There are many fine centers of learning here. I am sure you'll find what you are looking for."

"You speak very good Indonesian, brother Ibn. Perhaps we can exchange lessons. I can speak with you in Indonesian, and you can help me learn Arabic. My name is Wayan." The Balinese extended his hand. Al-Saudi hesitated for a moment before he shook it.

The Arab asked, "Which part of Indonesia are you from?"

"I am from Bali."

He appeared taken aback. "Oh! You experienced a major event there last month, did you not?"

Wayan had anticipated this remark, and he had prepared his response. "Yes, the bombing at the hotel. Anyway, they were mostly non-believers who perished. Christians and Jews. Americans. Ironic too that they were travel agents. We need to cleanse Bali of those filthy tourists. They pollute our beaches with their frolicking, half-naked women." He completed his statement with a grimace.

Al-Saudi chuckled. "Well put, Wayan. The local sheik would agree with you. He has said as much to his followers here."

"The local sheik? Who is that, brother?"

The Arab paused, as though considering whether to reply or not. At last he said in a low voice, "The imam, Abu Najib. He concurs with your sentiments. I may introduce you to him."

"I would like that. Perhaps he can assist me with my studies. I plan to reside in Surakarta. As I said, I only recently converted to Islam."

"I will inform the sheik. Though you may be too old to attend his *madrassah*, the boarding school. He might arrange private lessons. Where do you stay in Surakarta?"

"I am staying in a small hotel. Temporarily. I do need to find an affordable boardinghouse. Can you suggest one?" Wayan made brief eye contact with the Arab.

"Why don't we have tea or coffee together? We can discuss your situation. There is a *warung* nearby. Walking distance. Follow me."

The two men walked together south on Jalan Gajah Mada.

The tall, bearded Arab continued to query the swarthy and muscular Balinese about his political opinions and his plans. Wayan suspected he was being subtly assessed for recruitment. And so he played along, hinting of his disgust with the depraved conditions on his island. "Bali was once a paradise before the foreigners destroyed it," he commented as they ambled along a sidewalk. "Perhaps now, after the bombing last March, conditions will return to what they were. What do you think, Ibn?"

"I believe you are correct, brother Wayan. And we need to continue our militant, Salafi jihad against the infidels—be they foreigners or Indonesian non-believers. We require more soldiers like the ones who sacrificed themselves in Bali." The Arab spoke with a fierceness in his dark eyes.

They entered a small *warung* and sat at one of the six tables. Al-Saudi ordered tea and sweets for them both without asking his new acquaintance what he might prefer.

Al-Saudi informed Wayan that he was living in a boardinghouse, which had been arranged by Abu Najib. He would inquire if there were any vacant rooms. He asked for Wayan's cell phone number.

"I will phone you later today. Or perhaps I'll see you after *Isha* about a room at the boardinghouse," the Arab said, referring to the late evening prayers at the mosque. "I suspect the sheik can find a place for you."

"I cannot thank you enough, brother Ibn," Wayan exclaimed.

They met later following *Isha*, the final, late-night call to prayer. Ibn Al-Saudi waited outside the mosque and gestured with a wave to Wayan as the Balinese exited the hall.

"I have good news, Wayan," the Arab said. "A brother vacated his room at the boardinghouse earlier today. He departed Surakarta on a mission for the sheik. I took the liberty of reserving it for you. How soon can you move in?"

Wayan replied, "Excellent. I can move in tonight. I'll go to the hotel and pack. Can you give me the address of the boarding-house?"

"Better than that. I will help you move. Let's flag a taxi." Without waiting for a reply the Arab turned and faced the traffic on Jalan Gajah Mada. In less than a minute he had stopped a taxi, and they took off for the hotel. As they packed the Arab made a none-too-subtle point of scrutinizing all of Wayan's personal effects.

Wayan's room was on the second floor of the boardinghouse and directly across the hall from the room of the Arab. It occurred to Wayan now that Al-Saudi and Abu Najib were conspiring in a shrewd effort to recruit a Balinese Muslim into their organization, Jemaah Islamiyah. The boardinghouse was located one block from Abu Najib's *madrassah*.

The next morning at four o'clock, Al-Saudi knocked on Wayan's door.

"Join me for prayer, brother?" he asked when the Balinese opened the door.

Wayan had bathed and was dressed. "Yes, Ibn. I was about to see if you were still in. We can go together."

As they walked, the Arab mentioned that Abu Najib was looking forward to meeting Wayan later that morning. The sheik had suggested that they take breakfast together at his home. "You'll be able to discuss your studies with him. I believe he will embrace you into our faith and offer you guidance in carrying out our duty— to establish sharia law throughout the archipelago, and all of Southeast Asia. Are you willing to pursue that quest with us, brother?"

Wayan did not hesitate. "Oh, yes. If the sheik can instruct me in the creed of sharia, I would be most thankful, Ibn. There are many potential converts to Islam among the men and women of

Bali. They only need to be taught the truth about the universal fairness of sharia law. I will make it my mission to return home one day to carry out the sheik's good work." The Balinese managed to maintain a poker face as he spoke this nonsense.

"Abu Najib will be delighted to hear that, brother Wayan. I believe he will welcome you into his circle in due time."

The modest home of Abu Najib was at the rear of his boarding school. Al-Saudi knocked three times on the solid hardwood front door of the two story abode. A massively built and armed Indonesian security guard opened it, glanced at Al-Saudi, and stared for several moments at Wayan.

"The imam is expecting us for breakfast," the Arab said to the guard in his accented Indonesian. "I bring brother Wayan with me. Kindly inform Abu Najib of our arrival."

The unsmiling bodyguard beckoned them to enter. "Wait here," he said, raising an open hand in front of Wayan and then pointing to a sofa. "The imam will be here shortly." The two visitors sat where they were told.

Al-Saudi whispered to Wayan, "I apologize for this lack of hospitality. Abu Najib cannot be too careful nowadays. Especially after the glorious event in Bali. He has bolstered his personal security during the past month. One cannot blame him."

"I get it," Wayan uttered. "We must be watchful about who we let into our lives. One never knows."

"You are perceptive, brother."

At that moment, Abu Najib descended the stairs slowly, with a fixed smile. Wayan experienced a cold chill when he saw the tall, slender, bespectacled man with thinning hair and a matching white beard walk toward them. The man appeared to be at least a decade older than his sixty-five years. As he reached the ground floor, he walked with a discernible limp and gripped a wooden cane in his left hand. He reached out to Wayan, who was now standing, and the two shook hands. The Balinese bowed and grit his teeth at the touch of the terrorist mastermind's dry, wrinkled skin.

The old man spoke to Wayan in Indonesian, never altering his thin smile. "Welcome, our friend from Bali. Al-Saudi speaks highly of you. Please, follow me. We will take breakfast outside, in the garden." A second armed bodyguard opened a door for them at the rear of the house.

Abu Najib continued, "You will excuse us, brother Wayan. I prefer to speak Arabic with our Saudi friend." He glanced at Al-Saudi.

"Yes, of course, imam. Al-Saudi may have mentioned I wish to study the Arabic language here in Surakarta," Wayan replied.

"Yes, so he tells me. You must know Arabic in order to read the Quran properly. How long has it been since you became a believer, Wayan?"

"I made the decision last year. I have seen how my island has been spoiled over the past several years by the invasive Western culture. I read about sharia law and decided that would be the solution to our problem. I converted to Islam four months ago. I trust you can guide me in my quest to become a good Muslim and to help liberate my island from the evil influence of nonbelievers."

The imam beamed and motioned for his guests to sit. "Come, let us take breakfast."

The table had been set for three. There were glasses of juice at each place, a bowl of fruit and a large platter of fried rice in the center of the table.

"*Selamat makan*," Abu Najib said, inviting his guests to eat.

Abu Najib and Al-Saudi spoke with each other in Arabic as Wayan ate slowly and considered his situation. He knew he was not fully trusted by either man, though he had one foot in the door. He was confident he could play out this act for as long as it might take the two jihadists to embrace him, and to reveal some of their secrets. Later he would phone Marc with an update and ask him to dispatch Bruno to Surakarta within the week.

AT LAST ABU NAJIB SPOKE TO WAYAN. "LATER TODAY I WILL introduce you to our Arabic language teacher at the *madrassah*. Al-Saudi tells me you wish to reside permanently in Surakarta. Excellent. Do you have financial resources, Wayan?"

"I must find work to live here. I have little savings," he replied.

Al-Saudi spoke. "The imam told me he may be able to assist you in finding work. And the Arabic lessons will not cost you anything."

Wayan expressed his thanks.

As they stood, Abu Najib said, "Return to the *madrassah* later this afternoon. I will introduce you to your teacher. And welcome to Surakarta. I am certain you will be content here. And you need not pay for your room in advance. We will wait until you find work."

Later in the afternoon, Wayan rode his motorbike through the dense traffic and side streets of Surakarta until he found a quiet cul-de-sac near the university. He parked there and speed-dialed Marc's burn phone. When Marc answered after two rings Wayan told the American that he needed another week to prepare for the Sicilian's arrival. The call took less than thirty seconds.

61

SURAKARTA

ONE WEEK LATER, THE ARAB INVITED THE BALINESE convert to join him for a ride through the Solo countryside. They mounted their motorbikes outside the boardinghouse. Wayan followed Al-Saudi as he made several abrupt left and right turns through the various streets of the city. At last they entered a highway at the northern outskirts of Surakarta. The Arab increased speed and Wayan pulled beside him. The two raced their bikes west until they arrived at a rural farming area. The four-lane highway ended there, and again Wayan followed Al-Saudi on a paved two-lane road. Finally the Arab pulled onto a dirt track that passed between two vast, green rice fields. He motioned with a hand for Wayan to follow. In the middle of the field, Al-Saudi stopped. Wayan pulled up beside the Arab. They switched off their engines and remained seated on the bikes.

The Arab spoke. "The sheik has asked that I speak with you in confidence, brother Wayan. No one can hear us out here."

The Balinese looked at Al-Saudi without replying.

"Abu Najib is impressed. You are doing well with your language lessons. You are well-liked, and you appear to be a team player. Would you agree?"

Wayan replied, "I am committed to the sheik, Ibn. I am thankful if he recognizes my efforts."

The Arab held Wayan's eyes and paused. Finally he asked, "I am going to be blunt. Can we trust you to perform jihad, violent jihad, against our enemies: the infidels and crusaders who are at war with us?"

There was a long silence, each man nurturing his own thoughts. They stared at each other. At last Wayan spoke. "I am prepared to wage jihad, brother. I only need your guidance and training."

"Excellent," the Arab exclaimed. He took Wayan's right hand in both of his. "You will be part of a growing and disciplined Salafi organization in Indonesia. You will not be alone, my friend. I will explain."

Wayan continued to make steady eye contact with the Arab.

"You will train to be a soldier in Jemaah Islamiyah. Your spiritual leader is Abu Najib. What I tell you now is highly secret. Violate your oath of secrecy and you would meet a very painful death. You would not be the first. Do you agree?"

"Yes, I can agree to that, brother. My wish is to contribute to the struggle against our enemies." Wayan placed his right hand over his heart. "What is my mission?"

"Abu Najib wishes for you to move to Jakarta upon completing your training here. He has a plan for you which, for the time being, we cannot reveal. Suffice to say we will make use of your good command of English and of your refined appearance in order to gain access to a gathering of Westerners. You will be expected to penetrate the target and do it more easily than some of our less sophisticated soldiers could. That is all I can tell you at this stage."

Wayan remained silent.

"We have vast resources at our disposal, Wayan. I am more than a mere tourist and student here in Surakarta, as you may have surmised. I am the personal representative in your country for an organization in Saudi Arabia that provides funds not only for Abu Najib's boarding school, but for *madrassahs* and militant jihadist groups along the Indian Ocean shoreline, including Somalia, Pakistan, Afghanistan, and Southeast Asia."

Wayan asked, "So your organization in Saudi Arabia provides the money for weapons and explosives, and we, in each country, provide the soldiers on the ground. Do I have that right?"

"That is a good summary," the Arab replied. "An example of our success was the bombing in Bali two months ago. We supplied the funds, routed through Al Qaeda. The soldiers of Jemaah Islamiyah, under the guidance of Abu Najib, implemented the plan. Flawlessly, I might add."

The two men were silent again. The Arab, expressionless, continued to stare at Wayan who gazed out at the verdant rice field. At last the Balinese turned toward Al-Saudi. "I met a man in Bali earlier this month. At a mosque. He is an Italian and a fugitive. He says he was drawn to Bali because of his fascination with the bombing. He told me he wishes to convert to Islam and carry out militant actions against the West. He saw I was a Muslim, and asked if I had contacts inside an Islamist organization. At that time, of course, I did not and I said so." He paused. "Would you care to interview him, Ibn?"

The Arab glared at Wayan. "Be careful, brother, with whom you associate. This Italian could well be a double-agent or *provocateur*. What is the man's name?"

"I only know a first name. He called himself Bruno. He claims to be a professional assassin, Sicilian Mafia, and he wishes to dedicate himself to our cause. He cannot return to Europe, as there are warrants for his arrest throughout the EU. He would be able to penetrate a Western gathering here in Indonesia better than I can. I have his cell phone number if you would like me to contact him. He speaks broken English."

"All right. I suppose it would not hurt to meet with him over tea somewhere. You say he wishes to convert to Islam? He would have to."

"So he says. He was raised Catholic in Sicily. I doubt he is religious. The man mentioned he is attracted to Al Qaeda. He said he wants to live and operate in Asia, not in the Middle East."

"All right, arrange it, Wayan. See if he can travel to Surakarta. I'll meet with him and decide."

Wayan replied, "He may still be in Bali. I will phone him and ask him to take a bus to Jogjakarta. I will let you know when he arrives. You only need to tell me where you want to meet. Do you want me to attend your meeting?"

Al-Saudi shook his head. "No. I handle these assessment meetings alone, one-on-one. I don't need any distractions. And we must be vigilant."

"Right."

"If I accept him into JI, perhaps the two of you can work as a team during the imam's mission in Jakarta," Al-Saudi said. "We shall see."

62

SURAKARTA

BRUNO ARRIVED FOUR DAYS LATER. WAYAN MET HIM before midnight at the bus terminal and drove him on the back of his motorbike to the Syariah Hotel.

Marc Mancini had for three days briefed the Sicilian hitman on the relationships between Wayan, Al-Saudi and Abu Najib. The stage was set.

Bruno had grown a thick black beard and wore a three-quarter-length white tunic similar to Wayan's.

Wayan had casually mentioned Bruno to Al-Saudi on two occasions during the past few days. The Arab had shrugged his shoulders both times and said, "We'll see."

Now Wayan met Al-Saudi at five o'clock in the morning outside the mosque. The sky was still dark. "He's arrived, Ibn. Let me know your plans."

"Why are you so eager, brother Wayan?" the Arab demanded. "You know how careful we must be with strangers, especially Westerners. We do not trust any of them."

Wayan faced the Arab and said, "I believe we have a golden opportunity here, brother. Meet him and judge for yourself if this

Italian has the motivation to carry out our operations against the infidels. If not . . ."

"All right. You remember the *warung* where we had our first discussion over tea, the day we met each other?"

"Of course."

"Bring him there at 4:15 this afternoon, after prayers. I will sit at a table in the back. Then you vanish. I will conduct a preliminary interview. I'll phone you when you need to return. Satisfied?"

"He'll be there. Have you mentioned him to the sheik?"

"Certainly not," Al-Saudi exclaimed. He turned to see if anyone had overheard his outburst. In a low voice he continued, "I do not bother Abu Najib with these matters. If I decide your Mr. Bruno has potential, only then would I mention him to the sheik."

"All right." Wayan reminded himself to be patient.

"Leave me now. I have work to do. Deliver him to me following afternoon prayers as I have instructed."

Wayan met Bruno in front of his hotel at four in the afternoon. They rode through the side streets of Surakarta for fifteen minutes before arriving at the *warung* on Jalan Gajah Mada.

During the fifteen minute counter-surveillance tour of the city streets, Wayan reminded the Italian to pretend he understood little English. He should not allow the Saudi to trick him with an in-depth back-and-forth. Nor should he appear too cosmopolitan. In short, the Arab must never suspect the Italian of being a double-agent. Bruno needed to listen closely to Al-Saudi and declare in broken English how he wished to offer his talents to the cause of Al Qaeda. He was *not* to mention Jemaah Islamiyah, as there would be no reason for him to be familiar with the local terrorist outfit. He would explain to Al-Saudi that he'd specialized in covert murder-for-hire in Europe, and that he was prepared to live in Asia and apply his trade here. Al-Saudi would no doubt ask the Italian if he had converted to Islam. Bruno would reply in the affirmative.

Wayan pulled up in front of the *warung* and spotted the Arab at a table against the back wall. Bruno dismounted, and Wayan motioned with a nod of his head in the direction of Al-Saudi. "The man alone in the back. I'll meet you here when you're finished." He put the motorbike in gear and took off. In the rearview mirror, he saw the stocky bearded Italian walk into the restaurant. Wayan smiled to himself as he cut into the heavy traffic. He would await the Arab's phone call inside his room at the boardinghouse.

Forty-five minutes later, Wayan's cell phone rang. He noted the number of Al-Saudi in the display. Wayan let the phone ring four times before answering. "Yes."

"Pick him up," the Arab ordered.

Bruno waited on the sidewalk outside the *warung*. Al-Saudi had already left the area and returned to Abu Najib's *madrassah*, where he assisted with the teaching of religious studies to the young Indonesian students enrolled there. Wayan pulled up in front of Bruno and the big Sicilian straddled the bike's rear seat. They took off into the late afternoon traffic.

Neither man said a word as Wayan navigated the streets of Surakarta, heading north. He reckoned there was a good chance Al-Saudi was having them followed, so he dropped Bruno off in front of his hotel and continued on to the boardinghouse. Wayan decided to wait until Al-Saudi mentioned the subject of Bruno, and agreed to brief him about his meeting with the Italian. They would meet each other as usual at the mosque for the night's final call to prayer.

The Balinese exited the mosque and waited on the sidewalk nearby. Approximately fifty men left the small building at the same time. A few of them smiled at the Balinese and bid him good night as they passed by. At last Al-Saudi emerged, the last man to leave. Wayan raised a hand. The Arab spotted him and motioned for Wayan to approach.

"Good evening, brother Ibn." Wayan offered a hand. Al-Saudi gave him a perfunctory handshake.

"Let's go," the Arab said as he turned away. Wayan walked beside him. After a few moments, Al-Saudi remarked, "As you know I interviewed the Italian earlier this afternoon."

They walked in silence for a few moments.

Al-Saudi continued, "He strikes me as a nasty creature. An angry man." He made a face that indicated disdain.

"Yes, he seems to be looking for a fight," Wayan observed. "I wouldn't want to have him as an enemy."

"Hmm. Question is . . . what do we do with him?" The Arab continued walking and staring at the ground.

Wayan asked after several moments, "What's your idea?"

"I would need to interview him again," Al-Saudi replied. "You were correct, Wayan, in bringing him to our attention. He is evidently a man who has been betrayed. If we can control and channel his anger, perhaps we will enlist him as a soldier in our cause." He hesitated before speaking again. "I will mention him to the sheik. Abu Najib will want to observe him in his home. We have a special room for this."

"I will await your instructions, Ibn."

"Yes, I will let you know what to do about Mr. Bruno after I discuss this matter with Abu Najib."

63

THE WHITE HOUSE

THE PRESIDENT OF THE UNITED STATES AND HIS NA-tional security advisor, Harvey Katz, sat alone inside the small, tidy office in the family residence. The president studied the four photographs in the order they had been shown to him by Katz.

"You're positive, Harvey, no one else has seen these?"

"I'm sure of it, Mr. President. Walter Sarkies at the *Institute* is the only other person who has them. He received them two days ago from an Iranian double-agent that he's handling. I had a meeting with Sarkies this morning after he phoned me. He said these photographs are for the president's eyes only. Smart decision."

The president stared at each of the four photographs again for several seconds. "Pretty gruesome. Who are they?"

Katz reached for the photos. He handed one back to the president. "This one, the terrorist with the bullet through the head, was named Jeko Rusdiana. He's the first one they captured."

Katz placed the photograph on the coffee table in front of them. He handed the second color photo to his boss. "This was the team leader. They called him Ghazali."

The president commented, "It looks like he's laid out on a pile of life vests. They slit his throat. Marvelous."

"Right." Katz handed a set of two photographs to the president. "You'll like these. It's the bomb-maker himself. A skydiver without a parachute. Being tossed out of a helicopter. And this one shows him floating in the sea before the sharks got to him."

The president shook his head. "Who would have imagined we would ever cooperate with the Iranians?" he said. "Pour yourself a drink, Harvey, and explain this to me again, in detail. From the beginning."

The national security advisor mixed a vodka and tonic with a twist of lemon and a lot of ice. The president, a teetotaler, hadn't yet touched his Coke.

When Katz returned to his seat, he took a sip of his drink and shuffled again through the photos. He repeated to the president the story told to him by the deputy director of the *Institute*.

Sarkies, said Katz, had been handling an Iranian double-agent in New York. The agent was operating undercover as an Iranian diplomat at the U.N. The FBI knew he was the senior Iranian intelligence officer in the U.S., and the Feds had him under surveillance. Sarkies debriefed him once a month in New York."

"So we're running an Iranian agent at the United Nations? That's news to me, Harvey. Go on," the president interjected with a chuckle.

Katz explained how Walter Sarkies had recruited two Iranian agents when he was a rookie CIA case officer in Beirut. And one of those agents, Ramin, had risen high enough in the ranks to be posted in New York.

Katz summarized Sarkies's background. He had been recruited into the CIA after receiving his law degree from Stanford. He was fluent in English, Arabic and Armenian. Coincidentally, Sarkies and Katz had been classmates at Stanford. They had not known each other well, though there was a bond between them that was typical among Stanford grads.

After his training at the Farm and an initial stint at Langley, Sarkies had been posted under diplomatic cover to the U.S. Embassy in Beirut. Three years later, the CIA sent him to Cairo. He was pirated from the CIA by the *Institute*. Sarkies operated undercover in the Middle East for the super-secret DOD HumInt agency where he had a series of successes in the region. He'd been promoted to deputy director of the *Institute* in 2001.

A week ago, he said, Sarkies held a meeting with Ramin in Central Park. That's where he collected the photos. The Iranian revealed that an asset of theirs in Jakarta sent a report to Teheran that the Indonesian president had ordered the U.S. president to keep his hands off the Bali bombing investigation.

Sarkies said the Iranians were tracking and assassinating the bombers because of a mutual enemy—radical Sunnis. The Iranian hit men had already killed three of the Indonesian terrorists as evidenced by the photographs.

"No shit," said the president. "Why in the world would the Iranians want to help us with anything?"

"According to Walter, the head of intelligence is a secular Persian, a closet moderate. President Khatami appointed him to run the agency over the objection of hardliners in the Revolutionary Guard. Sarkies thinks Khatami may be reaching out to us through his new chief of Intelligence.

"As he explains it, the intelligence boss, his name is Afshin, was dismayed by the inclusion of Iran as a member of the Axis-of-Evil in your State of the Union address. Oh, there's one other thing. Afshin was undercover at the U.N. in New York back in the eighties."

"The United Nations again?" The president shook his head. "We provide these guys with everything they need for their cover stories, don't we?"

Katz continued, "That we do. At any rate, Afshin is a real pro and has distinguished himself in the spy business over the years, and so President Khatami, a moderate reformer himself, elevated him four months ago to lead the Iranian Ministry of Intelligence. Afshin and Khatami wish to establish their *bona fides* with you by eliminating the Bali bombers. That's Walter Sarkies's take."

As Sarkies explained it to Harvey Katz, they requested the president of the United States abstain from labeling Iran as a member of the so-called Axis-of-Evil. The evil actors, Afshin insisted, are the Sunnis, specifically those from Saudi Arabia, and not the Persian Shiites. Al Qaeda and their Arab enablers—all Sunnis—were America's true enemies. The government of Iran, like the Americans, had a vital interest in neutralizing them wherever they are in the world.

Katz continued, "This agent told Sarkies that Iran will not resist the American invasion of Iraq. Their desire is to replace Saddam with a Shia government, friendly to Teheran. Afshin and Khatami believe that the removal of Saddam will positively affect the balance of power in the Middle East."

The president asked his national security advisor, "So the Bali bombers were Sunnis? And that's what's motivating this fellow Afshin to get involved in Indonesia? It's a Shia-versus-Sunni thing."

"Yes, sir. The terrorists' spiritual leader, a man named Abu Najib, has links to Osama bin Laden. We know his school in Central Java is financed by Saudi petrodollars, as are scores of radical *madrassahs* around the world. These schools preach anti-Shia and anti-American propaganda. The Iranians have an interest in crippling Abu Najib's organization, Jemaah Islamiyah, and so do we.

"The agent in New York, according to Sarkies, says Iranian assets are tracking and killing the Indonesian Sunni terrorists, those pictured in these photos. Iranian money is financing the operation. Only you, Mr. President, me, and Walter Sarkies at the *Institute* are privy."

"I like it, Harvey. This Iranian operation achieves our objectives in Indonesia," the president exclaimed. "Hell, I'm not the first president to play footsie with Teheran. Iran-Contra and all that."

"I agree, Mr. President. We achieve our goal of bringing the Bali bombers to justice. Our hands are clean."

"And they expect a *quid pro quo*. Right?"

"Yes, sir. They want us to recognize that President Khatami is doing the best he can as a reformer, given the difficult job he has of bowing to the wishes of Ayatollah Khamenei, their Supreme Leader. This is a backdoor operation in the true sense."

"So bottom line, President Khatami wants to play nice and wants us to reciprocate."

Katz glanced at his notes. "They have one more request, Mr. President. The Iranians want us to disband the Iraqi army. Send the soldiers home to their families. My recommendation is to go along if it keeps the Iranians out of our hair in Iraq.

"We don't need further complications over there. The Sunnis and Shias have been mortal enemies for ages. We removed Saddam for them. And they're returning the favor in Indonesia. For the time being, let's see how this plays out."

"Do it, Harvey. Dissolve Saddam's army." The president smirked as he ordered this. "Now let's go join the ladies. You're staying for dinner, right?"

64

BALI AND SURAKARTA

ARC HIT SPEED DIAL. ROY ANSWERED AFTER SIX rings. "What is it Marc?"

"You need to send your cop to Surakarta. Things are moving fast. Where are you?"

Roy snickered. "Putting on my tank. Brewster and I are going scuba diving. We're on his boat. By the way, funds have been received in Labuan. Sent from the mystery source in the Caribbean. Your hit number three has been acknowledged."

"I'm going to send you an email after we disconnect," said Marc. "I'll summarize the op plan for Surakarta. I wanted to give you a heads-up. Time to move!"

"I'll tell Brewster to postpone the dive. Anything else?"

"That's it. Log in to your email in about twenty minutes." Marc closed the connection.

Twenty minutes later, Roy Mancini opened the email in the privacy of the cabin inside *Jambalaya*. What he read caused him to delay the dive trip indefinitely.

Marc repeated that Roy needed to summon Hotman Pardede and his team to Surakarta ASAP. Bruno had undergone an initial interview with an Arab operative named Ibn Al-Saudi. A second interview was imminent, and that meeting would be held at the residence of Abu Najib. Al-Saudi would have to be neutralized before then so Wayan could escort Bruno to the meeting instead.

Roy deleted the email after reading it. He took his Indonesian cell phone and speed-dialed Hotman. The police officer answered after one ring. He said, "Talk to me."

They spoke in Indonesian. The American explained the requirement. He provided addresses in Surakarta for Bruno, Al-Saudi, and Wayan and told Hotman the plot against Abu Najib was entering the final stage. The Indonesian listened in silence before finally muttering that he understood.

In Bali, Hotman Pardede gathered three police officers he trusted. The trio were fellow Batak Christians from North Sumatra. They spoke to each other now in the Batak dialect. Hotman briefed them on the barest details of the operation. They would flesh it out once they spotted their targets and evaluated the situation on the ground in Surakarta. Hotman booked flights to Jogjakarta for the four of them. Before departing police headquarters for the airport in Denpasar, he discussed the operation with General Agung and received the commander's blessing.

The four policemen, attired in civilian clothes, rented a sedan upon arrival in Jogjakarta. Their automatic weapons had been checked on the flight and were now stowed in the car's trunk. Each man carried a 9mm pistol and spare magazines. The drive from Jogjakarta to Surakarta took a little over an hour. They arrived at the Syariah Hotel in the late afternoon and took separate rooms.

Hotman phoned Wayan, who was waiting in a coffee shop two blocks from the hotel. Marc had alerted the Balinese, and he was expecting the call. "Where are you?" asked Hotman.

Wayan gave the policeman the address of the café. The Bataks entered the coffee shop and looked for a young man wearing a red baseball cap that had *Bali* written across the front of it. After identifying Wayan, the men left the café carrying their coffees back to the hotel. They knew the address of his boarding-house. And they knew it was the same building where Al-Saudi lived. Now they knew what Wayan looked like without having to make contact with him.

Hotman's task was to keep Al-Saudi under surveillance. The team split up. Hotman and Sergeant Jonathan Silitonga followed the Arab from the time he left his boardinghouse at four-thirty in the morning, walking to the mosque, until he returned to his room following the fifth and final call to prayer at night. The two other men on the team kept Bruno and Wayan under discreet surveillance throughout the day to uncover if either of them were being followed by Jemaah Islamiyah operatives. Bruno visited the mosque occasionally to give the appearance that he was a convert.

Twice a day, Wayan phoned Hotman to report on his discus-sions with Al-Saudi. He revealed that the Arab would introduce Bruno to Abu Najib after the imam returned from a clandestine recruitment trip in Aceh. The Saudi would act as the interpreter for the meeting because Abu Najib was not fluent in English. The two of them would, as usual, speak Arabic. Wayan was not invited to the interview.

At five in the morning, four days after the arrival of the po-lice team in Surakarta, Wayan phoned Hotman and asked for an urgent meeting. The two met for the first time face-to-face in the policeman's hotel room thirty minutes later.

"Today is the day. Al-Saudi has scheduled Bruno's meeting with Abu Najib at midnight," Wayan said as soon as he entered the room. "He informed me this morning. He ordered me to de-liver Bruno to the imam's home."

Hotman stared for several moments at the Balinese before asking, "Are you ready for this, Wayan?"

"Tell me your plan." He returned the stare.

Hotman explained to Wayan how the hit would go. The Balinese would take the gun and silencer to the house on the assumption that Wayan was now trusted by Abu Najib's bodyguards. He should be able to enter the home without undergoing a thorough inspection of his bag.

Wayan asked, "What about Al-Saudi?"

"Leave him to me," the Batak replied. "You prepare to be the interpreter in place of the Arab. The Italian will make the hit *after* you escape from Abu Najib's house. Disappear as quickly as you can. You cannot be involved in a murder, Wayan. I'll arrest Bruno outside the house, and drive him out of town where I'll set him free. Got it?"

Wayan hesitated. "I've got it," he uttered.

65

SURAKARTA

HOTMAN AND HIS TEAM OF BATAKS SLIPPED QUIETLY into the boardinghouse soon after sundown. They knew Al-Saudi and Wayan were in their rooms on the second floor. Hotman knocked on Wayan's door. When the Balinese opened it, the four policemen slipped into the room.

Hotman explained that all Wayan needed to do now was knock on Al-Saudi's door across the hall and ask to have a word with the Arab. When he opened the door, the team would take over. Wayan would go to the Syariah Hotel and wait there with Bruno.

"Who is it?" the Arab called out from inside his room after hearing the soft knock on his door.

"It's Wayan, brother Ibn. I need to discuss something with you. May I enter?" the Balinese replied. Two Bataks stood on each side of the door.

"Give me a minute," came the sharp reply.

Each of the policemen held a Glock 9mm pistol. Wayan stepped out of sight before the man inside the room opened his door. By the time the Arab appeared in the doorway, the Balinese had vanished. Hotman shoved his weapon at Al-Saudi's chest, as his two colleagues grabbed the man. "Throw him onto the bed. Gag and handcuff him," Hotman ordered.

Hotman bent and glared into the Arab's eyes. He spoke in Indonesian. "Where's your passport?"

The man's eyes opened wide with fear. The policeman slapped him hard on his face. "Your passport!"

Al-Saudi motioned with his head toward a chest of drawers. Hotman opened the top drawer and discovered a pistol and a full magazine. He lifted the weapon toward the man. "This is illegal. You will go to prison." He searched each of the drawers until he found the man's diplomatic passport.

"So you are a Saudi Arabian, and you are carrying a gun in Indonesia." Hotman motioned for one of his men to remove the gag from the Arab's mouth. "Who do you work for? Al Qaeda?"

The man replied in English in a hoarse voice, "I am accredited to the Saudi Embassy. I demand to phone my ambassador. This is an outrage."

Hotman understood enough of the man's English to comprehend that he was dealing with an intelligence officer under diplomatic cover.

"Yes, Mr. Al-Saudi. Or whatever your name is. I see you are a diplomat. And rather than make a phone call and disturb your ambassador, I will escort you to Jakarta tonight and leave you at your embassy's front door. First you will write a short note to Abu Najib explaining to him that you had to make an unexpected trip to your embassy, and that brother Wayan will replace you as the translator for the meeting tonight."

At that instant, Al-Saudi realized he'd been deceived. The scheme to recruit Bruno had been a subterfuge, and the Balinese had all the while been operating covertly. His eyes narrowed with an expression of pure hate. "Never!" he shouted. Hotman drove his fist into the man's face and jammed his pistol into the man's mouth, cracking his front teeth.

"We have several hours until midnight to change your mind, Al-Saudi." Hotman sneered. He forced the gun deeper inside the Arab's mouth. "We call this '*deep throat*'. Breathe through your nose. You have a choice. Write the note and leave here alive. Or cause me to write the note, and you can die a painful death in a rice field outside Surakarta. Either way, your career as a terrorist and spy in my country is finished. You have ten seconds to give me your answer." Hotman counted backward slowly from ten.

The Arab raised his hand in a pantomime of holding a pen and writing.

"Smart choice." Hotman removed the muzzle of his gun from inside Al-Saudi's mouth and aimed it between the Arab's eyes. He ordered a policeman to remove the man's handcuffs. "I'll ask you again. Who do you report to?"

He shook his head. "I am a diplomat. A consular officer. I work at the Saudi Embassy. Phone the duty officer."

Hotman stared into his eyes and grinned. He lifted Al-Saudi to his feet and marched him to the desk. He removed a sheet of blank paper from a drawer and took a pen from his own pocket. "I dictate, you write." The Arab nodded.

The Arab's note was written in Indonesian:

Dear Brother Najib,

This afternoon I was called to the embassy for consultations. I am entrusting this note to Wayan and appointing him as my replacement to translate for Mr. Bruno. I do not know how long I will be obliged to remain in Jakarta. I will contact you when I return to Surakarta.

Faithfully, Al-Saudi.

The letter was sealed in an envelope and addressed in Al-Saudi's handwriting to Abu Najib.

Hotman turned the Arab around and faced him. "Now Al-

Saudi, we have one question that you haven't answered truthfully." He pointed his Glock between the Arab's eyes. "I want to know the connection between your embassy, Al Qaeda, and Abu Najib."

Al-Saudi hesitated for a moment before replying. "We provide money for his boarding school."

"Is that all you pay for?"

"Yes." The Arab closed his eyes and sealed his lips.

"I don't believe you. The Saudis would not involve an undercover intelligence officer if all they did was pay for a *madrassah*. What else did you finance? The Bali murders? Bombing Christian churches?"

The Arab shook his head.

Hotman Pardede turned and looked to Sergeant Silitonga. He spoke in the Batak dialect so the Arab would not understand. "Take this asshole to the rice field. Get answers. I need to take this note to Wayan."

The three undercover policemen and their prisoner left the building through the back door and emerged into an alley where they had parked the car with a policeman waiting in the driver's seat. They tossed the Arab spy into the back seat and forced his head out of sight. Jonathan Silitonga drove the two blocks to the hotel where Bruno and the policemen were staying.

Hotman got out of the car in front of the hotel, entered the lobby, walked directly to the elevator, and ascended to his floor. He took the stairs from there to the room where he knew Wayan was babysitting Bruno.

Hotman rapped on the door and faced its peephole. He could sense movement and heard the chain being unhooked. As soon as Wayan opened the door a crack, Hotman pushed it open, entered, and immediately closed it.

He handed Wayan the envelope addressed to Abu Najib.

"Take this. The Arab has been detained and won't join you tonight. You are replacing him as the interpreter. The letter explains it."

Wayan took the envelope with an expression imploring clarification.

"That's right. Make sure this envelope is delivered to the imam *personally*. Get past the bodyguard and be prepared to explain to Abu Najib that Al-Saudi was called to Jakarta. You don't know why. Only that you were instructed to translate Bruno's English to Indonesian."

Wayan whispered, "The silencer and the gun are inside my bag, beneath a polo shirt. The handle is easy to reach. Bruno has practiced removing it. He is quicker than he looks. Fast on the draw, in fact. I don't think we'll have any problem with the bodyguards in the event they become curious and ask to search my bag."

"Let's hope that's so. A shame I won't be around to see it." Hotman gave a malevolent chuckle. "Remember, you need to get out of there fast. My men won't be able to help you. We'll be outside conducting the arrest of Bruno."

Wayan said, "I have the camera in the bag. I expect you'll see the results of tonight's work."

"Do your job, Wayan. This will end well. Trust me."

66

SURAKARTA

WAYAN AND BRUNO ARRIVED AT THE SMALL ROAD that ran behind the *madrassah* five minutes before midnight. Somewhere, a cat in heat howled. Otherwise the area was eerily quiet. The windows in the boardinghouse were now dark, with only a dull yellow light above the back door. There was likewise only one light shining at the back of Abu Najib's nearby house. Wayan parked the motorbike under the shadow of an acacia tree in the imam's back yard. The moon was full and afforded sufficient light for the two men to find their way along a narrow path that ran beside the imam's house and to the front.

Wayan whispered to Bruno, "Muslims hate dogs. Rarely do they have them in their homes. Lucky for us."

The Italian appeared to sneer in the dark. "We have the silencer don't we? A guard dog wouldn't be a problem."

At precisely twelve midnight, Wayan knocked on the imam's front door. They waited for a minute. The Balinese rapped again, louder. At last they heard movement inside. A deadbolt was turned, a chain was unfastened. Someone opened the door slowly.

The large, dark, brush-cut bodyguard emerged from behind

the door and stared first at Wayan and then at Bruno. It was apparent that he had a gun secreted inside his loose fitting, button-down batik shirt. He squinted as he asked Wayan, "Where is the Arab? We were not expecting you."

Wayan removed the envelope from a side pocket of his bag and showed it to the man. "I must deliver this letter to the imam. It was given to me by Al-Saudi."

The guard reached for it and Wayan held it back. "I am sorry, brother Muhammad, but the Arab instructed me to hand it to Abu Najib personally."

The guard and Bruno stared malevolently at each other for several seconds. At last the Indonesian shifted his gaze to Wayan. "Wait here. Sit. I will inform the imam." The man made a quick about face and climbed the stairs. When he was out of sight, Wayan unzipped the main compartment of the bag. He nodded at Bruno and indicated he was providing access to the pistol in the event the bodyguard returned and insisted on inspecting the contents. They remained standing. Wayan whispered to Bruno that there should be a second bodyguard in residence. He assumed Ali was off watch and sleeping somewhere inside the house.

After five minutes, Muhammad led Abu Najib down the stairs, making a point of placing himself directly in front of the old man. There was an awkward silence as the two men descended. When the imam arrived at the bottom of the stairs, he stared at Wayan and said in a soft voice, "Good evening. This is a surprise. You have a note for me?"

"I do, imam. Al-Saudi asked me to deliver it to you." The Balinese handed the envelope to Abu Najib. His instructions had been to appear ignorant of the letter's content.

"Let us see." Abu Najib took the envelope. At the same time Muhammad placed his hand at his hip in a ready position for drawing his weapon. Bruno moved closer to Wayan. The imam tore open the envelope, unfolded the letter, and withdrew reading glasses from his tunic. After reading the letter, he looked at Wayan and Bruno for several seconds. "Most unusual. Al-Saudi could have phoned me." He turned his head and gave an almost imperceptible nod toward his bodyguard.

There was a long pause during which Wayan looked at the floor and Bruno stared at the bodyguard, before Abu Najib finally spoke. "He says you will translate for us tonight, brother Wayan. I intend to interview this friend of yours. Bruno, is it? I'm not sure how much you know of our plans for Mr. Bruno. Tell me, please."

"No, imam. I know nothing about your plans. I have only recommended Bruno in case he can be of service to you and to our cause of ridding our nation, through the grace of Allah, of the pernicious influence of infidels."

Bruno noticed that Muhammad was now staring at the partially opened gym bag. The large, bearded Italian flexed his fingers. Wayan watched for Ali, the second bodyguard, out of the corner of his eye.

"Very well. Follow me to the interview room," Abu Najib said. "Muhammad, you join us. Call Ali and tell him to come down."

The imam led the group to an area behind the staircase. As though he had heard Abu Najib's directive, Ali called out from the second floor and began walking down the stairs, "I'm on my way, sir."

Abu Najib raised a hand. "We'll wait for Ali."

Wayan glanced quickly at Bruno, who maintained a stoic expression in the face of the new odds.

"Which one of you has the key?" the imam asked, looking at each of the guards in turn.

Muhammad replied, "Here." He unlocked the door and swung it open. The room was pitch dark. The imam motioned with an open hand for the four men to enter ahead of him. No one turned on the lights. As his eyes adjusted to the darkness, Bruno brushed beside Wayan, who carried the bag in his left hand. The Italian dropped his right hand into the bag's partial opening and thrust the tips of his fingers beneath the shirt, and around the handle of the gun.

Abu Najib spoke. "Muhammad, inspect brother Wayan's bag. We cannot be too careful, can we? Ali, switch on the light, please."

Wayan instantly translated the imam's order into English for Bruno.

The following action happened in less than five seconds. Bruno, anticipating trouble ever since entering the dark room, whipped out the gun, spun around, and fired twice, point blank, at Muhammad's head, killing him instantly. At the same time, Ali, having flicked the light switch, and walking behind Muhammad, crouched and drew his pistol, aiming it squarely at Wayan's midsection. Bruno, seeing the threat, drove rugby-style into the bodyguard, knocking him to the floor before he could get off a shot. The two giants fought for each other's pistols.

Bruno turned his head and shouted, "Wayan, go! Get out. Grab Najib."

The distraction allowed Ali to wrest Bruno's gun away from his hand. Bruno turned and yelled once more, "Get out of here, Wayan." The bodyguard pointed his own gun at the big Italian's head and fired, killing him with one shot.

Wayan had hurdled over the two struggling men on the floor and sprinted after the fleeing imam, who limped to the front door, where he tripped on the threshold and fell onto the pavement outside. Wayan jumped on top of the man and grabbed his scrawny neck with both hands. At the same time, there was the explosion of semi-automatic fire above them. Wayan looked back and saw Ali fall on his face with a half of his head missing.

"On your feet, Wayan. Go back to your room now! That's an order." It was the strained voice of Hotman Pardede. "Throw Najib in the car," Hotman called to Sergeant Silitonga. Two members of the police team lifted Abu Najib to his feet. "Gag him." Hotman placed his gun back into his jacket.

"Here," Wayan shouted, tossing his camera to Hotman. The policeman caught it with one hand and waved at the Balinese, motioning for him to run away.

The old man was thrown into the back of the sedan, where he was held down by two policemen. Sergeant Silitonga ran to the driver's side, hopped in, and started the engine. Hotman was already seated in the passenger seat.

"Where to, Colonel?" asked Silitonga in a calm voice as he accelerated along the side street.

"The rice field," Hotman replied. "Two heads are better than one."

67

CENTRAL PARK, NEW YORK CITY

WALTER SARKIES STROLLED ALONG A PATH THAT led into a dark tunnel. Ramin would be waiting on the other side. He was aware the Iranian intelligence officer was under discreet surveillance by an FBI team. The agents were easy for him to spot, as they made no real effort to disguise themselves. Sarkies was nonchalant about it owing to the nearly twenty-year pretense that he was running Iranian agents, and not the other way around. If they only knew.

Ramin displayed the safety signal when he saw the American approach the eastern end of the tunnel—he held the Wall Street Journal in his left hand. Had he held the newspaper in his right hand, Sarkies would have continued walking without making contact. All part of the reverse tradecraft for the benefit of the watchful Feds.

Sarkies did not break stride as he made eye contact and nodded toward the Iranian who now walked beside him.

"Did it fly, Walter?" asked Ramin. He glanced back at the mouth of the tunnel, an act once more for the benefit of the agents who kept him under surveillance.

"As planned," Sarkies replied. "I met Katz late last night at his home in Georgetown after he dined with the president in the private residence. They're on board. Tell Afshin his scheme has been swallowed, as we say, hook, line, and sinker."

"Hook, line, and sinker?" The Iranian furled his brow. "I don't get it."

"It means the president and his national security advisor believe our tale—that you Iranians are going around Indonesia assassinating the bombers, one-by-one. The president has agreed to reciprocate, to return the favor. He will refrain from berating Iran as a member of the Axis of Evil. In addition, he'll order the disbanding of the Iraqi Army, as Afshin requested."

Ramin smiled broadly. "Excellent."

Sarkies continued, "You've said President Khatami and Afshin believe the overthrow of Saddam Hussein and the dissolving of his army will benefit Iran. That it will rearrange the balance of power in the Middle East."

Ramin nodded his head and said, "The circle will be complete, Walter, once we have a Shia government in Baghdad. We trust your government's administrator there is temporary. He appears to be rather clueless. At any rate, America's invasion has turned out to be a windfall for my country. Afshin said the least we could do is tell your president that we are killing those terrorists in Indonesia for him, as a favor. It's not a total fiction. After all, we *are* financing the mission."

"Yeah. And had President Hartono not ordered our president to keep his hands off the Bali investigation, we wouldn't be having this conversation. We'd be working with the Indonesians. An interesting twist of fate."

Sarkies continued, "But you know, without the Iraqi army and the Baath Party there to keep order, and with this neophyte American governor in charge, the country may soon go to hell. I'm not sure that's what you want on your doorstep."

"Walter, we Persians have been operating in the Middle East for well over two thousand years. Long before those artificial Arab nations were sketched onto a map. We know a thing or two about the area. Soon enough we will rule the region"

They walked in silence, Walter Sarkies digesting Ramin's last statement with some trepidation. At last the Iranian spoke. "Afshin wishes to express his gratitude to you."

"Oh?"

"He believes there would be mutual benefit if we can figure a way to enhance your reputation with the President of the United States. It so happens we have information that will make you a superstar." The Iranian grinned as he looked at Sarkies.

Sarkies turned and looked Ramin in the eye. "I'm listening."

"Are you familiar with the Ace of Hearts and the Ace of Clubs?"

"Of course. Those are the code words for Saddam Hussein's sons: Uday and Qusay, respectively. America's most wanted."

Ramin chuckled. "And if we told you where they are hiding?"

Sarkies stopped in his tracks and held the Iranian by the arm. "No one knows where they're holed up. Do you . . .?"

"Indeed we do. They are in Mosul. The precise location . . . no. That would be for you to find out. What we suggest is that your government offer a reward of several million dollars to whomever reveals their hiding place. Broadcast it all over Mosul, because we can assure you that is the city where the two of them are hiding. Everyone has a price, Walter, and if the price is right, the person who is protecting them will contact you. This bit of intelligence should make you a hero in the eyes of the NSC."

Sarkies could not help but smile. "There is nothing more fun in life than this secret game you and I have been chosen to play."

Ramin stopped walking and looked askance at his American agent. "Oh, and before we part, one further word from Afshin.

What matters to us is that Abu Najib be eliminated. The other actors were small fry. He is the evil godfather, the Sunni leader who propagates so much anti-Shia rubbish throughout Indonesia. Kill him, Walter."

"A work in progress, Ramin."

The two men separated, and walked away in opposite directions.

68

THE COMMUNICATIONS CHAIN WENT FROM COLONEL Hotman Pardede to General Agung in Bali to Walter Sarkies in Northern Virginia. At home, before breakfast, Sarkies entered the encryption code into his laptop and checked email. The message from Agung had arrived two hours earlier. He clicked open the attachment.

The deceptively bucolic scene pictured two dead men in the foreground: Abu Najib and Al-Saudi, a.k.a. Khalid Muhammad. Khalid/Al-Saudi, it turned out, was a forty-five-year old Saudi Arabian intelligence officer, fluent in the Indonesian and Malay languages. He'd been posted in the Philippines, Malaysia, and recently, Indonesia. Both men were naked, their feet and hands were bound. And their throats had been slit. Blood streamed down the men's chests and between their legs. They were sitting on the ground in the middle of a recently harvested rice field. The photograph showed three black crows flying overhead in the distance.

Agung explained in the body of the email that under circumstances of enhanced interrogation, Khalid had admitted to being the master bomb-maker who had trained the Indonesian, Omar.

He claimed to the very end that he was a rogue operator. The Saudi diplomatic corps, he said, had no knowledge of his terrorist activity. His official role was to spread the Wahhabi creed throughout Malaysia, Indonesia and Mindanao, and to funnel money to Abu Najib.

Sarkies stared at the photograph for several seconds. He would phone Harvey Katz at the White House and schedule a meeting at the café in Springfield, Virginia where they discussed these matters. He'd present the photo and brief him regarding the results of the interrogation. Proof the Iranians were living up to their commitment. The president should be pleased the JI godfather, the spiritual leader for the Bali bombing, had been eliminated. The president would not be as happy when he learned of the Saudi Arabian diplomat's involvement in the bombing.

Sarkies sent the downloaded photograph to Roy Mancini. God knew where Mancini was hanging out these days. Wherever he was, he had coordinated the intelligence and finances for the operation with aplomb. An unsung, behind-the-scenes hero. He included in the email the news he'd received from Agung about the heroic death of the Italian hit man. Finally, he told Mancini he should now disband his *ad hoc* team of assassins. Mission accomplished. And he wished him luck.

He next emailed the photograph to Ramin in New York. He knew the Iranian "diplomat" would forward it to Afshin. Life should be so simple. Sarkies chuckled to himself.

Walter Sarkies kissed his wife goodbye and ruffled his ten-year-old son's hair before he left the house for the *Institute*'s office in nearby Alexandria. As he walked to his car in the driveway, he reflected on the double life he'd led for the past nineteen years. No one else at the *Institute* had a clue about *Operation Java Sea*. He'd orchestrated it from home every morning, over a second cup of coffee, before going off to work. A sixth sense, accurate as it turned out, told him his work as an agent for the Iranian Intelligence Ministry was coming to an end. It was only a matter of time.

As he drove east on the 495, he thought of the players in *Operation Java Sea*. He'd make a point of meeting Roy Mancini's son. Offer him a mid-level job with the *Institute*. And during his next inspection tour of the *Institute*'s offices in Southeast Asia, he'd take a side trip to Bali and visit the Bali Sea Resort in Amed. He wanted to meet the heroic brother-and-sister team in the flesh.

69

AYU LIKED TO RIDE ON TOP. AS HER PISTON-LIKE tempo increased, she called out Marc's name. He held her behind in both of his large hands and drove himself deeper with each of her thrusts. He sensed it was time, from deep in his loins, he felt the impending climax.

"Now, Marc, now," she cried out. He exploded inside her. Once again, a case of perfect timing.

Moments passed while the spent couple embraced and caught their breath. At last Marc spoke. "So, honey, we'll have the traditional Balinese wedding in Ubud. Do we have a date?"

Ayu kissed his lips. "Next month, darling. You haven't forgotten?"

"No. I wanted to hear you say it again. Music to my ears."

"And lest you forget, speaking of music, your father will play trumpet at the reception. He's bringing a band with him."

"Yeah, the best jazz musicians in Indonesia will be there."

Marc's cell phone vibrated on the bedside table. He'd switched off the sound when Ayu awoke, forty-five minutes earlier. He glanced at the caller ID and frowned. "Looks like it's from the States. I'd better take it."

Ayu got out of bed. "I'll be in the bathroom," she said as she wrapped a batik sarong around her waist. Marc watched her walk away and marveled again at her extraordinary, dark-skinned, long-haired beauty.

"Hello," he said, answering on the sixth or seventh ring.

"Marc Mancini?" the voice asked.

"The one and only." He was impetuous after the best sex he'd ever had in his life. "Who's this?"

"My name is Walter Sarkies. Your father and I are associates. He said I'd find you in Bali. I'm staying at a hotel in Nusa Dua. I presume you're home in the villa at this hour." It was past eight o'clock in the morning.

"Right."

"I spoke with your father thirty minutes ago. Before we continue, I suggest you phone him. You'll want to establish my *bona fides*."

Marc recognized the spook lingo—establishing *bona fides*.

"All right. You want me to phone you back?" Marc asked.

"No. I'll call you in twenty minutes."

"Your name again?"

"Sarkies. Walter Sarkies." They disconnected.

Ayu walked into the bedroom. She wore the black negligée Marc had bought her at Victoria's Secret during a recent trip to San Francisco. "Who was that, hon?"

"Not sure. Someone who knows my Dad. Give me a minute. I need to call and ask him to vouch for the guy."

"I'll bring coffee." Ayu left the room.

Marc speed-dialed his father's number. He glanced at his watch, did the math, and knew it was a few minutes after four in the afternoon in San Francisco. Roy Mancini answered after two rings.

Roy spoke first. "You're calling about Walter?"

"Yeah. And that answers the first question. Sarkies a friend of yours?"

"Marc, we haven't spoken since the recent bombing in Bali."

Roy Mancini referred to the two suicide bombings in Bali two days earlier, on October 1st. The first bomb had exploded at 6:50 p.m. at a popular beach, Jimbaran, where tourists and locals gathered around a food court to order freshly cooked seafood. Ten minutes later, another bomb detonated in the heart of the Kuta tourist belt. All told, twenty people were killed and over one hundred seriously injured. Jemaah Islamiyah had struck again, two-and-a-half years after the bombing in Nusa Dua.

Three days prior to the bombings Marc and Ayu had dined at Jimbaran beach at the exact location where the two suicide bombers had detonated their bombs.

"Yes. Tragic. It brought back a memory of that night two years ago," Marc said. "So what's going on? This guy a friend, a business colleague?"

Roy hesitated for several moments.

"Dad, you there?"

"Yeah. Listen Marc, you never knew him back in 2003. He operated behind the scenes, as I did. He arranged the money."

"*Java Sea!*"

"Yes. You recall the funds were sent from a mysterious shell company in the Caribbean. I never explained the source to you."

"Walter Sarkies was behind that?"

"Right. The money came from the *Institute*. It was funneled through there."

"Okay. What does he want now? That was two years ago," Marc said in a lowered voice.

"That I don't know. He phoned and asked me if I knew where you were. How to contact you. I hadn't spoken to him in over two years. His call came as a surprise," Roy explained. "I gave him your number. After all, we did work together, in a manner of speaking."

"All right, Dad. He's going to phone me in a few minutes. Let's see what he has to say."

"Get back to me."

"Will do."

Ayu carried a tray with two mugs into the bedroom. They sat at a table and looked out the floor-to-ceiling window at the ten acre green field adjacent to the villa where farmers had been harvesting rice since sunrise. "He'll call me back."

Ayu cocked her head with a questioning look. They took their first sips of Sulawesi coffee as the phone rang. Marc recognized the number and answered.

"Sarkies?"

"Yes. You can call me Walter," he replied. "You spoke with your father?"

"I did, yes. What's on your mind?"

"I'm arranging a reunion for some people you worked with a couple of years ago. I believe you referred to it as *Operation Java Sea*. Some of them you didn't know, but they knew you. Me, for example. I was impressed."

"A reunion?"

"Well, I might have called it a celebration if it weren't for the bombings two days ago. We may, in fact, never be able to claim victory over these bastards."

"You're talking in circles."

"That's because we're speaking on the phone. And I doubt that yours is secure. When can we meet, Marc?"

A moment passed. "Marc?"

"Yeah. I was thinking. Do you know where our villa is? We're north of Nusa Dua."

"I know exactly where it is," Sarkies replied. "Is Ayu with you?"

Marc was taken aback. "How do you know Ayu?"

"Because at one time, not that long ago, we all had roles to play. She played hers magnificently. I want her to be part of the reunion."

Marc glanced at Ayu and told Sarkies that they'd be able to meet him at the villa at four o'clock in the afternoon. "I'll bring a friend," Sarkies said. "Nothing formal. We'll have a short, confidential discussion. Do some planning and be on our way. I trust you can provide absolute privacy."

The van drove along the dirt road and past the rice field at precisely four o'clock. Earlier, Ayu had instructed the villa's entire staff to take the afternoon off. Each of them lived within walking distance, in the nearby neighborhood known as the *banjar*.

Marc saw the vehicle approach and went out to open the gate. Ayu stood fifty meters behind him at the front door. She saw two men through the tinted windows of the van as it approached. When it arrived and stopped in front of her, she was stunned. The man in the passenger seat was the popular Governor of Bali, Ida Agung. They got out of the van as Marc approached them. The men shook hands.

"And you are Ayu?" Walter Sarkies asked with a broad smile, as he turned to the young woman.

She returned the smile and offered her hand to the American. She bowed to Agung and greeted him in the high-caste Balinese dialect. Conforming to tradition, he answered her in the language of her lower caste as he shook her hand.

They entered the large, tastefully decorated living room. Cold drinks and fresh fruit had been laid out on a large, polished-mahogany coffee table. Marc switched off the stereo, which had been playing the music of Chris Botti in the background. They sat on adjacent sofas, Ayu and Marc facing the two men.

Walter Sarkies glanced around the room to be certain of their privacy, and spoke. "You will recall that General, now Governor, Ida Agung was the officer in charge of the bombing investigation two years ago." He glanced at Agung. "The Governor is aware of your roles in meting out justice to the Jemaah Islamiyah terrorists. Unofficially, he signed off on your project, *Java Sea*, in the first place."

Ayu and Marc, speechless, stared at the Governor of Bali. Agung looked Marc in the eye as he spoke. "And now, another bombing," he said quietly. "Walter has my consent to organize a new team. I'll step outside and let the three of you discuss the matter. Given my position, it is better I'm out of the loop." Agung took one last sip of his drink, and stood, before adding, "And this meeting never happened." He walked out of the house without another word.

Marc asked Sarkies if this had anything to do with the recent bombing on the island. He answered that it did not. He had been planning on this so-called reunion for the past two months. The terrorist bombing that same week was coincidental.

"All right, Walter. You have my attention. What's the plan?" Marc asked. He looked at Ayu. "By the way, we're getting married next month."

Sarkies replied with a grin, "You're a lucky man, Marc."

"I know that. So whatever you have in mind, it's got to wait. That is, if we do agree to it."

Sarkies looked hard at the two of them for several seconds before replying. "Thirty years ago, during the Cold War years, Roy Mancini worked undercover for my outfit, the *Institute*. His coffee export business proved to be an effective cover for his clandestine activity. It enabled him to visit any country in the region, legitimately."

"Yes, he mentioned something about that. He said he's still

doing odd jobs for you. I wasn't aware you're with the same agency."

"I'm the current deputy director of the *Institute*. I report to the commanding officer, a navy admiral. And from what I understand, you have joined Roy's coffee-trading business, running the overseas end of things."

"Right."

The three of them sat in silence for a moment. Ayu passed the fruit plate. Marc sipped his mango juice and stared at Sarkies, who speared a papaya chunk into his mouth.

Finally the visitor spoke. "So. Here we are. And I hear Amed is a nice place."

"To say the least," Marc replied. He saw where this was going.

"I'd like to meet Kadek and Wayan. I've already booked two rooms. Can you make reservations for yourselves at their hotel." Sarkies looked from Marc to Ayu. "Do it for this weekend. We'll arrive there separately, Saturday morning. Book the room in your name and I'll pay the bill in cash when we check out on Sunday. No need, Marc, to tell anyone there that we met today."

Marc phoned the Bali Sea Resort and had a short conversation with Wayan. There had been several room cancellations since the bombing on the first of October. The hotel was nearly empty.

"All right. It's confirmed," he told Sarkies.

"Excellent. I'll see you there before lunch on Saturday. And remember to pretend that we're meeting each other for the first time."

Walter Sarkies stood, said good-bye to his hosts, and walked out the front door to the van where he hopped into the driver's seat. Agung had opened the gate. Ayu and Marc stood at the front door, speechless, and watched the vehicle disappear.

The couple arrived in Amed on the east coast of Bali at ten o'clock Saturday morning. The scenic drive from the villa had taken over two hours. The winding, two-lane road passed through lush forests, and below Bali's largest active volcano. The route was familiar to them. They had been the Surya's guests at the Bali Sea Resort on several occasions during the past two years.

Kadek and Ayu had become "soul sisters." Wayan and Marc were close friends and confidants, two men who had shared the experience of a violent covert operation. They rarely spoke of their deeds in Central Java and North Sumatra. Nevertheless, there was a trust grounded on the secret world they had navigated together two years earlier.

At the reception area, Ayu and Kadek embraced as Wayan and Marc shook hands.

"Hey, brother," Wayan said. "The suite has been prepared for you two newlyweds."

The four of them laughed. "Not so fast, partner. There's a bachelor party," Marc said.

"Oh yeah. Almost forgot." Wayan grinned. "By the way, someone is waiting for you in the dining area. An American. He checked in an hour ago."

Marc's and Ayu's expressions turned solemn. "What's his name?"

"Mr. Sarkies," Kadek replied. "He claims to be a friend of your father's. Says he's looking forward to meeting you."

Wayan added, "He's sitting with a man from the Middle East, Lebanon, who arrived a half hour before you did. Nyoman can take your luggage to your room if you'd care to meet with the two gentlemen now." The member of the staff took the couple's luggage. Wayan led them to the patio, which served as the resort's outdoor restaurant.

Two men were seated at the edge of the patio. They were the only guests. Marc sized up the stranger sitting with Sarkies. He had the appearance of one from the Middle East or Mediterranean.

He looked to be in his fifties or early sixties. He was well-built, clean-shaven, had an olive complexion, and a full head of neatly-combed black hair. The kind of appearance where it was difficult to guess one's ethnicity. Walter Sarkies stood when he saw the three of them approach.

"Hello," Walter Sarkies said. The other man remained seated and expressionless.

Marc greeted the American. "You're Mr. Sarkies?"

The man grinned. "The one and only." Marc smiled as he recalled how he had likewise answered the phone when Sarkies had called him earlier that week.

Marc Mancini and Walter Sarkies shook hands.

Sarkies said, "I hope Wayan can arrange a boat for this afternoon after lunch. Pack some drinks and put it on my bill."

The Balinese nodded. "I can do that."

Sarkies motioned toward the man seated at his table. "I'd like to introduce you to Mr. Eskandari." The man got slowly to his feet and shook hands with Marc. He nodded toward Ayu.

Sarkies looked toward Wayan. "I trust your sister, Kadek, can join us on the boat."

Wayan gave a puzzled look and squinted at Marc, wondering how the American, Walter Sarkies, knew his sister's name? He replied, "Yes, sir, she should be able to get away for the afternoon."

Marc commented, "I believe Mr. Sarkies would prefer not to engage a pilot for the cruise. Wayan, perhaps you can skipper the boat?"

"Yes, of course." The Balinese was now even more perplexed. How would Marc Mancini know of Mr. Sarkies' wishes? "We can meet on the beach around two o'clock. Would you like me to load snorkeling gear?"

Sarkies replied, "By all means. Let's go diving."

Wayan arranged to have one of the resort's thirty-foot long motorsailers boats rigged and provisioned by two o'clock. The craft was anchored twenty meters offshore. The pristine blue-green sea was flat. The wind was light, the sky cloudless. A cargo ship steamed to the north, between Bali and Lombok Island.

"We'll swim out to the boat," Wayan told the other five. "You see the ladder on the side. Masks, fins, and snorkels are on board."

The two Balinese women wore bikinis. Each of the men wore trunks. The taciturn Mr. Eskandari continued to wear a T-shirt. The six of them swam the short distance to the boat and climbed aboard.

Wayan switched on the inboard engine and guided the craft out of the small bay, around a headland, and out to sea. He explained that in another bay there was a skeleton of a sunken Japanese trawler that had run aground during World War II. They would motor to that location for their dive, as the coral-encrusted Japanese boat was always chock full of tropical fish. As they glided south, the man named Eskandari sat alone at the bow, his back to the others. Wayan glanced at him occasionally, unsure of how he fit in.

Twenty minutes later, Wayan steered the boat into a small bay. The white-sand beach was deserted. "This is the spot," he called out. "We'll drop anchor here. The sunken trawler is just offshore."

The six of them spent the next forty-five minutes diving to a depth of fifteen feet to the coral floor and snorkeling along the surface above the trawler. The view below of a myriad of colorful tropical fish and undisturbed coral was spectacular.

At last Walter Sarkies called out, asking the others to join him for refreshments on the boat. He pulled himself aboard, removed his fins, and opened a bottle of Bintang beer for himself. The others followed. Mr. Eskandari helped himself to a bottle of mineral water and sat on the deck with his back against the main mast. Sarkies invited the others to sit near him on cushions in the boat's cockpit.

Sarkies looked first at Kadek and then at Wayan. "I have known you both for over two years. Let's see. I made your acquaintances in April of 2003."

There was a silence that lingered for several seconds. Wayan and Kadek regarded each other. Had one of them forgotten to introduce Sarkies to the other? They both looked at Marc for an answer.

"Oh, you never knew me. I can assure you of that," continued Sarkies.

There was another long pause. "First, I need to let you in on a secret. Eskandari is not this gentleman's true name. My friend's name is Afshin. That won't mean anything to you. Let me explain."

Sarkies took a large slug of his beer before launching into a discourse on the recent career of Afshin. The Persian had been, at the behest of former President Khatami, the Director of the Ministry of Iranian Intelligence for three years beginning in 2002. Khatami was voted out of office earlier in 2005, and replaced by the radical ideologue, and former mayor of Teheran, Ahmadinejad. Afshin was summarily fired and accused by the Revolutionary Guards of being an ally of Khatami, and thus too moderate to be the nation's intelligence chief. Afshin was replaced at the ministry by an RG hard liner.

The rumor circulated two months earlier that Afshin would be placed under house arrest, and investigated for corruption, among other concocted crimes. He got in touch with Walter Sarkies and requested his help in fleeing Iran. Long story, short, Sarkies provided Afshin with false documents—a U.S. green card and a Lebanese passport—a disguise, and a round-trip economy-class ticket from Teheran to Malaysia. Afshin had no intention of ever using the return portion of the ticket.

Earlier, before he vacated his position at the intelligence ministry, Afshin deleted from the record all evidence of the shell company and bank account he had personally set up in Antigua to fund Iran's North and South American clandestine intelligence activities. Prior to removing the records, he topped up that company's bank account with several million dollars, transferring black ops petrodollars from Iran's treasury. There was now more money in that Caribbean bank account than Afshin could ever spend on himself. He had been divorced years ago, and he had no children.

One month earlier, Afshin and Sarkies had put their heads together during a meeting in Penang and decided to use the fifty million dollars to fund an off-the-books operation in Asia, targeting Al Qaeda-linked terrorist groups: Jemaah Islamiyah and Abu Sayyaf.

What Walter Sarkies didn't reveal was that earlier that year he had terminated his clandestine, twenty-one year affiliation with Iranian intelligence.

Sarkies explained that his organization, the *Institute*, was chartered to collect strategic military intelligence for the joint chiefs of staff. It was *not* in the business of running covert counterterrorist operations. This newly created enterprise, funded from Antigua, would have no direct connection with the American intelligence community.

Wayan looked at Marc and then stared at Sarkies. "Care to explain why we're discussing this? And why you're in Amed?"

Sarkies slowly put down his bottle of Bintang. "I'll let you in on another secret. Roy Mancini's scheme to assassinate the Bali bombers and their sheik, Abu Najib, was wholly financed by Afshin and the Iranian intelligence ministry. Every cent. I'll let that sink in for a moment."

Marc, Wayan, Ayu, and Kadek looked from one to the other in disbelief. Afshin gave a tight-lipped smile.

"That's right," Sarkies continued. "Your father, Marc, believes to this day the money for the assassinations was sent from the *Institute*'s black ops account. No such thing."

Marc began to speak, but Sarkies raised a hand, interrupting him. "Now, as to Wayan's question. Why are we here? Let me ask each of you. Do you ever miss the natural high you got while plotting and achieving your successes two years ago? The challenge and your victory of pulling off the kills? Stimulating, wasn't it, despite, or perhaps because of, the immense risks you took?"

Kadek was the first to nod her agreement. "Revenge was sweet," she replied softly.

Wayan looked at his sister and then at Sarkies. "I second that. The rush was addictive," he said.

"Marc? Ayu?"

"I'll admit, coffee trading doesn't provide the same rush that I experienced two years ago while planning and executing *Java Sea*." Marc replied. Ayu nodded her agreement.

"Yes," Sarkies chuckled. "The extrajudicial slaying of evil murderers like Ghazali and Abu Najib must have been thrilling. I'm in Amed to recruit each of you to carry on the freelance work you did after the first Bali bombing two years ago. Our job is not finished. The killer, chief planner, of Kadek and Wayan's parents is still at large. Hambali is hiding in Thailand. Do you agree to join Afshin and me in this undertaking? Mind you, we're strictly off the books. As with *Java Sea*, there is no government sanction or support of any kind. Our goal is the elimination of Sunni terrorists in Asia."

At that point Afshin stepped down into the cockpit and spoke for the first time. He said he had decided to reside in Ubud, Bali and that the chain of secure communications would be from Sarkies to himself. Sarkies would surreptitiously forward actionable intelligence he gathered from the CIA, the DIA, and the NSA. Afshin would supply the money for the missions from his bank account in Antigua. He would guide the team and contribute the expertise he had gained during a lifetime of worldwide covert operations. Marc would use his coffee trading cover to travel throughout the region, develop leads, recruit agents, and pass targeting information from Afshin to the other members of the team. Ayu would continue to fly and perform as a courier. Wayan and Kadek would go under deep cover as they had two years earlier.

After several moments of silence, and as the boat continued to rest at anchor, each of them, one after another, raised their bottle in a toast and to a solemn pact.

Wayan started the boat's engine and steered out to sea. Barely a word was spoken during the short trip back to the Bali Sea Resort.

ACKNOWLEDGMENTS

I want to thank my team. I found both my copy editor, Rebecca, and my cover designer, Jimmy Gibb, on FIVERR. Rebecca did a super job and Jimmy was wonderful to work with.

Dorothy Ingebretsen is not only one of my oldest friends, she is the finest proofreader an author could wish for. Thank you, Dorothy, for identifying those typos and for your suggestions about how some things could be said differently.

And Stacey Aaronson, my book designer, formats and produces a book from cover to cover that an author can indeed take great pride in.

About the Author

STANTON SWAFFORD was born in Los Angeles and grew up along the beaches of Southern California. He attended the University of Colorado and the University of the Philippines, where he majored in economics and Asian Studies. He speaks Indonesian, Tagalog, and Mandarin Chinese.

Stanton served aboard submarines in the United States Navy during the Cold War era, one of which was the *USS Nautilus*, the world's first nuclear submarine. During his period living, working, and playing in Southeast Asia—in the Philippines, Singapore, Malacca, Malaysia, and Bali, Indonesia—he operated undercover as an intelligence officer, ran a timber export company, and performed throughout the region as a jazz musician. *Java Sea* and his debut novel, *China Sea*, portray plots and settings derived from that experience.

Stanton is an avid tennis player and sailor, as well as a self-taught musician who continues to play piano and lead his jazz band, the Blue Notes. He lives in Southern California with his wife and son, Louie.

www.asianaffairsblog.com
www.Facebook.com/SASwafford